MW00464082

DEATH
IN
THE
DETAILS

DEATH
IN
THE
DETAILS

A NOVEL

Katie Tietjen

CROOKED
LANE

NEW YORK

Published in the United States by Crooked Lane Books, an imprint of The Quick Brown Fox & Company LLC.

Crooked Lane Books and its logo are trademarks of The Quick Brown Fox & Company LLC.

Library of Congress Catalog-in-Publication data available upon request.

ISBN (hardcover): 978-1-6391-071-8
ISBN (ebook): 978-1-63910-719-3

Cover design by Amanda Shaffer

Printed in the United States.

www.crookedlanebooks.com

Crooked Lane Books
34 West 27th St., 10th Floor
New York, NY 10001

First Edition: April 2024

10 9 8 7 6 5 4 3 2 1

To Matt, Liam, and Sean.

CHAPTER 1

Wednesday, October 16, 1946

"Twelve dollars and sixty-seven cents?"

Maple Bishop squinted at the check the lawyer had just handed to her. It had been eight weeks since her husband had died in a field hospital in France, and she still felt out of step with the pace of the world around her. Her eyes slid across the desk to the two lawyers seated there. They resembled a mismatched set of bowling pins. One was very tall and the other very short, but both sported round midsections. She stared back at the check in her hand, which shook ever so slightly, and then again at the taller man, Mr. Cross, the one who'd handed it to her.

"Yes," he confirmed, averting his eyes.

There was a rushing in her ears. Her outstretched hand dropped to the desk like an anchor.

Maple found her voice. "But that's impossible. There must be some mistake."

The portly man on the right, Mr. Higgins, slid a paper across the desk to her. As Maple lifted her hand again to reach for it, she saw that her fingers left smudges on the desk's surface, and she caught Mr. Cross's almost imperceptible frown.

Time sped up. The early afternoon light streaming in through the squeaky clean windows brightened. Her scalp prickled. Her eyes skipped over most of the words on the sheet, bouncing off them, unable to absorb their meaning. The only words she could focus on were at the top of the sheet: *William and Mabel Bishop*. So formal. So . . . odd. She'd been "Maple" ever since a plumber misheard her introduce herself when she was two, and Jamie had thought it was so cute that he made sure the nickname stuck. And together, they'd always been Bill and Maple. Seeing their full names written out like that looked surreal, like something out of someone else's life.

"So, what you're saying is that the amount left to me from the settlement of my dead husband's estate is *twelve* dollars?" she said.

Mr. Higgins cleared his throat and offered helpfully, "And sixty-seven cents."

She blinked and turned to him. He, too, looked away.

Heat rose to her cheeks. "Explain to me, please, how this is possible. How is the estate of a successful practicing physician who died defending our country"—her voice was getting shrill; she paused, took a breath, and then finished—"worth just under thirteen dollars? I gave you his ten-thousand-dollar life insurance check from the government yesterday, and you're giving me back *this*?"

The lawyers exchanged an uneasy glance. Finally, Mr. Higgins spoke.

"I understand your consternation, ma'am. We didn't have much of a chance to get to know him before he left for war, of course, but Dr. Bishop was starting to make an impression on townspeople."

This attitude was one of the things Maple resented about Elderberry—if you hadn't been born and lived your entire life within these arbitrary geographic confines, you weren't truly a member of the town, nor would you ever be. She and Bill had fled the noise and filth of Boston for a peaceful rural life nearly three years ago only to find it came with its own set of disappointments.

And the ghosts of the past she'd tried to leave behind had followed her, too. She tugged at the cuff of the worn blue peacoat that used to belong to her brother, realizing she hadn't even had a chance to remove it after entering the office. Mr. Cross had been so quick to hand her the check.

The lawyer mumbled something about nonviable business habits and said Bill's practice had been "in the red."

Maple pictured Bill at the dinner table each evening, loosening his polka-dot bow tie and chatting about the patients he'd seen. He was a hard worker, but Maple knew all too well that his big heart always outweighed his financial savvy. He'd treat anyone who walked in the door of his home office, whether they could pay or not.

Maple had been surprised the first time freshly baked bread had appeared on their doorstep, but quickly learned it was people's way of paying Bill when they couldn't do so in a more traditional manner. This, her husband had told her proudly, was how things were done in Elderberry. The townspeople had been doing this for the recently retired Dr. Murphy for decades, and Bill found it charming. Maple wasn't so sure, but regardless of her misgivings, eggs, cookies, and even casseroles soon followed.

But casseroles wouldn't pay her bills now.

Maple closed her eyes and swallowed her pride. "Are you . . . quite sure you can't use my services here?"

Maple, who'd arrived in Elderberry ready to put her law degree to work, had found that the men in charge were not ready to put *her* to work. She'd responded to The Law Offices of Higgins and Cross's "help wanted" advertisement right after she and Bill had moved to town. They'd politely declined to hire her. On her way in this morning, she'd walked right by the desk of the young man they'd hired instead.

"We're quite sure." Mr. Cross smiled tightly. "We're very sorry for your loss, Mrs. Bishop—for *all* of our loss, in fact, as the entire community mourns Dr. Bishop's death—but there are other clients. If we could wrap this up . . ."

Maple's cheeks went hot with shame. And to think she had felt rich mere minutes earlier, striding into this meeting expecting that the government's insurance payment, inadequate though it may have been in exchange for Bill's life, would provide her with a comfortable living while she figured out her next steps.

Now, she thought of her dollhouses—all those tiny, silent replicas of real life that she spent hours painstakingly constructing—and of the dolls inside them, created from cotton and buckshot, damned to smile for all eternity because she, Maple, had painted their mouths onto their tiny, porcelain faces.

Trapped.

And now Maple was trapped too, stuck in a small town where her brain and legal training would fester, where memories of Bill were everywhere. It didn't matter that she'd worked herself to the bone to become the first female graduate of Boston City Law School. Her diploma and her training meant nothing if no one would hire her because of her gender.

It had been a mistake to come here. There was no such thing as a fresh start after all. She glared from one man to the other.

"I have a mortgage to pay," she said, her voice rising, "twelve dollars and sixty-seven cents to my name, no source of income, and no husband."

The men exchanged a sideways glance.

"Perhaps your father or a brother—"

"Gone. Dead." A lump rose in her throat, and she gripped the cuff of her jacket again.

"Our condolences." Mr. Cross tapped a folder twice on the table and checked his watch. "Well, Mrs. Bishop, it's been a pleasure meeting with you, but I'm afraid it's time for us lawyers to embark on an important part of our day: lunch."

He chuckled at his own joke.

Maple tilted her head. "But you've already eaten lunch."

A flush spread across Mr. Higgins' neck. "Pardon me?"

She pointed at Mr. Cross's chin. "There's a dab of mustard just there." She turned to Mr. Higgins. "And you have what appears to be a bit of roast beef stuck in your mustache."

"Well, I—" Mr. Higgins sputtered.

"Not to mention the crumpled napkins in the trash can near the door," Maple went on. "And the fact that it's already one thirty in the afternoon, and the sign on the front door says your office closes from twelve to twelve forty-five for lunch. You're just trying to get rid of me."

"We are doing no such thing," Mr. Cross said, swiping at the mustard on his chin. He stood up fast and knocked his chair over. Then he strode to the door and yanked it open. "Good day, Mrs. Bishop."

She'd done it again—been *too honest*, as her friend Charlotte would tell her. She'd said just that on numerous occasions when Maple had bluntly pointed out something others would leave unsaid—or fail to notice at all. Maple pictured the exasperated expression Charlotte reserved just for her, just for situations like this, and heard her gently chiding voice: *"Don't antagonize them, Maple. You'll catch more flies with honey than vinegar."*

But it was too late. For better or for worse, vinegar had always come more easily to her than honey. Given her nickname, the irony was not lost on Maple.

She wanted so badly to leave that check lying there, along with her fingerprints, to stand up and stalk out with her last shred of dignity intact. Instead, she grabbed the check, shoved it in her pocket, and pressed her arms to her sides so the lawyers wouldn't see the sweat dampening the armpits of her shirt.

She rose from her chair and held her shoulders high. She pointed at Mr. Cross's chin.

"You missed," she said as she swept past him and out into the hall.

CHAPTER 2

The door slammed behind Maple. She stalked down the hall, past the desk of the man they'd hired instead of her, and pushed open the office's door. The mid-afternoon air was warm for October, but it still felt cool on her hot cheeks. Even though she was a relative newcomer to Vermont, Maple already knew better than to expect this weather to last. The steel blade of winter lurked, ready to fall with a mere moment's notice.

She tugged at her jacket, a faded cornflower peacoat that was too big around the shoulders and clearly meant for a solid man, not a petite woman. Maple knew from the raised eyebrows and pointed looks that people thought it looked ridiculous, but she didn't care. She'd started wearing it right after Jamie died, when it still smelled like him. Inside the collar, there was a smear of Jamie's dried blood, a last remnant of the night he'd died. She inhaled now, trying to recover a little of her big brother's scent. Her practical brain knew the smell was long gone, but she couldn't stop hoping.

From the pockets, she retrieved her gloves. Unlike the coat, the gloves were dainty and fancy. They had little maple leaves embroidered on the wrists and had been a birthday gift from Bill, one of the last things he'd given her before he left for war. Her gaze lingered on the tiny leaves for a long moment before she set off again.

Main Street in Elderberry, Vermont, bustled. Other shoppers strode past with purpose, carrying their parcels. Despite her resolve not to wallow, Maple's legs faltered underneath her as the thought hit her: *What's* my *purpose?* She reached a hand out to the wall to steady herself and saw that she was outside Hamilton's Grocery. A newspaper in the window screamed, *"TEN HANGED AT NUREMBERG: NAZI WAR CRIMINALS EXECUTED."* Underneath, a photograph of a stern man wearing a gray suit glared at her, a reminder that the harsh reality of the war wasn't actually that far away from sunny, quaint New England.

As though she needed that particular reminder. She moved her hand from the store's brick exterior to her throat, where she felt her pulse racing.

Maple stepped back and caught sight of her own reflection in the window, her face hovering like a ghost over the dead Nazi's picture. She should have felt vindicated—triumphant, even— about these executions, which had been carried out after a trial the whole world had observed. These men, after all, were the reason Bill was dead. If it hadn't been for their despicable actions, her gentle husband, who'd been just over the age limit for the draft when the war started, wouldn't have felt compelled to volunteer to go overseas and treat wounded soldiers as the war was winding down. For some reason, though, reading about the executions just left her feeling cold.

She took a deep breath and dropped her hand from her throat. Her face was flushed, and her unruly brown hair, which fell gracelessly somewhere on the spectrum between wavy and straight, frizzed out as usual. Maple detested hats, only deigning to wear one if the temperature dropped below twenty degrees. She cocked her head, taking in the lines around her eyes and the pinch of her forehead. She looked older than her thirty-one years.

The grocer's door flung open, and a man burst out, nearly knocking her over. Maple pressed her back to the window and looked to her left and right. There were no other people on this stretch of sidewalk. The man, clad in overalls and a flannel shirt, turned his head and shouted over his shoulder back into the store: "You're a liar!"

Another man, his face mottled behind his brown beard, followed him onto the sidewalk. This man towered over the first by at least a head, and both of them looked vaguely familiar to Maple. Out of the corner of her eye, she saw the owner of the grocery store peek his head out the door and then quickly duck back in.

The bearded customer stuck his pointer finger right into the first man's face. "Now, you see here, Elijah Wallace! I know you killed her."

Maple gasped. She clapped a hand to her mouth and pressed her back harder into the glass display. In front of her, the two men glared at each other. Behind her, she could feel the dead Nazi's unseeing eyes bore into her back.

Elijah Wallace's thin face was mean and pinched. He hissed, "You can't prove a thing, Mooreland."

Mooreland thrust out his chest in a move that reminded Maple of a photograph she'd once seen of a silverback gorilla. He curled his meaty hands into fists.

Wallace smiled, but it didn't reach his eyes. "You gonna hit me in front of a witness?"

The bigger man turned and saw Maple for the first time. The rage in his eyes pinned her to the grocer's wall.

She wanted to run, but she was frozen—a motionless doll at the mercy of the man in front of her.

Mooreland dropped his hands to his sides. He looked back at Wallace. "Get out of my sight," he growled, "and stay off my property."

With that, he turned and stalked over to a large rust-red pickup truck. He hopped in and roared away, leaving a cloud of dust. Elijah Wallace smirked, and then turned and winked at Maple. She shrank back. He set off in the opposite direction, his gait uneven and halting.

Maple peeled herself off the wall, her heart thudding, and pressed a shaking hand to her throat.

CHAPTER 3

Sheriff Sam Scott's dead-eyed stare didn't alter in any way when Maple finished telling him what she'd just witnessed.

She sat across from him in his tiny office. It was the first time she'd met the county sheriff in person, though she'd seen him sometimes out and about. From this close up, she noticed that what had undoubtedly once been a crisp, bright, khaki uniform was now faded at the collar and the cuffs. The patches on the shoulder that designated him as the county sheriff were frayed around the edges.

Maple recalled her last experience with police officers. That had been back in Boston, and those officers had sharper, crisper uniforms, but possessed similarly cold stares even as they'd informed her that her brother was dead. That memory ratcheted up her impatience with the reaction of the law enforcement officer seated across from her now.

"Did you hear what I said? Mr. Mooreland accused Mr. Wallace of murder! Someone might be dead!"

The sheriff gave a long-suffering sigh, looked up at the ceiling, and ran his hand through his thick brown hair. He needed a haircut. Gray flecked the temples and also his thick eyebrows and bottlebrush mustache, which twitched as he answered.

"Those two are the bane of my existence."

Maple blinked. Were all police this uncaring? Her anecdotal experiences with them thus far indicated that they were. Anger rose in her. "But Mr. Mooreland said—"

"I know what Mooreland said," the sheriff replied, moving his gaze from the ceiling to Maple's eyes. "Don't get your pantyhose in a twist."

Again, the face of that Boston policeman flashed to the forefront of Maple's mind. Though it had been three years, she still recalled clearly how he, too, had addressed her in a condescending way, clearly having pegged Jamie as a lowlife and his death as a boon for society.

The sheriff's voice pulled her back into the room. "Let me ask you this: Were you the only one who overheard this argument today?"

Maple pushed down her anger and forced herself to consider this question. She hadn't thought about it before, so consumed had she been by what she'd overheard. Closing her eyes, she replayed the scene in her mind as though she were watching her own private picture show, able (as always) to recall the most minute detail of anything she'd seen. *"Photographic memory,"* her mother had always called it. Now, sitting safely in the sheriff's office, she realized there had been two other men—they'd worn faded overalls and flannel shirts, just like Mr. Mooreland and Mr. Wallace—standing just off to the side, but well within earshot. In her mind's eye, Maple saw them shake their heads and shrug their shoulders, not appearing the least bit concerned. And the altercation had happened just outside the grocer's door, but he hadn't poked his head out to investigate . . .

Her eyes snapped open. The sheriff was looking at her expectantly.

"There were two other farmers!" Maple said, her heart thudding. "Why haven't they reported this as well?"

The sheriff inclined his head and made a "there-you-go" gesture with his hand.

"Because they know these guys. And they're probably just as tired of them as I am."

Maple was working herself into a state of righteous indignation. "How can you be so . . . so *callous* about this?" she demanded.

He sighed. "Look, it's not what you think. Mooreland's talking about Bessie, his prize cow. He found her dead in the field two days ago, her throat slit. He's convinced Wallace did it in retaliation for Mooreland filing a dispute over a property line. They're next door neighbors. This is just the latest in years of back and forth."

Heat rose in Maple's cheeks. She felt relieved and stupid at the same time. There were many subtleties of small-town life she was unfamiliar with. Gruff disputes between rural neighbors was one she'd need to add to her mental list.

The sheriff leaned back in his chair and stretched his arms over his head. She heard his back crack in several places. He then folded his arms across his chest and pursed his lips, as though asking if there was anything else.

"Oh, my," was all she managed to say.

The sheriff sighed. "They're troublemakers, the pair of them, but I'm months away from retirement, and those two will soon be Carl's problem."

Fleetingly, she wondered who Carl was, but at the moment the sheriff's attitude was her overwhelming concern. It didn't sit right with Maple. A law enforcement officer—even one so near retirement—should aggressively and proactively pursue crime and criminals. Anything less was unacceptable—even if her experiences in Boston had taught her that they were still common. If Wallace really had murdered Mooreland's cow, well, that was wrong. He ought to be punished, and Maple wasn't going to let the sheriff off the hook so easily.

"But shouldn't you—"

The sheriff frowned and raised a hand to stop her mid-sentence. In a bored tone, he recited, "The accusation has been investigated, and there is no conclusive evidence of who slit the cow's throat. It's Mooreland's word against Wallace's."

Maple frowned. Where was his dedication to upholding the law? His compulsion to right wrongs? His *conviction*?

She opened her mouth, but he half rose from his chair and spoke again, "Ma'am, my advice is to try not to let this spoil your day. Get on with the business of your afternoon. I'm sure you have dinner to prepare, childr–" He caught himself before the word was fully formed and at least had the decency to blush.

Maple and Bill had no children. Bill had been sad about this fact, ruefully telling people that God hadn't seen fit to bless them yet whenever anyone looked meaningfully at Maple's midsection, which happened with astonishing frequency. Maple herself had been secretly relieved when children had failed to appear, having no desire to produce more humans in a world that, in her experience, treated them so shabbily.

Now, there was no chance there'd ever be any children for them, and clearly the sheriff felt awkward about his verbal blunder.

Just then, the door burst open, and a young man tumbled in. "Sheriff—oh." He blushed upon seeing Maple. "I'm sorry, I didn't know you were in a meeting."

The sheriff rubbed his temple. "Mrs. Bishop, meet Kenny, our officer in training. This is his first week on the job."

Kenny ducked his head and shook Maple's hand. His palm was clammy.

"What do you need?" the sheriff asked Kenny in a long-suffering tone. "Mrs. Bishop and I were just finishing up."

Kenny's words tumbled out so fast they ran over one another. "Well, you see, a man just came in and, uh, you're not going to believe this, but he just walked right into a cell and lay down."

Maple looked from Kenny back to the sheriff.

"Guy with a long beard? Black hair turning gray? Cell on the right?"

Kenny nodded, looking perplexed.

"That's Willy. He comes in whenever he needs to sleep it off."

Maple's eyes shot back to Kenny, who stood with his mouth hanging open. "But—"

The sheriff waved dismissively. "He's harmless. Would you see Mrs. Bishop out, please?"

When Maple turned back to the sheriff, he had picked up the telephone. "If you'll excuse me . . ." he said, gesturing to the receiver.

Maple was sure he wasn't actually making a call, but she was too weary to point this out. She'd used up all her energy on the lawyers. The adrenaline spike that had hit when she'd witnessed the argument between Mooreland and Wallace had waned, leaving her too exhausted to be too honest.

Charlotte would be pleased, at least.

Kenny escorted her out of the sheriff's office. On the way to the exit, they passed the small hallway where the county's two jail cells were located. Sure enough, there was a rumpled man curled up on the cot in the cell on the right, emitting alcohol fumes so potent Maple could practically see them. He snored softly. The cell's door was wide open.

Kenny shook his head and muttered something under his breath. Maple knew how he felt.

CHAPTER 4

Maple's heart sank when she opened the mailbox at the end of her driveway and saw the envelope from the local bank. She knew what was inside before she opened it; sure enough, it was a notice that her mortgage payment was overdue. At the bottom, in capital letters, was a stern warning: "KINDLY REMIT PAYMENT OF $52.75 BY NOVEMBER 1 IN ORDER TO AVOID POTENTIAL FORECLOSURE ACTION."

Her hands shook as she unlocked the front door and let herself inside. She had thought, when she earned her law degree, that she would never face the kind of financial uncertainty that had held her own mother hostage for Maple's entire childhood. She'd been proud that she had clawed her way out of that neighborhood, had made something of herself, yet here she was—qualified for a job no one would hire her to do and in danger of losing the home she and Bill had been so proud to own together.

Ruminating on these thoughts, Maple was hanging Jamie's coat in the front hall closet when she heard rustling just outside the front door. Charlotte, who'd informed Maple shortly after Bill left for war that friends didn't need to knock, had her own key to Maple's door, as Maple did to Charlotte's. Maple never used hers. Charlotte often did. Maple barely had time to close the closet door before Charlotte bustled in, baby Tommy clutched to her chest and a bag dangling from her hand. She stopped just short of bowling Maple over and frowned.

"What are you standing in the foyer for?"

The sentence wasn't even complete when Charlotte thrust the baby at Maple as she leaned in to kiss her on the cheek. Before Maple knew what was happening, she was holding the squirming boy.

"Lottie—" she started, her elbows stiffening as her friend pulled away.

"Just hold him for a minute!" Charlotte called over her shoulder, disappearing into the kitchen. Maple could hear the exasperation in her voice.

Maple gripped Tommy under his armpits and regarded him from arms' length. He scrunched up his nose and forehead.

She frowned at him. "Don't cry."

Tommy's little face rearranged itself instantly into a smile. He giggled and flailed his little fists.

"Yep, that's me, kid. Downright hilarious."

Tommy chortled even harder.

Charlotte reappeared, took Tommy back, and whirled him around. He trilled with laughter, and Charlotte smiled.

"Always happy, this one," she said. "Not like his grouchy auntie." She pretended to check a nonexistent watch on her wrist. "Wow, you were alone with him for a whole minute and a half, and look at that: you both survived."

"Barely," Maple said. "He was threatening to cry. You know I'm not equipped for that."

Charlotte leveled an "I'm-not-buying-it" gaze at Maple, complete with pursed lips and a raised eyebrow.

"Oh, Maple. You're equipped for more than you think."

Maple suppressed an ironic laugh.

"So . . . you made more of them, huh?"

Her tone was too casual. Maple turned and saw Charlotte looking into the living room. Maple moved behind her and looked over her shoulder. The first thing Maple saw was the vivid red, white, and blue of the crisply folded flag on the mantel. When the grim-faced young soldier had presented it to her at Bill's funeral, Maple had been surprised at how heavy it was. It still looked heavy resting up there.

But the flag wasn't what had caught her friend's eye just now. Since Charlotte had last visited a week ago, Maple had completed two more dollhouses, which rested on the floor in front of the couch. She'd had to place them there because every other surface was already occupied by other houses.

"Yep."

Charlotte turned and gave her the tight-lipped, raised-eyebrows look. "Don't you think—"

"What?"

Charlotte stepped up close to one of the new dollhouses and studied it for a long moment. "Is this the Murphys' house?"

Maple and Bill had first met each other in Boston because of Dr. Patrick Murphy, the kindly older man whose practice Bill had taken over. An advocate for implementing a nationwide medical examiner system to replace the outdated—and often corrupt—practice of governors appointing coroners with zero professional training or credentials, Dr. Murphy had been leading one of his regular seminars on legal medicine. Maple and Bill had both attended out of professional interest and had happened to sit next to each other. They'd instantly bonded with one another and also with the man running the seminar. Bill and Maple began dating that evening and kept in touch with Dr. Murphy over the years, connecting with him every time he visited the city. When he'd told Bill he'd be retiring from the family practice side of his job and encouraged him to relocate to Elderberry and replace him, Maple's mother and Jamie had just died in rapid succession, and Maple and Bill were ready—desperate, even—to leave the city. The timing had seemed perfect. Maple wondered now whether it had all been a terrible mistake.

"Maple?" Charlotte was looking at her with concern.

Maple shook herself out of her reverie. "Yes, I made this as a gift for Dr. Murphy. It's for his birthday. I'm actually planning to deliver it a little later today."

Charlotte picked up a teapot from the dollhouse kitchen table and examined the intricate, miniscule painting of blue hydrangeas. "All those tiny details! How did you paint the flowers on here?"

"A toothpick," Maple replied. "It's an exact replica of Mrs. Murphy's favorite one. It was handed down from her grandmother."

Though Dr. Murphy had been a widower for nearly five years now, he still cherished his late wife's possessions, and her influence lingered in their decor.

"Astonishing." Charlotte looked at her in wonder. "Just when I start worrying that maybe you've got an unhealthy obsession, Maple, you surprise me. He's going to love this." Charlotte replaced the teapot carefully and then looked at Maple and smiled. "You have a singular talent for capturing what's big in what's small."

Before Maple could reply, Tommy grabbed one of his mother's curls and gurgled. Charlotte gestured for Maple to go into the kitchen and then followed her.

"Come on. I only have a couple minutes before I have to get back."

Charlotte and her husband, Hank, ran the local diner. Maple knew what a sacrifice it was for her to pull away from the diner just before lunchtime. Maple walked across the kitchen threshold and saw a tiny cake, immaculately decorated, on the table. With sugar still all but impossible to get because of ongoing rations and maple syrup prohibitively expensive due to high demand, Maple knew Charlotte would've had to go to extremely creative lengths (and probably use up her family's allotment of corn syrup for the month) to make such an impressive confection. Two plates, two forks, and a knife sat neatly next to the cake.

Charlotte had been finding excuses to drop by more and more often, usually with some treat or other from her diner across town. Normally, Maple had a voracious sweet tooth and appreciated the baked goods more than she could even express to her friend. Today, though, her stomach was knotted so tightly she couldn't imagine eating even a single bite.

"New recipe," Charlotte said, expertly juggling Tommy onto one side of her lap as she sliced and plated the cake with her other hand.

Both women sat. Maple picked up her fork, but her stomach recoiled.

"Oh, Lottie—"

As Maple suppressed a sob, she saw the concern etched on Charlotte's wide, friendly face. A few blond curls had escaped from the bun she always wore. Not able to face telling her about

Bill and the money just yet, Maple instead recounted the fight she'd witnessed.

"Elijah Wallace's been in the diner a time or two," Charlotte said, and Maple could hear the frown in her voice. "He lost part of his leg in a farming accident a few years back, before you and Bill came to town."

Maple nodded, remembering the man's awkward gait as he'd stalked off. He must have a prosthesis.

Charlotte continued, "They lost a lot of their farm business after the accident. They're down to just a few fields and a handful of goats. They operate a little shop at their property, selling goat milk soap and vegetables."

The baby made a fussing noise, and Charlotte moved him to her shoulder and began rubbing his back. "Elijah Wallace is the type who's not happy unless he's miserable," she added, arching an eyebrow.

Maple heard the implication, though Charlotte didn't say it aloud: Maple, too, wasn't happy unless she was miserable.

It felt like a sign.

"That's not all." Maple blew out a breath, retrieved the check from her purse, and handed it to the other woman. When she finished reading, Charlotte looked at Maple, her mouth in a grim line.

"I guess Bill was worse at managing finances than I thought," Maple said, her voice wooden.

Baby Tommy let out a wail.

"Oh, Maple, I'm so sorry." Charlotte patted her son's back. "Well, if you need help . . ."

Maple waved a hand to stop her right there. The diner was popular, but Maple knew Hank and Charlotte worked their fingers to the bone for miniscule profit margins, and with five-year-old twins, plus the baby, they had three extra mouths to feed. There was no way Maple would allow Charlotte to help her financially.

Charlotte took one of Maple's hands in hers and squeezed. Maple had the disconcerting sense that, had it not been for Charlotte's hand, she might have floated away.

Maple squeezed back.

CHAPTER 5

An hour later, Maple knocked on Dr. Murphy's door. When he answered, she was surprised at how . . . well, how *old* he looked. His face broke into a smile when he saw her, but his eyes stayed sad, just as they'd been ever since Darlene's passing.

"Happy birthday," she said.

"Thank you, my dear. Seventy years young."

The words were cheerful, but his heart clearly wasn't in it. He stepped aside so she could enter. The table was set for two. She placed her gift on the sideboard next to a framed picture of Dr. and Mrs. Murphy at their wedding. Then she turned and gave the doctor a hug.

"Please sit!" He scurried off to the kitchen, returning shortly with several bowls. "Spaghetti," he announced, whipping the cover off one. "My specialty."

They tucked in. Maple, feeling much lighter since telling her troubles to Charlotte, didn't deem it necessary to recount her entire sad morning to the doctor; she didn't want to burden him with her troubles, especially on his birthday—and especially when he looked frailer than she'd ever seen him. So, when he asked how her day had been, she decided to tell him about Elijah Wallace and Russell Mooreland.

"Oh, my," Dr. Murphy said after she finished recounting the scene from the sheriff's office. "That must've been distressing to you."

"Yes," Maple said, concerned that his face had gone even paler. "But after the sheriff explained the situation, I was mostly embarrassed, I suppose—a silly woman, wringing her hands over what turned out to be nothing."

Dr. Murphy frowned and put down his fork. "You are not a silly woman, and don't ever let anyone make you think you are."

His sad eyes blazed. Maple, not sure how to react to this sudden fierceness, changed the subject.

"Here," she said, retrieving the dollhouse from the sideboard. "Open your present."

He pulled off the sheet she'd draped around it. When he took in the miniature replica of his home, his expression was stunned. It was several moments before he could speak, and when he did, tears were pooling in his eyes.

"I . . . oh, Maple. Look at the detail. The teapot! The loveseat she reupholstered . . . how did you . . .?"

Maple looked away from the raw emotion on his face, feeling as though she might cry too.

"Oh! And you've made—well, you've made us, haven't you?"

She glanced back to see that he'd picked up the two dolls from their seats at the tiny kitchen table. One had tufts of unruly white hair and round, wire glasses, just like Dr. Murphy himself. The other sported soft gray curls and a yellow polka-dot dress—a perfect rendition of his late wife in her favorite outfit.

"Thank you," he said, his eyes shining as he clutched the pair of dolls. "You have no idea how happy you've made me."

As they enjoyed tea and fruit for their dessert, Maple couldn't stop thinking about those words. Had her gift really made Dr. Murphy happy, or had it reopened a wound that would never truly heal by reminding him of the life he'd lost and would never have again?

As she put on her coat, spotted with her dead brother's blood, she wondered whether Dr. Murphy's joy would ever be untempered by his grief.

Would hers? Or would she, like Dr. Murphy, end up living a shell of the life she'd once had?

The quiet in her empty house was deafening.

Maple hung up her coat and went to the counter where the cookie jar sat. It had never held cookies. Maple used it for another purpose entirely. She opened it and pulled out a photograph that had been taken over two decades ago and was worn around the edges. It was the only photograph Maple had of her brother. In it, Maple was seated on a sled, with Jamie in her lap. Their faces were flushed from excitement and the cold. Maple remembered the day well. There had been a blizzard, and the children from her neighborhood had raced to a nearby hill. One family had a sled that all the children took turns using. Maple smiled as she studied the look of anticipation on both of their faces. It had been Jamie's first time on a sled, and the ride had been perfect. The cold air had bitten into their cheeks as they raced down the hill, her arms wrapped firmly around him, keeping him secure. Their mother had not been there to see it. She couldn't get the day off work; despite the storm, the factory still expected its employees to trudge in to work. Maple, no stranger to caring for her younger brother, had bundled him up herself and taken him out with the other children. After the sledding, there had been a snowball fight, and then hot chocolate provided by a local businessman who'd been charmed by the children's enjoyment of the day. That same man had taken this photograph, which he'd later printed and given to Maple the next time he saw her near his shop. When she'd brought it home, her mother had begun to cry.

Maple, who'd thought it a lovely picture, hadn't understood her mother's tears at the time. Now, though, she had more of a context for her other memories of home—the nearly empty shelves, the amount of times her mother had insisted she wasn't hungry and piled nearly all their food onto Jamie and Maple's plates instead of her own, the threadbare clothes she stitched and patched until they disintegrated . . . This shop owner had thought nothing of handing them a photograph—in fact, he probably thought he was being nice—but for the people like Maple's family in the next neighborhood over, a photograph was an almost unimaginable expense. Now, Maple reflected that seeing her children's joyful moment captured on a piece of paper had probably reinforced for her all the things she couldn't give them herself. There would be no other photographs to document their childhood. There would be plenty of moments their mother missed while working long hours at the factory.

And then, she'd ended up in an early grave, her lungs ravaged by the poor working conditions in the factory.

Maple ran her fingers over the image.

A muffled meow pulled her out of the past. She replaced the photo in the cookie jar and opened her back door. There, his tail swishing side to side, stood the stray orange tabby who'd started visiting Maple a few months back.

"Well, hello." Shutting the door behind her, she reached down to pet his head, and that's when she noticed the dead creature lying on her stoop. The cat sat proudly beside it, curled his tail neatly around his back legs, and purred.

"Very good," Maple said, wrinkling her nose. "That mouse never had a chance, did it?"

She scratched the cat's ears, and he leaned his head into her touch. She felt the purr vibrate through his whole body. She pulled her hand away and turned to open the door. The cat wended around her ankle and tried to follow her in, but she moved her foot to block him.

"No, silly. You stay out here."

She stepped over the threshold and closed the door in the cat's face. As she started toward the front closet for a dustpan, her gaze swept across the dollhouses displayed on every available surface in the living room. There was something satisfying about building little people and their objects, creating an entire world out of scrap wood and pieces of fabric. It made Maple feel powerful. Useful. It filled the hours while Bill was away. When Maple lost herself in creating a house, she could easily work from breakfast through dinnertime without even noticing the time that passed.

Now, it almost felt suffocating to look at them all. Charlotte's unspoken disapproval made sense.

She returned to the back steps with the dustpan, scooped up the critter, and went back into the house. The cat mewed again, more plaintively this time. The dead rodent was a stark contrast to the scenes of domestic bliss she'd spent the last year constructing. She paused and zeroed in on one of her dolls, a man clad in a doctor's coat and perched on a loveseat. Specifically, this was a doll-sized version of Bill; the loveseat and the rest of the house were replicas of their home. This was the first dollhouse she'd made after arriving in her new home in Vermont.

Glancing back at the mouse, she realized that its size in relation to her dolls was grotesque; it looked like a monster next to her one-foot-to-one-inch scale replicas of humans. Irrationally, she wondered whether the mouse had dashed through her dollhouses before meeting its demise. She shivered at the thought of the rodent invading her tiny houses, winding its body around the carefully built chairs and tables.

Feeling the need to check on her creations, she peeked into every house in turn. Row after row, room after room of undisturbed domestic tranquility met her gaze. Men, women, and children, frozen in moments of everyday life, sat just as she'd left them. Not a single chair was out of place, and she detected no evidence of mouse droppings anywhere in any of the houses. She felt her shoulders drop the tension she hadn't realized she'd been holding. Her gaze lingered on the doll version of her late husband. She nodded once, stepped back from the house she was examining, and turned again, intending to dispose of the mouse, but instead caught sight of her newest dollhouse, the one that was still a work in progress.

Still standing in the doorframe, she tilted her head and examined the wooden frame. It was the outline of a house right now, the promise of something warm, inviting, and pristine that did not yet quite fully exist.

The cat mewed again from the other side of the back door, and Maple remembered there was still a dead body to deal with. She pulled herself out of her reverie and went back through the house, out into the driveway, and into the garage, where there was a trash can that would serve as the little mouse's final resting place.

She had to squeeze past the maroon 1941 Chrysler Saratoga, still nearly as shiny as the day Bill had brought it home. He'd been so proud to drive it to his house calls and to take Maple for rides around the picturesque Vermont countryside, but it had sat dormant since he'd left for war. Maple had been unable to drive it because of gasoline rations anyway, and so she'd donated all four tires, plus the spare, to the rubber drives. Now, the car sat there on its bare rims, beautiful and useless.

Maybe not totally useless.

You could sell it, said a voice in her head, not for the first time. Bill had paid over a thousand dollars for it new. Now, even if she could get back a fraction of that, it would go a long way toward paying her mortgage and other bills. It would ease her stress. It would be the sensible thing to do.

She deposited the poor mouse in the trash can, returned the small shovel to its space on the tool bench, and climbed into the passenger seat of the car. She ran her hands over the smooth fabric of the seat and touched the steering wheel that Bill had handled so many times. She closed her eyes and remembered the first time they'd gone for a ride. He'd taken her upstate to see the foliage. It had felt so grand, holding his hand as he'd steered and the motor had purred beneath them. It'd seemed like they were in control of their destiny, that joy and success were possible after all, that she could escape the tragedies in her past—that her mother's dreams for a better life for at least one of her children had not been in vain.

Maple squeezed her hands together in her lap, remembering her mother's anguished face on her deathbed and the way she'd held one of Maple's hands and one of Jamie's as Bill had looked on somberly from behind them, his stethoscope dangling around his neck. There'd been nothing more he could do for his patient by then.

"Get out of this neighborhood," her mother had said, making eye contact first with Jamie, then with Maple. Her voice was wheezy and barely recognizable thanks to the chemicals from the factory she'd toiled in for over a decade.

"Mom, don't try to talk," Maple had said.

Her mother had frowned, shaking her head, and had spoken again. "Whatever it takes, get out." She'd closed her eyes then, and the next morning she hadn't opened them again.

Now, Maple's eyes snapped open. No, she decided. She wouldn't sell the car.

At least, not yet.

Back in the kitchen, she pulled a piece of leftover turkey breast out of the refrigerator and shredded up half of it. She took it to the back door, where the orange cat waited, hopeful, and placed it on the ground. He tore into the meal, his tail swishing merrily, and Maple shook her head, rueful at her own weakness; if she kept feeding this stray, he'd keep coming back, and she didn't need any more mouths to feed when she could barely feed herself.

She returned to the kitchen and prepared the remaining turkey for her own dinner. While it was warming up on the stove, Maple glanced around. The kitchen was neat and clean, but behind the cupboard doors, her shelves were nearly empty and her mortgage was due in mere days. At least she'd have fruits and vegetables from her Victory garden to last the winter. She, like all the other women in town, had learned to can their own produce during the war, and the results of her labor rested in neatly stacked rows of mason jars. But would she be able to keep her house?

She stared at the twelve-dollar-and-sixty-seven-cent check that was still sitting where she'd left it on the table. She couldn't help feeling that if she cashed it, those smug lawyers would win. The day might come—soon—where she'd be forced to cash it, but she wasn't down to her last twelve dollars just yet. Maple propped it up against the cookie jar, where it would be visible every time she walked through the kitchen—a motivating force, she hoped.

Then, she ate alone, lost in memories of a gorgeous fall day with Bill by her side and the wind in her hair, when the future had seemed so full of possibility.

CHAPTER 6

The next day dawned bright and cold, and Maple was up and about early. Having finished her tea and toast, except for one piece of crust that she put aside, she eyed the check, then emptied the small mason jar where she kept loose change. She'd heard people say, *"You've got to spend money to make money."* She hoped that it was more of a general guideline than a universal maxim: a mere smattering of coins rolled out onto the kitchen table, and until she cashed her meager check, it was all the money she had.

She thought about having a second cup of tea and glanced longingly at the empty sugar bowl that sat on the counter next to the cookie jar. She decided to skip the second cup, but remembered to wrap her crust in a napkin and tuck it in her pocketbook. She shot one last long look at the check propped against the cookie jar.

With visions of warm beverages dancing in her head and coins from the jar jangling in her pocket, Maple set off for the center of town. Two women who lived next door to each other on the other side of the street from Maple were chatting at the property line between their two yards. They paused their conversation as Maple approached. Maple didn't know either of their names. She smiled weakly and offered a halfhearted wave from her side of the street. One of the women crossed her arms over her chest. The other returned the wave with an equally lackadaisical one of her own. Both women were close friends of Ginger Comstock, the self-appointed town social chair whom Maple had inadvertently made into a nemesis.

When they'd first moved to town, Ginger had invited Maple to join her sewing circle. Eager to meet her new neighbors, Maple had gone to the first meeting with high hopes. However, it quickly became apparent that this was not the group for her. The women were insufferable gossips concerned with shallow, petty nonsense— and Ginger was the worst of them all. Despite their shared culinary nicknames, Maple had quickly discovered they had nothing else in common. She had disliked Ginger immediately, pegging her as an opportunistic gossip. When Maple had declined Ginger's invitation to attend future meetings, she'd been immediately ostracized from the social circle of women in town that Ginger seemed to feel, as the doctor's wife, was where Maple belonged. The two had had a frosty relationship ever since. Now, Maple was relieved when she was past Ginger's cronies on the street, but she was left with a familiar sense of resignation that she'd never fit in.

Puffs of breath exited her mouth and rose like small clouds in the cold New England morning. Maple was still not used to how quiet Elderberry was when compared to Boston. Smoke curled out of chimneys. Yellow, red, and orange leaves crusted with frost crunched beneath her feet, and Maple knew that winter would soon obliterate the brief, colorful burst of autumn.

When she got to Main Street, businesses were just opening for the day, and customers were trickling in. The usual array of posters reminding shoppers of their patriotic duty to stick to the ration rules were on display in shop windows, though most were starting to fade and curl. Maple saw one particularly aged paper entreating Americans to "make do with less so *they* have enough." It featured two panels: in one, a housewife smiled as she held a box of Kraft macaroni and cheese, and in the other a serviceman in uniform gave an approving thumbs-up. As the need for rations had diminished with the war's end, so had the production of such posters—and yet no one had taken them down. Maple wondered if it was carelessness or whether perhaps it had been a conscious choice to show the returning servicemen that those at home had supported them.

She frowned as she passed the lawyers' office, thinking of Mr. Cross and Mr. Higgins, but the only person she saw was herself, reflected in the shiny front window. The same frizzy hair ran wild, the same men's peacoat was wrapped around her torso, but something was different today. The lines were less noticeable around her eyes and on her forehead. There was a determined set to her shoulders. She moved with a new sense of purpose today. She looked more like her old self. Maple took a deep breath, enjoying the fresh, sharp feel of the fall air in her lungs.

She continued on a few blocks and entered the hardware store. A bell jangled cheerfully, and smells of fresh sawdust and oil greeted her. It looked like she was the first customer of the day.

"Morning, Mrs. Bishop," said Ben Crenshaw.

The hardware store owner smiled at her from behind the counter, his brown eyes twinkling. Ben always made you feel you were just the person he was hoping to see. Maple smiled back and returned his greeting. She heard a skittering behind the counter. A long brown nose appeared, followed by the wagging, well-padded body of Frank, Ben's dachshund mix. Maple crouched and unwrapped the crust from the napkin. Frank waddled over and gobbled it out of her hand.

"You spoiled boy," Ben said. He shook his head ruefully. "That dog is the only plump one in town. Everyone's been living on rations, but no one can resist giving scraps to him."

He shrugged good-naturedly and ran a hand through his silky black hair. Maple privately disagreed with him, at least about the people. An image of the rotund lawyers popped into her head, and she tried to suppress a scowl. She caught herself tugging at the waist on her own trousers, but quickly pulled her hand away and patted the dog's head. He flopped onto his side and turned his belly toward her hopefully.

"He *is* hard to resist," she said, rubbing his stomach as his back legs kicked the air with glee. "How are you?"

A shadow crossed Ben's face, and the wattage of his smile dimmed. His eyes shifted to the spot behind the counter where she knew he kept his cane. He twisted the gold ring he still wore on his left ring finger.

"I'm aboveground," he said. "How about you?"

During her many trips to the shop to buy dollhouse supplies over the past year, Maple and Ben had gotten to know each other pretty well. Maple wouldn't call him a friend exactly—more like a sympathetic acquaintance. She knew that Ben's wife, Annie, had died of a brain aneurysm shortly before Maple and Bill had moved to Elderberry. Annie had been four months pregnant with their first child. Since Bill's death, Maple had visited the store more and more as her dollhouse making helped keep her mind and hands occupied, and she and Ben had bonded over their shared grief.

Maple patted the dog one last time and rose to her feet. "I'm . . . about the same, I guess. Some days, maybe that's enough."

Ben pressed his lips together and nodded once. There seemed to be more silver speckled in his dark hair than the last time she'd seen him.

He took a deep breath, and Maple could see him pushing aside his grief; she knew all too well what that felt like.

Ben asked, "What can I help you with this fine fall morning?"

She stepped up to the counter. Frank lumbered back to his master.

"I need BB shot, loose cotton, and small amounts of red and blue paint."

That odd list would have taken most people aback, but Ben smiled easily.

"New dollhouse in the works?" he asked.

She nodded, then looked away, her stomach clenching as she said her next words aloud for the first time. "I, uh, was thinking I might try selling them. The dollhouses. The ones I already have, maybe, but I was thinking maybe I could make custom ones too, you know, if people wanted them a certain way."

She kept her eyes on her feet and hoped Ben wouldn't ask questions. Telling Charlotte about her money woes was one thing. Telling anyone else was quite another. She could easily imagine how the gossip would swirl and race.

"Bill left Maple with no money, did you hear?"

"A doctor's wife, penniless!"

". . . law degree, but no one will hire her."

". . . resorted to selling dollhouses, the poor thing."

When she finally looked up again, though, Ben wasn't looking at her with pity. He wasn't even looking at her at all. She turned and followed his gaze to the front window, past a pile of snow shovels stacked on a table. When he spoke, the words tumbled out fast, and his voice was higher pitched than usual.

"Maybe you could sell them here."

Maple stared at him. She realized her mouth was hanging open and closed it.

He gestured to the table in front of the window. "I've been trying to figure out what to do with that space," he said. "I'm underutilizing it right now. It's just my staging area for the next big display." He waved a hand to indicate the shovels that, Maple imagined, would soon be positioned on the display rack just inside the door, where a few lonely rakes now rested. "If we positioned the dollhouses on the table, people'd see them from the street," Ben said, excitement building in his voice. "It might even bring in new customers!"

He grabbed hold of his cane and clomped around the corner from behind his counter. Maple thought he was relying on it more heavily than the last time she'd seen him use it. Polio had stricken Ben in childhood; he had recovered but had suffered a relapse of symptoms after his wife's death. Maple drifted after him.

"You could even work on them here in the store! People would probably love to see the process behind them," he said.

Eyes bright, he turned to look from the table to her. He seemed to realize, then, that he had done all of the talking so far. The pink in his cheeks flushed a dark red, and he looked down at the tip of his cane.

"Uh, that is, if you'd like," he mumbled. "Business hasn't been great lately, to be honest."

Pity, fondness, and embarrassment all swirled in Maple's stomach. Ben was half Japanese; according to what Dr. Murphy had told them, Ben's father, a blond Vermont native, had returned from an overseas business trip with a dark-haired beauty—much to the shock and disapproval of many in the community. Maple had never talked about it with Ben, but it wasn't much of a stretch to imagine that his life had become more difficult in the wake of Pearl Harbor; she had a squirmy feeling that, though he'd lived in Elderberry his entire life, Ben's heritage made him an outsider just like her.

Mostly so she could avoid looking at Ben, Maple glanced again at the table near the window. Just then, Ginger Comstock appeared on the other side of the window. Her eyes widened when she saw Maple inside the shop, and her sharp gaze moved deliberately back and forth between Maple and Ben. Then, Ginger raised a white-gloved hand in a perky little wave accompanied by a knowing smile. Maple didn't return the gesture. Ginger switched her gaze to her own reflection, pursed her lips, and patted some loose curls into place before setting off down the sidewalk again.

Ben's cheeks had gone pink; there was no way he could've missed Ginger's insinuation that there was more going on inside the hardware store than a simple business transaction. Maple wanted to tell him to forget she'd ever mentioned dollhouses, and run out of his store as fast as she could. But the words caught in her throat, and her feet were rooted to the floor. Maple imagined what Ginger was already saying about the war widow and the tragic mixed-race widower, and what she'd say if they established a partnership and started working together every day. Then, she pictured her quiet house, which—despite the dollhouses that were multiplying faster than bunnies—was feeling more empty with every passing day. She thought of the paper Mr. Cross and

Mr. Higgins had given her yesterday, and how she'd never known how heavy a single sheet could be.

She thought about how maybe her dollhouses could help Ben as well as herself. Exhaling impatiently, she made a silent vow not to give Ginger any more power over her.

She heard herself say, "Yes."

The next thing she knew, Ben was clearing the snow shovels off the table. Maple made her purchases and left her paint, cotton, and BB shot on her new workbench; she would go home, gather supplies, and return in the early afternoon to set up shop.

She tried to discuss paying rent for the space, but Ben waved her off, saying her company would be reimbursement enough. The tips of his ears burned a bright red.

"I didn't mean—I don't want you to think—I mean, I'm happy for *any* company. I know people might think, you know, with Annie and Bill gone, that you and I—but I don't—"

He covered his face with his left hand and shook his head. His wedding band glinted under the overhead lights.

"Well, then," Maple said briskly, "we'll table the rent conversation for now. Thank you for your generosity."

It sounded stiff and formal, she knew. She'd never been good at emotional conversations.

Ben reached out a hand, and she shook it.

"See you after lunch, Mrs. Bishop," he said.

"Maple," she said. "We're colleagues now. I think it's time we were on a first-name basis."

"Maple," he agreed.

From behind the counter came the sound of Frank's tail thwapping against the floor.

Maple hitched her bag up on her shoulder and left, grateful for the walk home and the opportunity it offered to clear her head of the emotional mess swirling inside it. The sun warmed her already-warm face, a welcome change from the chilly morning of only an hour ago.

She spun her own wedding band around on her finger the whole walk home.

CHAPTER 7

Too excited to feel very hungry, Maple ate a small, hasty lunch. She decided she'd bring in one of her completed projects to display at the hardware store along with the one she was currently working on. Her fingers itched to move, to build.

In the living room, she selected the dollhouse with the figure of Bill in his doctor's coat, carried it outside, and loaded it into her wheelbarrow, where she'd already placed the wood scraps and a few other odds and ends from her existing stash of materials, and then repeated her journey to and from the garage with the dollhouse frame. She got into a rhythm as she neared town, her mind busy planning how she'd set up her new work area both to display her existing pieces and to leave herself a functional workspace to build the new ones. With her legs and her mind moving at a brisk pace, she felt happier than she had in a while, and before she knew it she was back at the hardware store.

She turned the wheelbarrow and pushed open the door to Ben's store with her behind. Scooting in backward with the wheelbarrow, she felt the door catch and heard Ben's voice welcoming her.

He held the door and they smiled at each other, reaching an instant unspoken agreement not to mention the awkwardness from earlier that day. She patted Frank's head, unpacked her things onto her new workbench, and hung her coat and hat on a hook nearby. Ben presented her with a plain apron and a simple piece of wood with two holes drilled in the top and a piece of rope in a neat loop.

"I thought you could use it as a sign," he explained. "Paint whatever you want on it. Just a little welcome gift."

She thanked him as she put the apron on. "I actually just thought of a name for my shop-within-a-shop: Maple's Miniatures."

They stood there smiling at each other for a long moment. Then Maple's stomach lurched, and she wondered whether something she'd eaten for lunch disagreed with her.

She steered the wheelbarrow outside and parked it around the back of the store, where Ben had suggested she leave it for the rest of the day. Humming to herself as she walked back, Maple realized she should call on Charlotte to tell her the news about her new business adventure. She pushed open the front door again and was surprised to see a man and a woman, their backs to her, standing in front of her worktable.

"Hello," she said, wiping her hands on her apron.

When they turned to face her, Maple recognized the man: Elijah Wallace, the grumpy farmer she'd seen just yesterday. Her heart jumped to her throat as she remembered the intensity of the fight she'd witnessed. Blushing a little, and with an uncomfortable jolt, she wondered whether Mr. Wallace recognized her from the scene outside the grocer's the day before.

"Are you in charge of this?" Wallace asked, inclining his head toward her table. His tone was belligerent, and his expression gave no indication he remembered her.

"Yes. I'm Maple Bishop. Nice to meet you," she said, keeping her own tone neutral.

She offered her hand. Wallace scowled and left his hands in the pockets of his overalls. Maple wondered whether those hands had, indeed slid a knife across the throat of that poor cow. Maple's gut instinct was that Wallace seemed more than capable of cold-blooded murder of an innocent animal. That feeling only increased when she looked more closely at the woman accompanying him, who was thin and pinch-faced. Everything about her looked faded—her milky skin, the floral dress that had seen better days, her straw-colored hair.

His wife shook Maple's hand and said, "We're the Wallaces. I'm Angela. This is Elijah."

Angela Wallace was soft-spoken and had a gentle grip. Maple noticed her forehead seemed permanently scrunched up, as though she were squinting into a bright light. As Angela shifted away from the handshake, the sleeve of her dress moved, revealing the edge of a nasty bruise on her upper right arm.

"Your work is beautiful," Angela said.

"Thank you." Maple smiled.

Angela continued, "It reminds me . . . Well, never mind. Is this one for sale?"

She brushed her fingers over the dollhouse containing the version of Bill.

"No," Maple said, her heart rate picking up at the idea of parting with it. "No, that's just on display. This one is for sale, though."

She pointed to the frame of the house in progress. Angela smiled and nodded. "I'd love it."

Maple's heart leaped. Had she really made her first sale within five minutes of setting up shop? She could feel Ben's grin from across the room.

"I'll just need to put some finishing touches on. What color—"

Elijah interrupted. "Look, just be upfront with me. How much is this all going to cost?"

He crossed his arms and gave Maple a dead-eyed stare. Maple heard Ben's cane tapping on the floor and knew he was coming over. She realized she hadn't even had time to think about what to charge. Keeping her tone and expression neutral, she ran through some numbers in her head.

"Three dollars."

Wallace slapped the table. "Why, that's highway robbery!"

Angela flinched. Maple felt Ben stiffen next to her. She placed a hand on his arm, hoping she was conveying the message *I've got this under control.* Though her nerves jangled, Maple stood up taller. As she'd learned early and well, and had taught her little brother, bullies responded to strength. If you were going to survive in their rough neighborhood, you needed to know that. The man in front of her may have been bigger than the boys who'd leered and jeered at her from dirty Boston street corners, but after what she'd seen yesterday and heard from the sheriff, Maple realized that Elijah Wallace was really no different from those boys.

Angela's voice was barely audible. "It reminds me of one I had when I was a girl."

Wallace exhaled impatiently. "A dollhouse for a grown woman. Ridiculous."

Frank let out a low growl, echoing Maple's own feelings. She decided on the spot, sale or no, that she would not bargain with this man.

"Three dollars," Maple said. "Firm."

Angela's fingers rubbed at the hem of her dress. She avoided her husband's gaze. Glaring at Maple, he pulled a rumpled dollar and two quarters from his pocket and tossed them onto the table.

"That there," he said, "is the down payment. You'll get the rest when you deliver the final product to our house tomorrow. Is that clear?"

Maple heard the quarter roll off the table and onto the floor. She maintained eye contact with Wallace.

"Crystal," she said.

Wallace eyed her for another moment, told Maple their address, and then turned and grabbed his wife's arm. As he pulled her out the door, Angela looked over her shoulder at Maple.

"Roses," she said shyly. "I don't care so much about the color, but I like roses a lot, if you could figure out how to put some in the house. And I have a sister—she has brown hair. Could there be two dolls?"

Maple nodded and thought she saw a spark flicker in the other woman's eyes, but just as quickly as it came, it went—and so did Angela Wallace, who was yanked out the door by her husband.

The silence when they left was tangible. Maple knew she should've been excited about her first sale, but mostly she just felt disgusted.

"What a horrible man," she finally said.

Ben's face was red. He shook his head in agreement. "He's got no right or reason to treat a woman like that."

"Did you see those bruises on her arm?" she asked.

Ben nodded. "And the deadness in her eyes. I have half a mind to report him to the sheriff."

"Well, you're a man, so maybe he'd actually *listen* to you." The words were out of her mouth before she could stop them.

Ben's eyes widened. "What—"

"Never mind," she said quickly.

Had the sheriff been inappropriate in his casual dismissal of her concern yesterday? Or had Maple really been overreacting? She wasn't sure, and the encounter with the Wallaces today had only muddied the waters.

Maple picked up the quarter and slipped it and the dollar into her apron's pocket. Then, she got to work.

She wasn't sure how many hours had passed when she finally took a break. The sky was darkening, and there was a pleasant ache in her shoulders. She sat back and admired the dollhouse, which had gone from rough draft to finished home all in one long afternoon. The highlight was the wallpaper she'd created by meticulously painting a repeating pattern of identical red roses over a deep navy background. She'd used paste to affix it carefully to the walls of the living room. It looked rich and elegant, but as she studied it, Maple felt a pang. She wondered whether meek, bruised Angela Wallace had ever felt elegant. Maybe, Maple thought as she untied her apron, this little house would give Angela that feeling for the first time; maybe Maple was making more than a dollhouse for Angela. The thought both pleased and saddened her. Tomorrow, she would furnish some basic furniture and a few dolls, and then it would be ready to deliver.

Ben had gone home with Frank already and left Maple with her own key. She hung her apron on a hook near her worktable, then gathered her things and left, locking the door behind her.

In spite of her feelings about her first customers, Maple walked home with a spring in her step. It had been a long time since she'd felt the satisfaction of a good day's work. She decided she'd treat herself to a slice of Charlotte's celebratory cake when she got home.

CHAPTER 8

The feeling of satisfaction stayed with her through Friday morning as she sewed cloth figures and stuffed them with BB shot to give them a little heft and cotton to round them out with softness. She made two girl dolls, one with brown hair and one with yellow like Angela's, and gave them dresses in different shades of green. Basing her measurements on an average-sized girl, Maple used her typical ratio of one foot to one inch and created dolls that were three and a half inches tall.

Ben's theory had been correct. Even though it was pouring rain that morning, which he'd told her usually put a damper on foot traffic to the store, as Maple worked, customers came in off the street, drawn by her window workstation, and paused at her table to watch her. She sold the two finished houses she'd brought in from her own living room and took two more orders before noon, one for a fully furnished house from scratch and one for some custom dolls. She had ten more dollars in her apron pocket before lunch, with the promise of more once she delivered the finished products that still needed to be made.

And while her dollhouse customers were in the shop, they bought other items as well.

During a brief mid-morning lull, Ben said, "My cash register hasn't been this busy in quite some time."

Maple's satisfaction was tremendous, barely even dipping when Ginger Comstock and a gaggle of cronies passed by on the street outside, making no attempt to hide the fact that they were scoping out Maple's new business. Maple reflected that, in some ways, being the only woman in law school had been easier than trying to navigate the female social circle in small-town New England.

🍁 🍂 🍁

Maple finished the rudimentary furniture for the Wallaces' order—kitchen table and chairs and a sofa and coffee table for the living room—in record time. By four o'clock, she had the house, dolls, and furniture loaded up in her wheelbarrow and was ready to make the delivery.

Ben frowned. "Are you sure you don't want me to come with you? I'm concerned about the temperature drop—all that rain from earlier is freezing now, and the roads and sidewalks are slick."

Maple shook her head. "I don't want to put you out. You've done so much for me already."

The truth was that neither of them had a functioning car, and the farmhouse was about a mile out from the center of town. Maple was concerned about Ben's ability to make it on foot, even under perfect conditions, let alone icy ones. Rather than embarrass him, she'd insisted she didn't want to put him out, but she was pretty sure he knew the unspoken reason. Also, though, she didn't want him—or any man, really—to feel compelled to protect her. She'd always been most comfortable relying on herself, for better or for worse.

"It's going to get dark," he said now, his face a little flushed as he leaned on his cane. "Be careful."

Maple promised she would, though she smiled ironically as she set off. The contrast between sleepy Elderberry and the rough section of Boston where she'd grown up made Ben's concern for her safety almost absurd. Moving at a brisk pace despite pushing the wheelbarrow, Maple knew she'd be at the farmhouse in under fifteen minutes. The smell of fresh paint drifted from the dollhouse back to her as she made her way down the sidewalk, mindful of slippery spots.

A familiar heaviness settled itself on her shoulders again, she fingered the worn cuff of Jamie's coat, and she found herself thinking of her brother, who hadn't made it out of that neighborhood. Maple would never forget the policeman who'd knocked on her door at eight in the morning to inform her of Jamie's death. He must've spoken in complete sentences, but most of his words had bounced right off Maple; her grief over their mother's death still so raw that it served as a sort of shield, not allowing her to fully absorb what the officer was saying.

". . . found unconscious on the sidewalk . . . outside a bar . . . brought into custody . . . two A.M. . . . dead this morning in his cell . . ."

Jamie and Maple had dealt with their mother's death in different ways. Maple had doubled down on her studying, more determined than ever to complete her degree, though her mother wouldn't be there to see her do it. She'd also just started dating Bill, the handsome young doctor who'd cared for her mother in her last weeks. Jamie, conversely, began spending more and more time with a rough crowd of fellow dockworkers, frequenting dive bars and drinking away most of his paltry salary.

That still didn't excuse the officer's attitude when he delivered the news. He'd looked down at Maple the entire time, his expression one of barely contained disgust. It didn't matter that her graduation gown, representing her ability to rise above the circumstances into which she'd been born, hung neatly on the closet door just outside the officer's vision. It didn't matter that her fiancé, a successful doctor, was on his way home at that very minute. To this officer, Maple and her family were trash—a problem to be dealt with, and nothing more. To him, her brother had deserved his fate and had brought it on himself.

Then, something caught her eye and yanked her out of her reverie. The last driveway she passed before getting to the Wallaces' house had "MOORELAND" written in big letters on the mailbox. Maple felt a jolt of recognition; this was where Russell Mooreland, the man she'd seen fighting with Elijah Wallace, lived, then. She could see a red farmhouse, set several hundred yards down the gravel drive, and a modest barn behind it. Out in the pasture beyond the barn, three cows munched grass. She wondered again whether Mooreland had been correct about Wallace murdering his prize cow, and the thought of it sent a shiver down her spine. She slipped on an icy patch as she took her next step. The road was more treacherous on the outskirts of town, where the elevation was a little higher and the traffic much lighter. Maple recovered her balance and kept walking, now quite eager to get the delivery done and be on her way.

But when she arrived at the edge of the Wallaces' driveway, she hesitated. Prickles ran up her neck and her feet refused to walk forward.

Ridiculous.

Though the sky was darkening in the early evening, Maple's sharp eyes had no trouble seeing that the large barn doors were open a crack. Across the driveway and to her right sat the house, gray with white trim, and it reminded her of Angela Wallace's appearance: faded and worn. Some scraggly bushes squatted in front of the house. The windows were dark. A crow cawed, and a gust of wind blew red and orange leaves across the driveway. There was no sign of human life.

But they're expecting me . . .

She flicked on her flashlight and pushed her wheelbarrow down the driveway.

"Hello?" she called out.

Her voice was barely recognizable—high and tight. She felt drawn to the barn with its open doors. The flashlight's beam bounced across the gravel. Her wheelbarrow creaked as she pushed it closer. The crow cawed again and flew across her path, headed away from the barn. Maple started to sweat despite the cool evening and wondered if she ought to turn around now and go get help.

She shook her head. Help for *what*, exactly? Temperamental customers who weren't home when they said they would be?

No. She was not some helpless damsel who got spooked by a bird and some breeze.

She pushed the wheelbarrow past the barn, navigating it over some ruts that had formed and frozen in the ground. There was some scuffling to her right, and Maple saw two goats poke their heads through the fence next to the barn. They bleated, and Maple thought they sounded perturbed.

Silly, she thought. That was probably just what goats always sounded like.

Leaving the wheelbarrow at the base of the front steps, she marched up to the front door and knocked. "Hello?"

There was no answer. She cupped her hands on the glass and pressed her face up close. She was looking into the Wallaces' small mudroom, and all she saw were some boots on the floor, two jackets hanging on a coat stand, and a wooden chair. No sign of life or movement.

She turned back to the barn and eyed the slightly open door. Sweat dampened the armpits of her shirt as she made her way across the driveway again, pushing the wheelbarrow over the ruts for the second time. The rough movement jostled the dolls inside. She parked the wheelbarrow just outside the barn and pulled open the barn door the rest of the way, wincing at the great creak it gave in protest. Her hand shaking, she aimed the beam of her light into the barn.

There, hanging from a noose on the barn's hay hoist, was Elijah Wallace.

CHAPTER 9

He swayed gently back and forth in front of her like a metronome. For a long moment, Maple was frozen, mesmerized by the rhythm. Then, in a rush like a rogue ocean wave, the reality of what she was looking at caught up with her. Maple whirled so her back was to Elijah and clapped a hand over her mouth. She went lightheaded and bent over, squeezing her eyes shut.

Maple's leg muscles twitched with an overpowering urge to flee. Without permission from her brain, her feet took two halting steps toward the barn door. Then, a thought stopped her: *What if he's still alive?*

She was the only one here. She had to check. Bile rose in her throat.

Hand still clamped over her mouth, Maple swung back around. Against her will, she took one step, then two, then three toward him. A moan escaped through her fingers. She forced herself to shine her flashlight beam ahead and look straight at Elijah— well, at the body that used to be Elijah; he was, on closer inspection, most certainly dead.

His head lolled at an unnatural angle above the rope that squeezed his neck. His arms and legs flopped off his torso like the limbs of a rag doll. A dark wetness stained the crotch of his overalls. The toes of his left foot pointed down, reminding Maple of a ballerina who'd never find the floor again. The toes of his right foot, the one with the prosthesis, remained rigid and straight, as though he were standing on a floor.

It was those mismatched feet that pushed her over the edge. A hot flash ripped through Maple's body. Her stomach heaved. She turned and ran out of the barn, just making it across the door's threshold before she vomited. She grabbed onto the doorframe to steady herself from her bent position, took a few deep breaths, and looked up at the house.

Still dark.

Where was Angela? Wiping her mouth, Maple stumbled down the path to the front door, feeling like a newborn colt on wobbly legs. She said a brief prayer and turned the knob. It opened, and she stumbled through the mudroom and clattered around the kitchen until she found the telephone and told the operator to give her the sheriff.

"What?" came a gruff voice.

"Elijah Wallace is dead," she announced.

"Who is this?"

"Maple Bishop."

There was a long pause. Maple thought she heard him chewing.

"You sure?"

Maple pulled the receiver away from her ear and looked at it.

Is he asking if I'm sure about the dead body or about my own name?

She shook her head in disbelief and put it back to her ear. The answer was the same either way.

"Yes," she said through gritted teeth. "I came to make a delivery. Elijah Wallace's dead body is hanging from a noose in his barn."

"No one else is there?"

"No."

"I'll call the county coroner and be right there. Stay put."

The county coroner was Dr. Murphy, who'd somewhat grudgingly agreed to fill the role even as he advocated for Vermont to switch to using the more formal medical examiner protocol. Relief flooded Maple as she realized a friendly face would be arriving in short order.

She wasn't sure how long she stood in the kitchen after hanging up, thinking not only of the dead body in the barn outside but also of her brother's, fresh in her memory, though it had been three years since she'd seen it. The house's silence pulsed in her ears until a crow cawed again, snapping her attention back to the present. She went back outside to wait for the sheriff and coroner.

As she closed the front door behind her, she noticed blood on the knob. She looked down at her own hand and saw a great smear of red. As if on cue, her palm began to sting. She examined it more closely and saw small, broken pieces of wood poking out. She pulled out her handkerchief and used it to pluck the splinters from her hand.

Where did that come from?

Maple looked at the barn. A knot of dread grew in her stomach. Nonetheless, she picked up her skirt and marched back over to where she'd vomited. She avoided looking at the corpse within and instead peered at the frame around the barn door. The entire surface was smooth and worn, except for one spot. She directed her flashlight and bent to look closer at the area, no bigger than a baseball, that had been smashed. Splintered wood stuck out in multiple directions, revealing the aged brown of the wood beneath the white paint. This was where she'd placed her hand to steady herself not ten minutes earlier; looking at it from this close, she could see a smear of her own blood.

She cradled her injured hand and swept her eyes across the barn's interior. Buckets, tools, and other supplies were stacked or hung. It was neat as a pin, a place for everything and everything in its place. The gash in the doorframe was the only imperfection— well, besides the dead body, of course. She couldn't imagine the fastidious Elijah Wallace tolerating such a blight for any amount of time. No, the gash had to be new, or else surely he'd have repaired it.

Her eyes fell to the ground in front of the barn, where the mud that had formed during the morning rain was now hardening again in the evening chill. Preserved in that mud, along with grass and fallen leaves, was the clear imprint of tire tracks. They were the source of the ruts she had steered her wheelbarrow over. She moved the wheelbarrow to get a better look at the tracks, and it tipped right over. The dollhouse fell out, landing on its side with a crack.

Before Maple could retrieve it, she heard the gravel crunch as a car turned into the drive. She saw the words "County Sheriff" emblazoned on the sedan's side. Maple waved her arms, and the car swung off the main drive and bumped onto the semi-frozen tracks Maple had been examining. The front passenger-side wheel connected with the fallen dollhouse, pushing it forward about a foot.

The sheriff, who wore a rumpled tan uniform, hitched his pants up as he heaved himself out of the driver's side, but a combination of gravity and his pot belly made it a losing battle; his belt settled back exactly where it'd been. A tall, slim man in a matching uniform stepped out of the passenger side, placing his feet carefully around the ruins of Maple's dollhouse. Her stomach sank.

"Mrs. Bishop," the sheriff said, removing his hat and raising his eyebrows. "We meet again." Maple felt herself flush. "This is Deputy Sheriff Carl Rawlings. Coroner's on his way. Might be a few minutes. Kenny's picking him up."

Rawlings nodded at her once and shook her hand. "A pleasure, ma'am. Sorry about your—is that a dollhouse?"

"It used to be," Maple said hollowly.

Rawlings stooped and helped her pick up the house, which had a long crack on the back, where it had made contact with the ground. They placed it back in her wheelbarrow.

The sheriff placed the hat back on his head and hitched up his belt again. Again, it settled right back into its original position.

"We'll just have a look," he said, gesturing for her to stay put.

The two men went inside the barn. Maple's stomach heaved at the thought of seeing the body a second time, but the idea of standing out in the dark next to a puddle of her own vomit was almost equally jarring. The goats brayed.

Maple gathered herself and stepped through the doorway for the second time in less than an hour, braced for the shock. This time, though, seeing the body brought only a small jolt. She stood next to the sheriff, who studied the body from a few feet away.

"I meant for you to stay outside." His eyes remained on the body even as he addressed Maple.

"I know." She was surprised at how steady her voice sounded.

The sheriff gave a long-suffering sigh. "Well, you're right. He's dead."

Maple eyes snapped to the sheriff's face, which wore an unreadable expression. "Are you making a joke?"

"Gallows humor." He kept his eyes on the body. "Funny," he went on. "With suicides, you don't usually see a drop hang."

Rawlings nodded his agreement.

Maple's gut twisted; his casual use of the term *suicides* struck her as callous and dehumanizing. "What?"

The sheriff pointed to the hayloft. "No chair or box or anything under his feet. He jumped from up there. Usually, suicides get a chair or something, stand on it, and kick it out from under themselves when they're ready to do the deed."

"True," Rawlings agreed.

"End result's the same either way, I guess." The sheriff sighed. "Paperwork for me."

When the other officer had conveyed a similar attitude while informing her of Jamie's death, Maple had been too stunned to react. This time was different.

"How can you be so heartless?" she demanded.

The sheriff's eyes locked onto hers, and she knew she'd gone too far. His voice was deadly calm: "Do you usually speak to officers of the law this way?"

"Do you usually speak about dead people so callously?"

Her voice sounded sullen, even to her own ears. Petulant. He stared silently at her, and she knew he was waiting for her apology. She didn't offer one and held his gaze, unwavering.

"Sam . . ." Rawlings said. "Come on. This is a traumatic experience, especially for a civilian."

Finally, the sheriff cleared his throat.

"Given the circumstances, I'm going to let bygones be bygones." The look on his face didn't match his words. His eyes were hooded, his cheeks stone. "What brought you to the Wallaces' property this evening?"

Maple explained about the dollhouse. "I was expecting Mr. and Mrs. Wallace to be home. They scheduled the delivery."

For the first time, she thought of the money the Wallaces owed her and realized she wouldn't be getting it tonight. She immediately chastened herself for thinking about money with her customer's dead body right in front of her.

The sheriff asked a few more questions about the details of the transaction and about what she'd observed on arriving at the Wallaces' property. Then, he glanced at his watch.

"Guess we'll have to cut him down," the sheriff said doubtfully. "Dr. Murphy won't be able to examine him up there."

As the two officers went to get a ladder that was leaning against the wall in a corner, Maple found herself alone near the body. Now that the shock had worn off a little, she noticed more details she'd missed on her first viewing. Elijah's fingers were swollen to the size of sausages, and raw red marks were evident on his wrists. His flannel shirt had come untucked on his left side, and Maple caught a glimpse of what looked like the top of a large, horrible bruise that likely spread farther down the side of his body.

Nausea rose in her. She didn't want to see any more. She decided she'd wait outside.

The crisp evening air felt good on her cheeks. She stood outside the barn and looked up into the darkening sky. The too-long sleeves of her coat slipped over her hands, and she gripped the cuffs hard, like she was holding on for dear life.

When they were children, her brother had always been good at spotting the constellations and pointing them out to her—that is, when they were visible among the lights and smog cluttering the Boston sky. Usually, the visibility was much better here in the clean air of Vermont. Tonight, though, a layer of clouds obscured the stars. Maple squinted until her eyes burned with tears, but she still couldn't see them.

Jamie had been the first one to show her the Big Dipper, guiding her eyes one evening with his steady finger. She'd always had a harder time than he had seeing past the immediate details of their life. While she was laser-focused on day-to-day survival and opportunities to make their way out of the life they'd been born into, her little brother had kept his eyes on the stars. When she'd recognized the constellation for the first time, it had surprised her to think it had been there all along, and she just hadn't known how to look for it.

Oh, Jamie.

A set of headlights appeared at the top of the driveway. Maple hastily swiped at her eyes with her sleeve. The car swung off the driveway proper and bounced across the lawn, screeching to a halt right next to her. Kenny, the young officer she'd met in the sheriff's office, bounded out of the driver's side. Dr. Murphy climbed much more slowly and deliberately out of the passenger's side, his gnarled hand shaking a little as he leaned on the door. He peered through his round spectacles and broke into a broad grin upon seeing her.

"Maple," he said, taking her hand in both of his. "I'm so sorry you got caught up in this." His brow wrinkled in concern.

"I could say the same to you." She relished the feel of his warm, reassuring hands: a doctor's hands.

He smiled ruefully. "It's not the same as sitting in a seminar room and listening to a lecture about legal medicine, is it?"

She shook her head, unable to speak past the lump in her throat.

Dr. Murphy sighed. "Well, to be honest, there's not usually all that much to it. We don't get a lot of mysterious or violent deaths here. That's why I agreed to stay on in the position after I retired from primary practice." He smiled ruefully. "I guess I'm not very good at retiring from *any* jobs."

Dr. Murphy had resumed his role as the town's family doctor, temporarily, when Bill had gone to war. Now, in the wake of Bill's death, *temporarily* had turned into something . . . well, less temporary.

Dr. Murphy let go of her hands so he could reach back into the car for his bag. Kenny bounded around to the doctor's side and tipped his hat to Maple.

"Good evening, Mrs. Bishop." He offered Dr. Murphy his arm. "Careful, Doctor—the ruts are no joke."

Dr. Murphy shot him a baleful look and clutched his bag harder. "I'm not an invalid, young man."

Kenny flushed bright red and dropped his arm. From inside the barn, Maple heard a dull thud and realized the men must've succeeded in cutting down Elijah Wallace's body. Kenny and Dr. Murphy seemed to have reached the same conclusion; both of their expressions became somber. They headed into the barn at the same time that Sheriff Scott emerged. The men paused for a brief conversation. The doctor continued inside, but Kenny and the sheriff came out again, Kenny wearing the glum expression of a puppy whose owner has just chastised it.

"Mrs. Bishop, Kenny here will give you a ride home. Thank you for calling this in tonight."

He pulled a pack of cigarettes out of his pants pocket and lit one.

"That's it?" Maple said.

The tip of the cigarette flared as the sheriff inhaled, then exhaled.

"What do you mean?"

Rationally, Maple understood that Sheriff Scott was not the officer who'd exhibited such disdain at her own brother's death scene. She also knew her emotions from that event, while less raw than they'd been three years ago, were still powerful. Still, she couldn't hold herself back.

"Why are you out here instead of in there with your victim?" she demanded.

"Oh, now—" Kenny shuffled his feet.

"Didn't want to smoke in the barn." His tone was bored, but his eyes flashed with anger.

She gritted her teeth. "But you're the sheriff. Isn't it your responsibility to investigate this death? Shouldn't you be observing the autopsy? Looking for his family to notify them?"

Her voice was loud, but her words evaporated into the evening fog until she questioned whether she'd actually spoken at all. The fact that the sheriff took several moments to reply didn't help.

"The good doctor's doing his examination now, and my deputy's in there. We'll locate his family. I have actually done this before, you know. But honestly, aside from checking off those boxes, what's to investigate?" he said.

Maple thought her eyebrows might shoot off her forehead.

"What's to investigate?" she repeated, throwing up her hands. "How about the fact that a man is dead, and we don't know how he got that way? Did you notice the gash in the doorframe? The bruise on his body? You—"

The sheriff's eyes blazed, stopping Maple mid-sentence. He dropped his cigarette butt and ground it out with the toe of his boot. He leaned in toward Maple and held his forefinger and thumb in a pinching motion with about a half inch of air between them.

"I am *this* close to retirement," he snarled. "You know what I mostly *investigate* these days? Stolen chickens. Not dead farmers. Dead farmers create a lot more paperwork than stolen chickens. And you know what I hate? Paperwork."

"Uh, is that really necessary?" Kenny smiled the nervous smile of someone vainly attempting to keep peace.

The sheriff twirled his finger in the air, ignoring Kenny.

"And you know what *everyone* in this town hates?"

Heart in her throat, Maple shook her head. Kenny sighed.

The sheriff pointed toward the barn. "That guy. I've gotten more complaint calls about Elijah Wallace than about any other individual in the entire county. So, aside from the hassle of hauling Wallace's body to the morgue and filling out the required *paperwork*, this right here is a win for this town."

He might as well have punched her in the gut.

"How dare you. This is so unprofessional. And you're only proving my point! The fact that a lot of people hated Mr. Wallace makes it all the more urgent to fully investigate his death. What if someone murdered him and staged it as a suicide? What about Mr. Mooreland? I saw them arguing, and you told me yourself—"

"Are you accusing Russell Mooreland of murder? You'd best watch yourself, ma'am. Flinging around half-baked accusations against a lifelong resident isn't exactly going to endear you to the rest of Elderberry."

Maple gaped at him, hit anew with the understanding that, in a town like this, unless you'd been born there, you'd always be an outsider. *She'd* always be an outsider. No matter what she did, the word or reputation of someone like Russell Mooreland would hold more value than her own.

And beyond that, the sheriff's words showed that he saw her position as outsider; he knew that she knew this reality of small-town life. By acknowledging it out loud, he'd made it worse. The sheriff had knocked the wind right out of her.

"I'm not *accusing* him," she managed to choke out. "I'm merely bringing up the idea that you should consider—"

"Okay." Kenny held his palms out in a placating gesture. "How about we just—"

"Listen, lady," the sheriff snarled. "I appreciate you doing your civic duty and calling this in. I really do. But your imagination is running away with you. I suggest from now on you stick to making dollhouses. Don't trouble your pretty little head about this guy's death."

Maple bristled and found her voice. "I happen to be a trained lawyer. I know what I'm talking about. Do you?"

As the words left her lips, Maple knew she'd gone too far.

Under his breath, Kenny muttered, "Whoo, boy."

The sheriff leaned in close to her, pointing a finger in her face. "I have half a mind to arrest you."

She forced herself not to blink. "For what?"

"Disturbing the peace. Interfering with a police investigation. Take your pick."

Outrage shook Maple's voice. "Interfering with *what* investigation?" She threw up her hands. "If anything, I'm the one *inciting* an investigation."

The sheriff pulled his handcuffs off his belt. Kenny placed an arm around Maple's shoulders and steered her toward his car.

"Okay, Mrs. Bishop, let's get you home," he said loudly.

Numb, Maple allowed the young man to bring her to the passenger side of his car. She sat inside and watched the sheriff light another cigarette as Kenny picked up the cracked dollhouse from her wheelbarrow and placed it carefully in her lap. Then, while he wrestled the wheelbarrow into the backseat, she looked up at the sky. All she saw was hazy darkness. Despite the presence of four living men and one dead man, she felt very alone under stars she couldn't see.

Maple looked out the passenger's side window as Kenny pulled onto her street, but her thoughts were far away. She rubbed her right hand along her left sleeve, feeling the smooth wool of the coat that reminded her of her brother.

Her brilliant, silly brother—the spark that lit up their family, until he didn't.

Now, she sat in the front seat, clutching the dollhouse that had, until a couple of hours ago, been pristine. Now, all she could see was the long crack running down the back. The blond and brunette dolls lay haphazardly on the living room floor, having been thrown unceremoniously from their perches on the tiny couch. The rose wallpaper she'd been so proud of now seemed almost trivial and looked far less elegant than it had back in Ben's store. What did interior decorations matter when there was no longer structural integrity in the house itself?

As he pulled into her driveway, Kenny seemed to Maple more like a nervous kid than an officer of the law. Now, after putting his truck in park, he turned to her and blurted, "That was my first dead body!"

"Well, it wasn't mine." She shot a sideways glance at her driver and saw his prominent ears turn bright red.

"I'm new on the job."

Despite his awkwardness, there was a clear note of pride in his voice. Because of this, Maple bit her tongue and resisted the urge to reply sarcastically, *You don't say.*

"I know. The sheriff told me it was your first week when we met in his office."

Kenny's face fell. Maple gripped the doll harder and thanked him for the ride. Before she could get out, however, Kenny spoke again.

"But even though I'm new and even though that was my first dead body, I'm already getting a sense of the way things work around here. I want to reassure you, ma'am, that we will investigate this death. The sheriff may have seemed callous back there, but he did everything he was supposed to. He brought in the coroner and had him do an examination, and Dr. Murphy's report will be an important part of the investigation. I don't want you to think that he won't give this matter his full attention."

She gripped the cracked dollhouse with both hands and studied Kenny's face in the moonlight. His eyes shone with the fervor of the optimistic and unjaded. Had she ever looked like that? Had she ever felt that level of righteous conviction that justice would prevail? That people were inherently good?

If she had, she decided, it had been a long time ago.

Kenny continued, "Sometimes, I've noticed, he and Deputy Rawlings talk in a kind of insensitive way about people they're investigating, but I think they actually do it to protect themselves. If they get too close to the investigation, it's not good, you know, emotionally."

He gave her a meaningful look and tapped the area over his heart with one hand.

For a moment, Maple was incredulous. Was this . . . this *kid* really lecturing her, of all people, on how to handle emotional trauma? Then, though, she felt a pang in her own chest. Had the sheriff, in fact, been doing exactly what he was supposed to do? Were his words and his tone in keeping with a lawman who needed to maintain a professional distance from his cases? Had she overreacted?

Kenny nodded once, solemnly. "Sometimes the wheels of justice turn slowly."

Maple barely restrained herself from rolling her eyes. *Enough is enough,* she decided. Self-reflection was one thing. Sitting here enduring earnest cliches from a kid was another. Steadying the dollhouse with her left hand, Maple opened the door with her right and climbed awkwardly out as Kenny scurried around to the back and pulled Maple's wheelbarrow out.

"Where can I put this for you, ma'am?"

He was so eager. It made her weary.

"Oh, just leave it there. Thank you, Kenny." She shifted the dollhouse onto her hip and pulled out her house key from her coat pocket with her free hand.

"Uh, actually, ma'am, it's Ken," he said in a deeper voice. "That's how my—the sheriff should've introduced me."

Maple's supply of patient niceties had officially run dry. She let herself in her front door and closed it on Ken-not-Kenny's goodbye.

She placed the cracked dollhouse on the kitchen table and returned to the hall, where she hung up Jamie's coat, kicked off her shoes, and padded back into the kitchen. After putting the teakettle on to boil, she turned her attention to washing the wound on her hand. She managed to pull all the splinters out, but the soap stung as she scrubbed and then bandaged it. She missed having Bill here to take care of her.

Steam poured from the kettle's spout, and Maple clicked off the burner, poured herself a cup of tea, and moved the kettle to a cool spot. She wondered where Angela Wallace had been tonight and who would be there for her as she picked up the remnants of the life she used to have.

Maple's eyes fell on the dollhouse again, and the two dolls lying prone on the floor, tossed from their seats after the night's violent events. They were supposed to resemble Angela and her sister, but it occurred to Maple that the brown-haired one resembled Maple herself. She replaced the blond doll on the couch and went to do the same with the brunette, but something stopped her.

Clutching the doll, Maple padded barefoot out to the garage, noticing the lack of a familiar meow. The cat must've obtained his dinner elsewhere tonight. She told herself she wasn't sad about it as she opened the passenger door of the car, climbed in, and curled up on the seat. She tried to breathe in Bill's familiar scent—tobacco and mint—but it was getting fainter and fainter. She'd hated his cigars when he'd been alive, and the mint was his attempt to cover it up for her with sticks of Wrigley's Doublemint gum. Now that he was gone, though, she found herself rather fond of the sweet, yet sharp, aroma. She wondered if there would come a day when she wouldn't be able to smell it at all, the way she could no longer smell Jamie on the blue coat.

Maple had lost just about everyone she loved, and now she had to wonder whether her own grief over these losses colored her perceptions. Had Maple allowed her frustration about the lack of investigation of her own brother's death to influence her interpretation of this evening's events?

Did she, in fact, owe the sheriff an apology?

She came to no conclusions, and when she finally went back into the kitchen and looked at her tea, it was cold and over-steeped. And, of course, there was no sugar to soften the resulting bitterness.

She put the doll down, dumped the tea in the sink, and started over.

CHAPTER 10

O ne satisfactory cup of tea later, Maple was tired of being alone with her thoughts. She grabbed the brunette doll and wandered into the living room, where the rest of her dollhouses sat on display. She moved her eyes over scene after scene of domestic bliss—perfect wallpaper, carefully crafted furniture, tiny people with smiles frozen on their tiny faces.

What she had seen tonight was the opposite of this. Death had wormed its way in, like it always did, and upended the orderly world. She clutched the doll in her hand more tightly.

It doesn't matter what you do. Death will always find you.

Maple gazed into one house, where a man and woman sat positioned at their kitchen table. The walls of the room were a bright yellow. No dirty dishes sat in the sink. Each doll had a tiny teacup and saucer in front of them. Anger rose in Maple swiftly. The scene before her was a sham. A lie. There were no happy endings. There was no such thing as closure. She was ashamed that she'd spent so much time creating these fake scenes of domestic bliss.

What a waste.

Before she even consciously knew what she was doing, she reached into the house and swiped the cups off the table. They clattered to the dollhouse floor, which she'd covered with scraps of linoleum left over from her own kitchen. The noise startled her, and her finger brushed against the male doll as she retracted her hand. He fell off the chair and landed on the floor near the teacup, legs akimbo.

A part of her itched to put the doll and the teacups back, to restore order to the chaos. Instead, with one flick of her hand, she swept him out of the dollhouse and onto her own living room floor, his wife still seated upright, the yellow walls as cheerful as ever. Nothing amiss except for the husband's sudden absence.

Still clutching the brunette doll, she moved into the hall and snapped on the light. Without really knowing why, she opened the door to Bill's office and paused. For a moment, she thought she could see Bill's silhouette sitting behind his big brown desk. Then, she saw the silhouette move and, with a jolt, realized she was actually looking at her own shadow, projected onto the wall behind Bill's desk.

Maple recovered her bearings and flicked on the wall light. She placed the doll on the desk next to a haphazard stack of papers and files and thought of Bill's kindness, of the respect he'd always had for his patients, even the difficult ones. It deepened her resentment of the sheriff's behavior. No matter what Kenny said to excuse it, she was sickened by how the men had talked about Mr. Wallace tonight—as a nuisance to be dealt with rather than a human being. Had police officers talked about her brother that way? Maple had a feeling she knew the answer.

Maple pulled back and noticed her fingertips had left ten small dots in the thin sheen of dust on the desk. It reminded her of how she'd left smudges on the lawyers' desk, and that reminded her about the money she still owed for her mortgage and other bills.

The dollhouse money she'd felt so proud of just hours earlier now seemed insignificant—a drop in a bucket.

Her eyes wandered to the bookshelf on the opposite wall, where Bill kept his medical texts. Bill's approach couldn't have been more different from the smaller, neater shelf on the other wall where Maple had meticulously shelved her law school texts. On Bill's shelf, hardcovers and papers were stacked haphazardly every which way. It had driven her crazy when he was alive, but since his death, she hadn't been able to bring herself to organize them.

Maybe it was time. She crossed the room and crouched to pick up a book that had fallen entirely off the shelf, having slid sideways off an avalanche of papers. She glanced at it and froze. The book she held in her hand was called *Death, Natural and Otherwise: A Physician's Manual*.

One thing was sure: there was nothing natural about Elijah Wallace's death. Had he hung himself, as the sheriff assumed? If so, why? What had tortured his soul in the hours, days, and years leading up to his death? Wallace struck her as grumpy. Angry. Bad-tempered. Downright mean. But suicidal? Maple had barely known him, and what she *did* know of him, she didn't particularly like; he'd been a bully. She just couldn't wrap her mind around the idea that he'd taken his own life.

But that would mean someone had killed him, and the idea of a murder in Elderberry was equally difficult to fathom.

Maple rocked back on her heels. She held the book in both hands and gazed at it for a long moment. She felt like a naughty child with a toy that didn't belong to her—an emotion that was very familiar to her from her days as the only female law student at Boston City College. She supposed she should've gotten used to being an outsider—of pushing her way into somewhere she was not wanted or welcomed—but the guilt of it was still palpable. She thought of the sheriff's words, mere hours ago, that had reinforced her status as a permanent outsider here in town.

And yet . . .

She gazed longingly at the book in her hands. How long had it been since she'd held her *own* textbooks?

Too long. Feeling a surge of adrenaline that came with rule breaking, she sat on the floor, her back against the shelf, and opened the book.

It was time to shake off the dust.

CHAPTER 11

The next morning, Maple awoke with a start to something tight pulling at her neck. She scratched at it, gasping, and opened her eyes. Half-formed images of Elijah's body swirled in the ether between sleep and consciousness, along with the photo of the hanged Nazi Maple had seen on the newspaper cover several days earlier. She blinked a few times. Jamie's face appeared in her mind's eye the way she'd last seen it: white and stark, lolled to one side on the slab in the coroner's lab.

She was surprised to find herself still propped against the bookshelf in Bill's office, her legs splayed out in front of her and the textbook in her lap open to the section on deaths by hanging.

There was nothing around her neck.

It took several seconds after her brain registered this to bring her hands back down to her lap. Early morning sunlight shone through the window and onto the examination table that had sat empty for a year now. From this angle, she could see the cobwebs that had formed underneath it.

She looked down at the book, where, in the history of hanging section, she'd learned the word *asphyxia* came from the Greek, meaning "pulselessness." Maple's own pulse was decidedly present. She felt the throbbing in her neck even without touching it with her hands.

Her eyes fell now on a reproduction of a painting from the scene in Homer's *Odyssey*: a row of nooses awaiting the maids Odysseus condemned to death for sleeping with the suitors. A quote below the image read:

> They would be hung like doves
> or larks in the springes triggered in a thicket,
> where the birds think to rest—a cruel nesting.
> So now in turn each woman thrust her head
> into a noose and swung, yanked high in air,
> to perish there most piteously.
> Their feet danced for a little, but not long.

Elijah Wallace's feet, too, had danced in midair. Like the maids, his had been what the textbook termed a "complete" hanging, in which the body is freely suspended.

Maple returned her hand to her own throat, which pulsed with fingernail scratches. In Elijah's barn, there had been no chair or box beneath the body. The logical conclusion, as the sheriff had pointed out, was that he'd climbed up into the hay hoist, fastened the noose, and then jumped. She shook her head. Something was bothering her about that scenario. Even the sheriff had said drop hang suicides were unusual.

She scrambled to her feet. Her whole body ached, and she couldn't imagine she'd gotten more than four hours of sleep, yet she felt invigorated. Holding the medical book now, in the bright morning light, didn't feel like the act of a naughty child. It felt . . . right.

She looked at the doll lying on the desk and then back to the medical text. She couldn't sit and read anymore. Maple's whole body itched to *do* something, to make sense of what she had seen and work out what was still troubling her.

She jumped up and went down the hall. She didn't have a plan or destination in mind; she simply needed to move. As she reached the entryway, there was a scuffling sound behind the front door. A moment later it opened, and Charlotte stood in the entryway.

"Maple," her friend said, moving across the hall and enveloping her in a hug. "I'm so sorry." Maple stiffened at the touch. All her nerve endings jangled with the desire to do something. Her friend's well-meaning attempts to comfort her irritated Maple, even as she was grateful for them. Charlotte pulled back and smoothed Maple's hair. "Are you okay?"

Maple always found this an odd question that she rarely knew how to answer. Many people had asked her this same question after her mother, her brother, and her husband died. What on earth did *okay* even mean?

Maple pulled back from the hug, deciding to sidestep the question. "How did you hear?"

She knew the answer before Charlotte could even open her mouth. Together, they said, "Ginger Comstock."

"That woman," Maple said. "How did she find out so quickly?"

"You know Ginger," Charlotte replied, shrugging. "I don't think she sleeps. Too busy having her ear to the ground, listening for everything anyone might be doing, saying, or thinking." She rolled her eyes, took a step back, and studied Maple. "Tell me about it. "

Maple complied, giving Charlotte a condensed version of what had happened last night, from her own discovery of the body to her argument with the sheriff.

"Men are the worst," Charlotte said, shaking her head.

"Well, only some of them," Maple pointed out. "Hank's an excellent man. So was Bill."

Charlotte gave her a half-exasperated smile. The doorbell startled them both. Maple saw a man's face pressed up against the narrow window to the side of the door.

"It's Harry Needles from the *County Tribune*," Charlotte said.

"Why on earth—" Maple started.

"If *I* heard about you discovering the body, you can be sure Harry did too. He wants the scoop," Charlotte said grimly. "Do you want to talk to him?"

Maple shook her head, wide-eyed. The last thing she wanted was attention from the notoriously aggressive reporter. Behind his back, people joked that Harry put on airs—that he thought he was an investigative journalist for the *Boston Globe* instead of the sole reporter and editor for a small-town rag. After Bill's death, he'd hounded Maple for a quote for his story even after she, stricken by grief, had repeatedly told him to leave her alone.

"He's not going to go away voluntarily," Charlotte warned.

Maple thought about how many times he'd rung her bell, approached her on the street, and called her house in the immediate aftermath of Bill's death, and she made a decision. She opened the hall closet at the same moment Charlotte opened the door.

Immediately, Maple heard the reporter's voice, combative and insistent. "I need to speak with Mrs. Bishop."

"She doesn't want to talk to you," came Charlotte's reply.

Maple found what she was looking for and closed the closet door just in time to see Needles, a bulky man with curly gray hair and thick black glasses, trying to push his way past Charlotte into the house. Charlotte placed her palm on the man's chest and shoved him back onto the stoop.

Undeterred, Needles called over her shoulder to Maple, "Is it true you found Elijah Wallace's body last night?"

"No comment," Charlotte snarled. "Go away."

Maple slung Bill's pump-action rifle over her shoulder. Harry's eyes immediately became the size of dinner plates. Maple stepped toward him. He backed down the steps, his hands raised in a calming gesture.

"Now, listen, there's no need to overreact—"

Charlotte, who hadn't turned around to see what Maple was carrying, said, "What?" and looked over her shoulder. Her eyes got as huge as Harry's. The reporter had made it all the way to the end of Maple's driveway.

"I'll just leave this here in case you change your mind! Call me! Whatever you do, don't talk to that chucklehead Ray Harrington from the *Burlington Daily Times*."

He waved a business card in the air, placed it in the mailbox, and took off.

Charlotte slammed the door and turned to Maple with exasperation. "Was the shotgun truly necessary?"

Maple returned the weapon to its spot in the closet. "I wasn't actually going to use it. I've never fired it. I don't even know how."

Charlotte sighed.

"What?" Maple felt a little indignant. "It worked, didn't it?" She was sure her face revealed her satisfaction at having dispatched the nosy reporter.

"It worked," Charlotte agreed, shaking her head and bending over toward the bag she'd brought. "Maybe you're getting used to rural Vermont life after all. Bet you never aimed a shotgun at anyone in Boston."

"That's true," Maple agreed, "but a bully's a bully, no matter what neighborhood you're in. You have to stand up to them."

"Maple Bishop, you are a wonder. You're better than anyone I know at boiling down the essence of a thing." Then, she stopped and pointed behind Maple. "It looks like something fell out of one of your houses, Mape."

"Oh." Heat rose to Maple's cheeks. She'd quite forgotten her childish ransacking of the little house the night before. Maple avoided Charlotte's eyes, but she felt them boring into her, nonetheless.

Maple moved imaginary dirt around on the floor with her toe, studying it with exaggerated interest.

"Must've been the wind," she said.

This lie, badly told, was met with silence. With a surge of stubbornness she didn't fully understand, Maple made no move to put the doll back. After several awkward moments, Charlotte retrieved the bag and brought it into Maple's kitchen, calling over her shoulder that it was leftover soup from the restaurant and she was putting it in the refrigerator.

Maple moved into the kitchen behind Charlotte and watched her friend close the refrigerator door and then pause, looking at the row of Kraft macaroni and cheese boxes lining the counter near the stove.

Charlotte flashed Maple a half smile. "Remember the first time we met?"

"How could I forget?" Maple mirrored her friend's smile.

"I was frantic. Matthew had that infection in his toe, and it had gotten so bad . . ."

"By the time you brought him over, it was bright red and oozing pus, and he couldn't walk on that foot anymore," Maple recalled.

"And he was spiking a fever."

"Bill wasn't home! He was out on a house call."

"I had Michael with me too, because Hank was already off at war—"

"—and both kids were screaming to beat the band," Maple finished.

"You were so calm," Charlotte said. "I was frazzled, all on my own with twin toddlers, and not sleeping and sick with worry about Hank. You brought us right into the exam room and gave the kids tongue depressors to play with."

"I was making it up as I went along," Maple said ruefully. "I didn't feel calm. I was panicking."

"We got out the rubbing alcohol and sanitized the toe and then we both prayed Bill would get back soon."

"Luckily, he did."

"Bill was so great, the way he talked to Matthew and calmed him down. He got us the penicillin, and the infection cleared right up."

Maple swallowed past the lump in her throat. "And then you repaid us by preventing our house from burning down."

Charlotte laughed, though her eyes sparkled with tears. "That darned macaroni and cheese," she said. "You forgot you had it on the stove, and all the water evaporated. Luckily, I smelled it in time and grabbed it."

"And luckily there was snow on the ground. I couldn't believe how fast you ran out into the backyard with that smoking pan and flung it right into the snowbank."

"Me neither. I didn't know I could move that fast."

They both smiled at the shared memory of that night—the infection, the screaming toddlers, the pan sizzling from its resting spot in the snowbank, the acrid smell of burnt instant dinner that had made their eyes water . . . The eventful night had begun and cemented their friendship. Though their personalities were miles apart, Maple and Charlotte had bonded that night and been fast friends ever since.

Finally, Charlotte broke the reverie. "I should go."

Bank in the entryway, Charlotte paused, glancing at the doll on the floor again. Placing one of her hands on Maple's, she said, gently, "Do you ever wonder why you build all those dollhouses?"

Maple twisted out of reach, and Charlotte's hand fell to her side. "What kind of question is that?"

"What kind of answer is that?" Charlotte retorted.

"A lawyer's answer," Maple admitted. They both laughed.

"I know," Charlotte said, "and you're extremely good at it—and by 'it,' I mean both evading questions and building doll-houses. I was just wondering . . . well, I was wondering whether it brings you joy."

Maple paused, thrown by this unexpected question. She recalled the sense of shame she'd felt last night that she had wasted so much time making all these houses. She wasn't ready to probe this emotion aloud with anyone, though—not even her best friend.

"It brings me satisfaction," she finally said.

"That's not the same thing. I'm worried about you. You've lost so much. You need something in your life that brings you joy. Otherwise, what's the point?"

This time, Maple stayed silent. She didn't know how to answer that question.

"It's okay if you don't know what that is yet, but you need to keep looking. Promise me you'll keep looking."

A lump rose in Maple's throat. They faced off silently for a long moment, and then Charlotte told Maple she had to get back—the kids, the restaurant—and just like that, she was gone again, with a stern promise that she'd check in tomorrow.

Alone again, Maple found herself drifting into the living room, looking at the scene she'd wrecked the night before. The tiny man was still splayed on the floor, his wife still seated at the kitchen table alone.

She took a step back and closed her eyes. Maple had always had the ability to call up a perfect image of anything she'd seen. She hadn't realized that other people's brains did not do this too, until she was in the fifth grade, when her teacher was distressed one morning because the janitor had cleaned the blackboard the night before. She had been planning to continue with the lesson and needed the information she'd put on the board. There had been notes, detailed diagrams, and a chart depicting the life cycle of a frog. Ms. Hancock, nervous and shrill on a good day, appeared to be on the verge of tears.

Maple had been early to school that day and was eager to be helpful. She'd jumped up and started re-creating the teacher's notes and examples. Standing on a chair, her tongue poking out as she concentrated, she was barely aware of her classmates trickling in. She didn't notice how quiet the room had become, even though arrival time was second only to recess as the noisiest time of day. The chalk scraping across the blackboard was the only sound. Maple finished, placed the chalk in the tray, and brushed off her hands, confident she'd reproduced her teacher's work exactly.

Almost twenty years later, Maple still remembered the awful sinking in her stomach when she turned to look at her teacher and saw the entire class gaping at her. She'd felt exposed, as though she'd been standing in front of the class naked and had only just realized it.

As a law student, Maple had realized that her photographic memory was an asset rather than an embarrassment. When her first professor told the class that good lawyers document everything, Maple had felt vindicated—documenting everything was her natural instinct. It seemed she'd pursued the right career.

Now, Maple cocked her head, appraising the collection of homemade dollhouses in front of her. Perhaps that's what she'd been doing with the dollhouses: documenting domestic life as it should be. She considered her response to Charlotte's question and wondered whether building these houses really did bring her satisfaction, as she'd said. Certainly, she took pride in her craftsmanship and her meticulous attention to detail. But now, with the image of Elijah's body fresh in her mind, she was forced to consider why she'd made so many of these happy dollhouses. Could it be that she was seeking something she had yet to find? Could she be attempting, over and over, to document something that simply didn't exist?

An idea began taking shape. She'd need more supplies: rough-hewn wood, coarse rope, bits of hay. She'd also need to learn some new skills, such as how to sculpt ruts and tire tracks into a muddy surface. Her brain whirred as excitement bubbled up in her. This was something new, but she could do it. She'd cleared higher hurdles. She'd graduated law school. She'd survived the deaths of her three favorite people. She'd scared away Harry Needles.

Documenting a death scene, by comparison, would be simple. After all, she decided, a barn wasn't really all that different from a house.

CHAPTER 12

Maple was in the garage, fitting boards together and sanding them down, when she heard the doorbell.

She frowned, annoyed at the interruption, and went to see who it was. Before she even got past the kitchen, though, she spotted Ginger Comstock's distinctive red curls and froze. The woman's nose was pressed up to the narrow window beside Maple's front door. Maple felt sick at the idea of Ginger trolling for gossip about a man's untimely death. She backed herself around the corner so she wouldn't be visible. The doorbell rang three more times before Ginger gave up. Maple exhaled gratefully and made her way back to the garage.

An hour later, the doorbell chimed again. At first, she ignored it, marveling at Ginger's persistence.

When she heard a familiar man's voice calling her name, though, she went to the front door again and opened it this time. Ben stood on her stoop, his forehead creased with worry. She squinted in the sun, realizing it was far up in the sky and headed for sunset. She'd missed lunch.

"You weren't expecting me, were you?" Maple blurted by way of greeting. "The store is closed on Saturday."

"No, it's not that," Ben said, frowning. "I heard the news about Elijah Wallace. Were you really the one who found him?"

Maple stepped out onto the front stoop, pulling the door swiftly closed behind herself. She saw Frank's head poke around from behind Ben's leg and begin sniffing at a plate covered with aluminum foil near her foot. His tail wagged hopefully. Immediately, she heard a hiss from her left. Her heart lifted when she saw the orange cat slink around the steps. His tail was thick as a bottle brush, and his mouth curled into a sneer. Ben and Frank backed down the steps as the cat leaped up to join Maple. He wound around her ankles, purring and rubbing his ear against her. Despite herself, she reached down to scratch his head. He purred louder.

"What's your cat's name?" Ben asked. Frank whimpered, his tail tucked neatly between his back legs.

"Mack," Maple answered before she could stop herself. She clucked her tongue. "He's not my cat, though. He's a stray that comes around sometimes. I just started thinking of him as Mack. You know, because he's orange like, uh, Kraft macaroni and cheese . . ." She trailed off, embarrassed to have revealed she'd named a stray cat after a boxed dinner.

"*You* may not think he's yours, but it looks like *he* has a different idea." Ben sounded amused.

Maple pulled her hand away and told the cat to shoo. Much to Frank's relief, the cat did just that, tearing off and disappearing into the woods. Ben's expression grew serious again.

"Are you—all right?" he asked tentatively, stepping forward again now that the fierce guard cat had gone. "That must've been quite upsetting."

She knew she should be glad her friend was checking on her. After all, Ben wasn't a gossip like Ginger. She felt a tug of annoyance, nonetheless. She had momentum with her project, but the physical representation didn't yet match her memory, and she was anxious to continue working on it.

Maple studied Ben's earnest face. Loath as she was to ask for help from anyone, she found Ben inherently trustworthy, and she could use his skills and supplies.

"Yes," she said after a brief pause, "but I could use your help with something."

"Sure," he said. "It looks like I'm not your first visitor today."

He pointed at the ground in front of him, where Frank had started sniffing excitedly. Maple bent and picked up the plate. She peeked under the aluminum foil and saw cookies.

"What is it?" he asked.

She wrinkled her nose. "A thinly veiled excuse. Come on in."

After admonishing Frank to stay put, Ben followed Maple inside. Maple led him into the kitchen, where she placed the plate on the table. Where on earth had Ginger Comstock gotten enough sugar to bake cookies? Maple had heard ladies were getting creative with corn syrup as a sugar substitute. Her stomach rumbled.

Maple led Ben into the garage, where he navigated the stairs carefully with his cane.

"Nice car." He patted the Chrysler's hood appreciatively.

"Not much use at the moment," Maple said shortly, embarrassed by the memory of herself curled up in the passenger seat, alone.

"Maybe it will be," Ben said. "You never know."

He turned and took in the partly assembled barn, the tools strewn around, and the multiple rolls of twine.

"What's all this?" he asked.

"It's my new project: Elijah Wallace's death scene, in a nutshell."

The wrinkle in Ben's brow deepened. "In a nutshell," he repeated.

"I need to make sense of some discrepancies," she said, "and creating an exact visual representation seemed like the best way to do it."

Ben still didn't reply. Maple plowed ahead.

"I know it seems on the surface that he committed suicide, but I'm troubled by several details: the bruise on his side, the scratches on his wrists, the gash in the doorframe. Whose car left those tracks in the mud? Why did he jump off the hayloft, when the sheriff himself said that most people who die by suicide don't do it that way? And there were plenty of people who disliked Mr. Wallace. I don't like loose ends. This"—she gestured to the dismantled dollhouse—"is the only way I can think of to wrap my head around what happened. To document it, I guess."

"You're re-creating the scene," Ben said, nodding.

His tone indicated that her decision made sense, that it was the most logical next step. Gratitude surged through Maple.

"In miniature," she agreed.

"What did you want me to help with?" he asked.

"Well, I want to make it so I can close the model up for easy transport, so I was thinking of having the driveway section attached by hinges so it can fold up, like this." She demonstrated by miming lifting a flap and closing it over the side of her model.

Ben nodded. "I have just the right material. I'll go work on it now."

"Really?" she said, hardly daring to hope that he'd get it done so quickly. "It's your day off. I don't mean to burden you with a silly project . . ."

His brow crinkled. "It's not silly. And besides, I have nothing else to do."

She walked him back out. As they passed the kitchen, she saw him glance at the plate of cookies and then away again quickly. Her conscience had a brief tug of war between her dislike for Ginger and her gratitude toward Ben. She grabbed the plate.

"Here," she said, opening the foil and holding it out to him.

His eyes brightened, and he didn't wait to be offered some a second time. He grabbed one and bit in. Maple did the same. They were, she was forced to admit (if only to herself) delicious—sweet, soft, and just a little crumbly. Whatever sweetener Ginger had used, Maple grudgingly had to admit, it was near perfection. She would've sworn these were prewar cookies.

"That made my day," said Ben.

His voice sounded happy, but his eyes were sad. He didn't look like someone whose day had been made, and something told her that he wasn't just talking about the cookies. Charlotte's voice popped into her head: *Does it bring you joy?* Maple wondered what sources of joy Ben had in his life. Her throat felt tight all of a sudden. She swallowed the rest of her cookie with some difficulty.

"Here." She thrust the plate at Ben.

"Really?" he said. "No, I couldn't."

"Take them," Maple insisted.

Ben smiled. "Thanks. What a treat! But you should keep some."

She shook her head, annoyed at herself for eating even a single cookie Ginger Comstock had made. Refusing to take no for an answer, Ben placed two cookies on her table, and then they walked out to the driveway, where Frank was napping in the sun.

"C'mon, boy," Ben said, and Frank reluctantly opened his eyes and staggered to his feet. It might have been Maple's imagination, but it seemed as though Ben leaned even more heavily on his cane than usual as he and Frank walked down her driveway and disappeared from sight.

She thought of Elijah Wallace's fake leg and, without consciously deciding to do so, looked down at her own feet. She was standing on a streak of mud—the track the wheelbarrow had made when she'd maneuvered it off the soft lawn. She looked to her right and saw the imprint of the wheel was still clear on the edge of her lawn. She cocked her head, and suddenly she wasn't looking at her own lawn anymore. Instead, she was recalling the tire tracks similarly imprinted on the earth just outside the Wallaces' barn.

She went back into the garage. There was more work to be done.

CHAPTER 13

Maple worked on her nutshell through Saturday and into Sunday. Sleep eluded her, whether because of her distress about finding the body or excitement about the nutshell, she wasn't sure. Regardless, she finished the frame in the early hours of Sunday, before the sun came up, and nailed pieces from the crumbling shed in her own backyard to the exterior. Using her usual dollhouse scale and her crisp memory, Maple figured out exactly where the gash in the doorframe was, and used a flat-head screwdriver to gouge out a chunk.

To re-create the tire tracks, Maple cut a piece of plywood to the exact dimensions of the front of the barn and warmed up some modeling clay. Once it was extra soft and impressionable, she'd mixed in gravel from her own driveway. Finally, she took a toy truck Charlotte's twins had abandoned at her house and drove it over the clay until the print resembled the one she'd seen in real life. Then, she let it set until it was hard, just like the frozen ground had been at the Wallaces' house.

The crowning touch, though, was Elijah himself. Maple estimated the dead man had been about six feet tall, so she made the doll six inches, filling him with buckshot and cotton. She took a porcelain head from her collection of old dollhouse making materials and painted a likeness of Elijah's face, including the bluish tint she'd seen when she discovered him. She fashioned tiny overalls for him out of blue fabric and cut up one of her own old flannel nightgowns for his shirt. She even created a tiny prosthesis by wrapping a small piece of tinfoil around a toothpick. When she placed the tiny work boot over it, the casual viewer would have no idea that a prosthesis, rather than a regular leg, lay beneath, as had also been true of Elijah in real life. If she was going to do this, Maple decided, then every detail had to match real life as perfectly as possible—even (especially?) the ones only she knew about for the time being. *Document everything,* her professor had said, and Maple was excellent at following rules. She positioned the other foot pointed down the way it had been when she'd found him.

As she painstakingly applied dark blue and purple paint to his side, she considered how he might've gotten that enormous bruise on the side of his body. The raw red patches around his wrists were curious too. She wondered whether Bill's medical texts might hold any answers. She held the book and read as she heated up the leftover soup Charlotte had brought from the diner, but found no information about mysterious bruises.

Back in her kitchen, Maple wrinkled her nose when she saw the two cookies Ben had left her yesterday. There was a funny jolt in her stomach, and before she could stop herself, she picked the cookies up and put them in the trash. Ginger Comstock and her cookies would not get any more of Maple's attention today.

After eating the lunch that also served as breakfast, Maple found that the paint on the doll version of Elijah had dried. She picked up the doll and carefully widened the noose with two fingers. She slipped the doll's neck through it gently and then let go. Her model of Elijah swung a few times before settling into the center of the barn. Maple shivered as she remembered Homer's description of the dancing feet. The bad feeling in her stomach was getting harder and harder to ignore.

True to his word, Ben had created the metal pieces she'd asked for and dropped them off. Maple was fastening the hinges to the barn doors with a screwdriver when Charlotte appeared, arms crossed, in the doorway to the garage. Maple looked up from the workbench, a little surprised—and not displeased—to see there were no children with her.

"This is a welfare check," Charlotte said. "When was the last time you slept? Or ate?"

Maple could tell that Charlotte was in what she privately thought of as "mother hen mode." From her experience with this particular mood, Maple knew there was no point in fighting it. She put down the screwdriver.

"I've slept each night," she said, which was technically true.

"For how many hours?" Charlotte threw back.

Maple nodded once, conceding the point. "Not very many."

"And eating?"

"I had Hank's leftover soup for lunch. It was delicious. The bowl is still in the sink, if you'd like to verify."

Charlotte's shoulders sagged a little. "I believe you, Mape. I just worry about you. Take a break. Have you seen anyone besides me all weekend?"

"Yes. Ben."

Charlotte raised her eyebrows. "Oh, really? And how's Ben?"

She said it in an overly deliberate way. Maple avoided her friend's gaze. "He's fine. He built those for me." She pointed to the metal pieces.

Charlotte's eyes followed Maple's finger. Her expression went from amused concern to shock as she took in the scene.

"Maple," Charlotte started. It sounded like she was struggling to exert great control over herself. "What on God's green earth is *that*?"

"In a nutshell, it's Elijah Wallace's death scene."

Maple was having déjà vu as she repeated almost verbatim what she'd said to Ben the day before. Charlotte's reaction, however, couldn't have been more different.

"Elijah Wallace's . . . you made a—a—*death dollhouse*?"

"It's not a dollhouse. It's a tool."

"A . . . tool? And Ben Crenshaw knows about this? *Helped* with this?"

Maple exhaled impatiently. "He came to check on me yesterday. I showed it to him and asked for help fashioning the metal pieces. He brought them back a little while ago. Why is this so horrifying to you?"

Charlotte tucked her chin and raised her eyebrows. "It's gruesome, Maple! Shocking and gruesome."

"Look, it's like I told you: I can't shake my feeling that there's more to Elijah Wallace's death. This is my way of working through my concerns, of documenting what happened. I'm sorry you find the replica so unpalatable, but imagine how *I* felt when I stumbled upon the real thing."

Tears formed in Charlotte's eyes, and she gave Maple a quick, fierce hug. "I'm sorry. You're right. I can't imagine how you . . . well, it's a lot to process, especially with everything you've gone through in the last few years. And you have such an analytical lawyer's mind, and such a talent for making miniatures, that I guess this . . . makes sense."

Maple didn't like Charlotte's tone. It sounded as if her friend was trying to talk herself into believing the words she said.

And maybe, a small voice in Maple's head suggested, *you're still mad at her for making you think about why you made so many dollhouses . . .*

"Anyway, thanks for checking on me, but I actually have a lot to do, so . . ."

Charlotte ignored Maple's strong hint that it was time to leave and cocked her head. "Okay, I don't want to hurt your feelings, but I have to ask: Are you sure this is really about Elijah?"

Maple bristled. "He's the one who's dead, isn't he?"

Concern filled Charlotte's wide eyes as she placed a hand on Maple's arm. "You know what I mean. Your brother—"

Maple shook her hand off. "This is *not* about my brother. It isn't the same thing at all."

"Your brother died alone in that jail cell. The Boston cops wrote him off as a drunk. You're understandably bitter about it. I can't help but see parallels here to Elijah Wallace."

At moments like this, Maple cursed her photographic memory. As she had innumerable times since she'd gone to identify her younger brother's body, Maple recalled in perfect detail his white face and still body laid out on the silver slab. She recalled the cops' dismissiveness when she'd pushed for more answers: *"He was alive when you arrested him, but dead in his cell the next morning. How did this happen on your watch?"*

Maple took a deep, shaky breath and pointed at her project. "This is what I need to do, Charlotte. I don't know exactly why, but right now, I really just need to do this."

"All right, Maple," her friend said, but her tone indicated she thought this was anything but. "Take care of yourself. Get some rest. Do something—anything—besides just work on this today."

"I will."

For once, Maple wasn't being too honest—quite the opposite, in fact. Charlotte saw herself out, and Maple went back to work.

CHAPTER 14

Monday morning dawned bright and cold. Mack meowed at the back door while Maple was sipping her morning tea, and she brought him a piece of her toast that she'd set aside. He swished his tail happily and peered hopefully into the house behind her, but Maple gave him a pat on the head, stepped back into the kitchen, and closed the door firmly behind her. Then, she put on her coat and hat, picked up her recently-completed project, and left through the front door, where she loaded her miniature into the wheelbarrow and set off.

Sometime late the previous night, as she'd finished fashioning tiny bales of hay, Maple had decided that simply documenting the scene wasn't enough. Something about the process of re-creating what she saw in her mind's eye compelled her to actually *do* something with it. Bringing the memory out and creating it in the real world for others to see had given her a sense of urgency. After all, good lawyers didn't document details simply for their own sake. They did it to build a case, and Maple believed she'd built a pretty strong case for a murder investigation.

Now, as she turned the corner onto the street where the sheriff's office was located, Maple felt confident she'd made the right decision. Today, in the light of day and in consideration of all the details Maple had painstakingly documented, surely the sheriff would be able to see reason.

After parking her wheelbarrow near the bushes to the side of the main entrance, Maple lifted her model out carefully. With the front folded up, it looked from the outside like a normal doll-house, the carnage within hidden from view. She pulled open the door to the sheriff's office, carefully balancing the miniature on her knee. Once inside, she held her shoulders back and her head high. If she looked confident, she figured, she'd have a better chance of talking her way in.

First, she just had to get past the severe-looking secretary, whose nameplate announced in capitals letter that her name was Mrs. Langley.

"Hello," Maple said. "I'm here to see Sheriff Scott."

Mrs. Langley peered at her over the reading glasses that perched on her long, thin nose. Then, her eyes slid to the nutshell Maple carried. She frowned.

"He doesn't have any appointments this morning."

"But if I could just—"

"You can't."

"He'll want to see me," Maple argued, though she wasn't at all sure this was true. "I have to show him this."

The woman looked up again and cocked her head.

"Oh," she said in a friendlier voice. "You're the dollhouse lady! I've heard about you." Mrs. Langley put down her pen, smiling now.

"I do make dollhouses, yes," Maple said, taken aback.

"I just loved mine when I was a girl," the secretary gushed. "Is that one for Sophie?"

"Sophie?" Maple echoed, confused.

"The sheriff's granddaughter. It's her birthday next week." She stood and made to move out from behind her desk. "May I see it? I bet Sophie will just love it."

Maple opened her mouth but paused when Charlotte's voice spoke inside her head: *"Don't be too honest, Mape."*

Maple gripped the nutshell tighter. "I'm not at all sure the sheriff would want me showing it to you."

That wasn't exactly a lie. It wasn't exactly the truth either. Whatever it was, it got the nosy secretary to retreat.

She put her hands up in a placating gesture. "Of course, of course. I wouldn't want to ruin the surprise."

She disappeared down a short hall behind the desk, and Maple heard a door open and voices murmuring. Her heart jumped into her throat.

The secretary reappeared and said, "The sheriff will see you now."

She gestured down the hall and made a show of covering her eyes when Maple walked past.

Maple was very aware of her heart pounding as she swept into the sheriff's office. She was so nervous she doubted her ability to speak. The sheriff, wearing a polite frown, started to rise out of his chair, his eyes at first focused on the dollhouse she carried.

"Did my wife order—" he started. Then he froze as his eyes slid to her face and recognition dawned. "You!" he said. He fell back into the chair and rubbed his temples. "What do *you* want?"

Maple swallowed despite the lump in her throat and said, "I have something you need to see."

Her voice sounded steadier than her hands looked as she set the nutshell on the desk between them and turned it so they could both see the front.

She swung the front panel down and opened the barn doors, revealing both the tire track imprints and Elijah Wallace's doll swinging back and forth from the hay hoist. For several seconds, the sheriff said nothing. He just stared. Then, he turned to Maple, his eyes flashing.

"What is this?" he growled.

"Elijah Wallace's death scene, in a nutshell," Maple replied crisply. "There are several things I'd like to draw your attention to. You see here—"

"You made this into a *dollhouse*?"

He looked up with an expression of horror and disgust that Maple would have assumed he reserved for murderers. Or chicken thieves.

Maple's stomach swirled uneasily. "It's not a dollhouse. It's a tool to help me show you where your investigation went wrong."

His eyes went dark, and he straightened up to his full considerable height.

Too honest, she thought, too late.

"Get out of my office."

Hot shame spread inside her like wildfire. She'd expected annoyance from the sheriff, but not this.

"But—" Maple started.

"I don't know what you think you're playing at," he said, his voice brimming with barely controlled fury.

He hitched up his belt, which, just as it had Friday night, immediately fell back to exactly the same place. Her shame transformed into indignation. She was taking his job more seriously than he was.

"I'm not 'playing' at anything," Maple said. "There are troubling details you need to consider before you close this case—particularly the gash in the doorframe—just here—and these tire tracks. And the scratches around his wrists point to a struggle, as does the giant bruise on his side. I think someone murdered Elijah Wallace."

The words surprised her. It was the first time she'd said them aloud, and she realized that all her work of the last two days had led her to this conclusion. Now, that word—murder—was out in the world, just like her death scene was. It was a bell Maple couldn't un-ring, even if she wanted to . . . and in spite of the furious look the sheriff gave her, Maple realized she didn't want to.

The sheriff placed his knuckles on the desk and leaned toward her, not looking at the nutshell.

"Well, the case is closed," he said. "Dr. Murphy made a ruling on the cause of death. We're done here."

Maple gaped at him. "Already?" She knew from Dr. Murphy's own seminars that the completion of an autopsy report, including a ruling on official cause of death, typically took far longer than a couple of days.

The sheriff thumped a fist down on his desk. "This isn't your concern!"

"Well, what did he—"

"Get out!" he thundered.

She made a move to pick up her miniature, but the sheriff added, "Now!"

Maple bit back a reply. Based on the sheriff's thundercloud expression, any retort at this moment would've been a bad idea. Having no desire to experience the dubious hospitality of one of the county jail cells, Maple left her creation on the sheriff's desk and hurried out. In the hall, she nearly crashed into Kenny. He'd been standing directly outside the door, and Maple wondered how much he'd overheard. In her other encounters with Kenny, his facial expression had broadcast his emotions quite readily. Now, however, it was unreadable.

He stepped aside, and she continued past him into the small lobby area.

"You work out of the hardware store, don't you?" Mrs. Langley called after her. "Maybe I'll come and order one of your dollhouses!"

CHAPTER 15

By the time she reached the hardware shop, Maple just wanted to put the whole morning out of her head and carry on filling her other orders. She stashed the empty wheelbarrow behind the store and entered through the front door.

Ben was listening to a news update. The newscaster's somber voice recounted details of the recent executions in Nuremberg.

Herman Goering, formerly the second-highest-ranking Nazi, eluded justice by swallowing a potassium cyanide capsule in his cell hours before he was scheduled for the gallows. The ten men who did hang mostly displayed stoic defiance to the end—this in spite of the fact that the hangman used rope that was too short and a trap door that was too small.

Maple felt a jolt in her belly.

The last man to go, Arthur Seyss-Inquart, used his last earthly words to say, "I hope that this execution will be the last act of the tragedy of the Second World War, and that the lesson taken from this world war will be that peace and understanding should exist between peoples. I believe in Germany." From Nuremberg, this is—

Ben switched off the radio.

"He's one to talk," Ben said darkly. 'Peace and understanding,' he says. That man was directly responsible for executing hundreds of political activists and throwing thousands of people into concentration camps."

Maple's sense of distress from her encounter with the sheriff deepened. Any news of the trials and subsequent executions left her cold, understandably—these men were horrible Nazi war criminals, and hearing their crimes recounted was chilling. She understood Ben's disgust at Seys-Inquart's final words too.

"I wonder whether they should have broadcast that," she said, frowning. "Sharing his final words like that gives him a solemnity and a . . . I don't know, a cachet he doesn't deserve."

Ben nodded. Maple pulled the coat tighter around herself. Clearly wanting to change the subject, Ben asked how her morning had been. Frank ambled over to sniff her ankles, and Ben listened with raised eyebrows as she recounted her decision to bring the nutshell to Sheriff Scott, and the subsequent disaster in his office.

"And so ends my career as a detective," she said in what she hoped was a lighthearted tone, "and on the very same day it began, to boot."

"I'm sorry. It's not right that he won't listen to you. You make some excellent points," Ben said.

She felt an awkward surge of gratitude.

"What was Dr. Murphy's finding for the cause of death?" he asked.

Maple shrugged. "The sheriff wouldn't tell me, but I assume suicide."

Ben nodded. "I wonder if you should show it to Dr. Murphy." Ben looked thoughtful. "After all, you have that professional history with him, and he clearly respects you."

She shook her head. "No, I don't want to waste his time. Plus, I don't have it anymore."

"Where is it?" Ben asked.

"Probably in the garbage. I left it in the sheriff's office."

Maple's heart gave a funny lurch. She pictured all the dolls she'd created over the years, perched silently in their wooden houses, surrounded by furniture and wallpaper, as seconds ticked by and minutes slipped into hours, days, years. Were they, in fact, any better off than Elijah and his nutshell in the trash can? They were displayed carefully in her home, but no one saw them besides her. No one played with them. They simply . . . existed. Maple had always been proud of her ability to craft miniatures, but now she was forced to wonder whether she'd inadvertently made her own life small too. Here she was, thirty-one years old, a failed lawyer and a bankrupt widow. What did it matter if she could make pretty dollhouses or "jarring" miniature death scenes if she couldn't pay her mortgage?

The fact remained, however, that making the dollhouses was her only viable path forward—financially, at least. Though her profits seemed like a drop in the bucket, at least it was a start. There was no use wallowing over things she couldn't change.

Ben frowned. "I'm sorry. That's a shame. You worked so hard on it." Then he looked thoughtful. "Hey, what are you calling it, anyway? 'Dollhouse' doesn't seem quite right."

"I've started thinking of it as my 'nutshell.'" Maple blushed, wondering whether this sounded silly. "You know, Elijah Wallace's death scene . . ."

". . . in a nutshell," Ben finished. "I like that."

Her shoulders released tension she hadn't known they were carrying.

"Thanks again for your help." She found she was unable to look Ben in the eyes. She concentrated her gaze on the large box of ribbons on the table in front of her. "I better get to work."

"I'm sorry, Maple. You tried."

Maple knew he meant for the words to be comforting, to indicate that he was on her side, but all she heard was confirmation of her failure. She waited for the sound of Ben's cane moving back across the floor. Several beats later, it came, and she looked up. His head was bowed and he moved slowly. Maple felt a pang. He'd been nice enough to help her, and now she felt she'd let him down too.

Despite her existential misgivings and the fact that working on dollhouses was more or less the last thing she felt like doing at the moment, Maple had committed to filling orders for customers, so she busied herself preparing the materials to finalize her next dollhouse, which was to be a birthday gift for a four-year-old girl. Her heart heavy, she began by creating two little girl dolls with red and pink dresses. Her hand still stung a little from where the barn splinters had pierced her skin, and she navigated carefully to avoid aggravating the injury.

She was just finishing up the first doll's dress when the bell over the door tinkled. She looked up and saw Deputy Rawlings enter the store, remove his hat, and move toward her table. He stopped in front of her and flashed a small smile.

"Mrs. Bishop," he said, dipping his head in greeting. "Sorry to interrupt you, but is there a private place we can talk? It's about a police matter."

Maple's mind swirled with anxious possibilities. The deputy hadn't been in the office that morning, but the sheriff must've told him about her visit. Her cheeks burned. Had the sheriff sent his deputy to . . . what? Arrest her? But, no, if she were being arrested, he'd have simply taken her into custody, not asked for a private meeting. And besides, Maple thought, getting herself whipped up into righteous indignation, what law had she broken? One couldn't be arrested simply for offending the sheriff with a dollhouse.

Maple turned and said in a voice that sounded much more calm than she felt, "Ben, could we use your office?"

Ben nodded, and Maple led the deputy to the cramped room behind the counter. Ben watched with concern. She tried to fake a reassuring smile but could tell it fell flat. Still, it felt nice to know there was someone in her corner.

Deputy Rawlings closed the door behind himself and flashed another tight-lipped smile. Then, he said, "Ma'am, we received a complaint about you threatening a man with a firearm."

Maple's jaw dropped. Harry Needles? This was about Harry *Needles*? He'd trespassed on her property and then complained to the police about *her*?

Rawlings held up a palm. "Now, before I say what I came here to say, I'd like to tell you something, but I'd need you to promise you'll keep it between the two of us. Can you do that?"

Taken aback, Maple nodded.

Rawlings leaned in and said in a conspiratorial whisper, "I can entirely sympathize with the desire to point a gun at Harry Needles. That man is more annoying than the most persistent mosquito, and he's louder too."

Before Maple could decide how to react to this statement, Rawlings pulled back and resumed his businesslike demeanor and tone.

"Now, I have to tell you that I am issuing you an official warning: stay away from Mr. Needles and please refrain from aiming any weapons at him in the future."

The corner of Rawlings's mouth twitched, and Maple realized the deputy was barely holding back a laugh. Her eyebrows knitted together as she tried to work out an appropriate response.

Finally, she said, "It's my husband's gun. I don't even know how to use it. I . . . I don't know what came over me. He wouldn't get off my front stoop, and I knew the rifle was right there in the front closet, and—"

Now, Rawlings held up both palms toward Maple. "Can you promise me you'll comply with that official warning?"

Maple blinked. "Yes."

"Okay, then. My business here is done."

The smile the deputy had been holding back broke across his face then, and he reached out and shook Maple's hand, which Maple noticed bore a long scratch from the top of his thumb all the way to his wrist. He saw her eyes flash on it and said simply, "My cat." Maple nodded, wondering whether the orange tabby would be there to greet her when she got home later. She hoped so.

"Maybe Mr. Needles will think twice from now on before he goes harassing his fellow citizens in their homes," Rawlings said

Rawlings thanked her for her time and showed himself out. As Maple watched him go, she could've sworn she heard him chuckling to himself as the door closed behind him.

She shook her head at Ben. "What a strange day."

She returned to her station, finished the doll she'd been working on, and started on the dress for the second one. When the bell above the door tinkled again a half hour later, she didn't look up—at least not until a throat cleared and a voice in front of her said, "Mrs. Bishop?"

Kenny stood in front of her. He held her nutshell out in front of him. Maple's heart lifted at the sight of it, still intact and most definitely not in the trash heap. She poked herself with the needle she was holding and dropped the dress she'd been sewing.

"Sorry," Kenny said, his ears reddening.

"What are you doing here?" she asked before popping her pricked finger into her mouth.

He put the nutshell down on her table and looked around. Ben, the only other person in the store, was behind the desk, on a phone call.

"I wanted to give this back to you," he said.

Maple pulled her finger out of her mouth, her forehead wrinkled in confusion.

"The sheriff told you to—"

"He told me to get rid of it," Kenny said, pulling off his hat and holding it at his side. "He didn't specify how. May I speak frankly, ma'am?"

The young officer eyed her more cagily than she would've thought him capable of doing. She nodded, suddenly at a loss for words.

He leaned in closer. "I think you're onto something. This may only be my first death investigation, but I have common sense. There are plenty of people who wanted Elijah Wallace dead. You're right that the gash and the tire tracks should be examined, to say nothing of the giant bruise on his side and the marks around his wrists, which look like rope burns to me. Maybe someone tied his hands against his will, and he struggled. But as you heard this morning, Dr. Murphy made a finding on the cause of death, and I found out an hour ago that they're closing the case."

He must've ruled it a suicide, then. Maple watched Kenny's knuckles go white as he clutched his hat in front of him with both hands. Conflicting emotions swirled inside her: elation that Kenny believed her, mixed with dismay at his confirmation that the investigation (such as it had been) was over practically before it had begun. Disappointment pricked her belly as she realized Dr. Murphy had gone with the surface-level conclusion rather than stepping back to consider all the possibilities. Then, she shook her head. If the professionals felt it was suicide, who was she to argue?

"Why did you bring this back to me?" Maple finally asked. "You could've just thrown it away."

Ken met her eyes. "Because someone needs to investigate. I can't do it. Not right under my—the sheriff's nose, and not when he's already closed the case."

"I'm no investigator," Maple protested.

Kenny nodded vigorously. "Oh yes, you are. I was at the scene. The level of detail you put into this"—he gestured at the nutshell—"well, it's incredible, ma'am, if you don't mind my saying so. You pay attention. You notice things. And you care."

His neck flushed red to match his ears. Maple looked down at her pricked finger just in time to watch a drop of blood plop onto the doll's face. She picked it up and dabbed the spot with her work apron.

He continued, "I could help you, but it'd have to be under the radar. If we can gather enough evidence, my unc—the sheriff—will have to reopen the case."

Kenny's boldness was short-lived. Suddenly, he seemed to find his shoes extremely interesting.

"Were you about to say 'my uncle'? You're related to Sheriff Scott?"

He rubbed the toe of one shoe over the top of the other, looking like a bashful kid again.

"Yeah. My mom's his sister."

Maple wasn't sure how to take this information. She scrutinized Kenny's earnest, bashful face.

"Why are you doing this? This could end your career practically before it's even begun."

Kenny's eyes flashed. "I believe in truth and justice, ma'am. For all. That's what my father went over there to fight for. If we don't take a stand for truth and justice, then we're no better than those Nazis." He balled his right hand into a fist. "And we *are* better, ma'am. I just *know* we are. We've *got* to be."

He practically whispered those last words, and Maple recalled her mixed emotions at the news of the hanged Nazis. She wondered what had become of Kenny's father. Had he returned from the war?

Kenny pointed at her nutshell. "We might be two small people in a small town, Mrs. Bishop, but we can make a difference. We can . . ." he looked at the nutshell and then back at her.

Maple recalled Charlotte's observation when she'd seen Mrs. Murphy's dollhouse.

Before she could stop herself, she finished the sentence for him: "Find what's big in what's small."

Tears shining in the corners of his eyes, Kenny said, "Exactly."

Uncomfortable with his raw emotion, Maple averted her gaze. Giving him a moment to compose himself, she looked down at the doll again and thought about what it represented: a way out of her financial predicament. Maybe (eventually) if she was very lucky, it could even represent a way for her to support herself—to have a comfortable life, not a "just-scraping-by" existence. And, after all, didn't she owe it to her mother, who'd worked so hard to give Maple a shot at escaping the city slum, to achieve that kind of life? Didn't she owe it to Jamie, who'd never gotten the chance to get out himself?

She looked down at her worktable, where the nutshell sat next to the sweet dollhouse in progress for the little girl's birthday: Which path would she follow? Maple had always had a strong moral compass. It was important to her to do the right thing. Sometimes, she was so devoted to this deeply ingrained sense of justice that it cost her friendships. After all, she'd quit Ginger Comstock's sewing circle after one meeting because the ladies there gossiped viciously, even though quitting had been her death knell in Elderberry's society of ladies. This time, if she stubbornly stood her ground and attracted the ire of the sheriff, the stakes were much higher: her very livelihood could be destroyed.

She closed her eyes. Her priority needed to be earning money, not Mapleing about with a side project that upset everyone. After all, she was already enough of a pariah in this town. For once, she'd follow Charlotte's advice and work on catching her flies with honey. She was going to forget about investigating this death. She'd return to creating pristine scenes of domestic bliss. Those were what brought people joy. Those were what people wanted to see, what they needed to believe in. Those would eventually, probably, make Maple enough money to survive. And survival was what mattered now, she told herself—not death.

When Maple heard Kenny clear his throat, she opened her eyes.

"I'm sorry. My answer is no."

CHAPTER 16

Maple watched Kenny's back as he exited the store, his shoulders slumped. She told herself it was ridiculous to feel guilty about refusing his offer. Turning her gaze to the nutshell, Maple fingered the rope that held Elijah. She pushed Elijah's chest and watched his body sway back and forth. She thought of her brother and then of Odysseus's maids, their feet dancing in midair. Then she thought of the hundreds of thousands of Americans besides Bill who hadn't come home, and finally of the Nazis just hanged in Nuremberg.

She'd made the right decision—the *sensible* decision. Still, though, her heart hurt as she closed the flap on her nutshell and tucked it behind her workstation. She picked up the doll she'd been working on before Kenny came in. The bloodstain from her pricked finger was no longer visible to the naked eye, but Maple knew the taint wasn't really gone. The little girl who received the doll would never know it—would probably play with it happily for years, never having any idea—but Maple knew traces of blood would be there forever.

The doorbell tinkled. As she swiveled her head from the table to the door, she barely had time to register her feeling of hope that it was Kenny returning again and refusing to take no for her answer. Instead, Ginger Comstock swooped in.

Maple didn't even try to hide her groan.

Ginger made a beeline for the craft table, tugging the hand of her eight-year-old daughter, Camille, who trailed behind her. Behind Camille was a trio of Ginger's cronies, eyes beady as they watched their fearless leader at work.

"Is it true?" Ginger's overly personal way of talking made it sound like you'd been her best friend for years. Maple hated that.

Ginger's green eyes gleamed, and her curls bounced a few times even after she halted in front of the table. She leaned forward, resting her hands near the dolls. Maple made a point of looking at Camille first and greeted the girl. Only then did she turn to Ginger.

"Is *what* true?"

Maple slid the dolls away from Ginger's fingers, which she began drumming on the table. Camille followed the dolls with her eyes. Ginger raised her eyebrows and pursed her lips.

"That his death was accidental?"

The floor seemed to tilt underneath Maple. "What?"

Ginger exhaled impatiently. "I heard Dr. Murphy ruled Elijah Wallace's death an accident. Was it?"

By this time, Ginger's cloying perfume had settled over Maple like an unwelcome cloud. Like Ginger herself, the scent she wore was over the top—fake gardenias, liberally applied. Maple's mind spun. Could Ginger be telling the truth? But how could that be? How on earth could Dr. Murphy have arrived at the conclusion that Elijah Wallace had hung himself from his own barn rafters *accidentally*?

Maple's tongue felt three sizes too big for her mouth. "Are you sure?"

Ginger arched an eyebrow. "Oh, so you *didn't* know."

The trio of ladies began whispering behind their hands.

Maple threw up her own hands into the air. "What makes you think *I'd* know anything?"

Ginger narrowed her eyes, and Maple could see the wheels turning. The woman glanced at her daughter, who was still gazing shyly at the doll. Then she arched her eyebrows and leaned in.

"You found the body," she hissed before she straightened up. "And I saw the officer leaving here just minutes ago!"

Maple's eyes slid back to the little girl, a miniature replica of her mother, except with blond ringlets instead of red, who peeked up at Maple and quickly looked back at the doll again. Maple returned her gaze to Ginger.

"The deputy was simply returning something that belongs to me."

"Well, what was it? I saw him walk back out holding the same box he was holding when he walked in."

Maple's good intentions evaporated. She threw up her hands. "None of your business, that's what it was! Do you *ever* keep your nose where it belongs? Is your life really so small you have to fill every waking minute delving into other people's private affairs?"

So much for honey instead of vinegar. Maple's face was hot and her breathing heavy. Camille flinched and retreated behind her mother's back. Ginger, however, looked perfectly calm. Positively serene. Her eyes glittered, and when she spoke, her voice was silky smooth.

"Really, Mrs. Bishop, there's no need to shout. You've frightened my daughter. I'm sure you wouldn't want word to get out that the dollhouse woman scares children. That wouldn't be good for business, now would it?"

The ladies stopped whispering and stared at Maple, waiting for her response. Then, she met Ginger's triumphant gaze again, realizing the other woman had gotten exactly what she wanted. By allowing her to get under her skin, Maple had played right into her hands.

Technically, Maple reminded herself, she'd only promised to refrain from aiming weapons at Harry Needles in the future, so that meant Ginger was fair game, right?

Swallowing her rage, Maple modulated her tone. "What makes you so concerned about Elijah Wallace anyway?"

Ginger straightened up and gave Maple a haughty look. "I'll have you know that Angela Wallace is my good friend."

Maple barely contained a snort. She doubted Ginger had ever even spoken to mousy, shy Angela Wallace.

"Then why are you here pumping me for information instead of comforting your *good friend* who just lost her husband?"

Ginger's cheeks flamed as red as her hair. "Well, it just so happens I'm helping her keep tabs on the investigation."

"She's the next of kin. She's going to get all her information straight from the sheriff."

Ginger straightened up and abruptly changed the subject. "I left you cookies."

"Oh," Maple said, raising her eyebrows at the other woman's verbal sidestep. "Was that you?"

To keep herself from grinning triumphantly, Maple picked up the doll Camille had been eyeing and held it out to her. "Here. This is for you."

The girl's eyes brightened as she took the doll, but Ginger immediately grabbed it and threw it back on the table.

"I'm not buying that."

"I'm not selling it to you. It's a gift for Camille."

"We don't need your charity."

"I never said you did."

They held each other's stares for a long moment. Ginger looked away first but picked up the doll and shoved it into the little girl's hand. She turned to leave, yanking her daughter's arm so hard that Camille nearly tipped over. Her cronies, whispering to one another, turned to follow her. Ginger called over her shoulder to Maple.

"Well, I must say I'm disappointed. I thought you'd be more helpful."

Maple swatted the air in front of her trying to dispel the cloud of artificial gardenias and said, just loud enough for the other woman to hear, "I'm sorry you thought that."

There was a hitch in Ginger's step, and for a moment Maple was sure she'd turn around and have the last word. But she didn't. Camille looked over her shoulder and mouthed, "Thank you," clutching her new doll. Maple smiled and gave her a small wave. Then Ginger yanked open the door, and with a cheerful tinkle of the bell, they were gone.

Maple looked down at the lone doll on her worktable. She'd have to start the second one from scratch and work double time to get it made before her paying customer came to collect it, but she didn't regret giving away the doll to little Camille.

An *accident*?

Maple replayed her interaction with Kenny in her mind, realizing he'd never said the death had been ruled a suicide; Maple had inferred it—incorrectly, it now seemed—when he'd said the investigation was closed.

Ben made his way over to the table.

"Do you think she's right? That Dr. Murphy ruled it an accidental death?"

Ben leaned a crutch against her table and rubbed his chin. "Much as it pains me to say it, Ginger usually knows what she's talking about when it comes to stuff like this—you know, straightforward information. And even though I usually disagree with her opinions about things, she's got a real knack for breaking news when it happens. Harry Needles could learn a thing or two from her."

"But how is that even possible?" Maple threw her hands up. "How could a person *accidentally* hang themselves?"

Maple positively itched to get up and go, but where? She certainly wasn't welcome at the sheriff's office. Kenny was too far away now to chase down by foot. Then it hit her: Dr. Murphy's house! If she walked fast, she could be there in ten minutes.

Suddenly, she realized Ben was staring at her. "Those are good questions, but it seems to me the doctor and the sheriff must've been able to answer them satisfactorily. Otherwise, why would they have closed the case?"

Maple had no answer. Her eyes flew to the nutshell under the table. Tucked away like that, it seemed to represent the case itself: closed. The adrenaline left her body as quickly as it had come. She sank back into her seat.

"I'll say this," Ben said mildly. "That Ginger Comstock is a piece of work." He turned, leaning heavily on his crutch. On his way back to the cash register, he added, under his breath, "But she makes a darn fine cookie."

CHAPTER 17

After Ginger stormed out, Maple made quick work of finishing the project she'd taken on for the custom furniture, including the feverish creation of a new doll from scratch. Despite the knot in her stomach from the morning's encounters with Kenny and Ginger, she finished just in time. She loaded the house, furniture, and two dolls into her wheelbarrow and made the delivery to a house a few streets away. The customer was thrilled with the results.

Energized and with three more dollars in her apron pocket, Maple wheeled around to start back toward the store. A gust of wind kicked up, and she stopped to put on her gloves. She pulled one of her gloves out of her pocket, but though she rummaged around, she couldn't find its mate anywhere. She yanked the glove back off her left hand and shoved it in her pocket again, annoyed at this uncharacteristic carelessness and distressed to think she might've lost half of the last gift Bill had ever given her.

As she rounded the corner onto Main Street, Maple nearly ran over a petite blond woman.

"Oh! I didn't see you there," Maple said, halting. "Sorry."

Maple attempted to maneuver around the blonde, but to her surprise, the woman didn't move.

"Are you Maple Bishop?" the woman asked.

Maple stopped and looked into the other woman's face. On closer examination, she looked very young—barely more than a girl. And as Maple watched, she pulled a notebook and pencil out of her raincoat pocket. Maple tensed up.

"Who wants to know?" Maple asked, narrowing her eyes.

"Ella Henderson, ma'am. I'm with the *County Tribune*."

The image of Harry Needles trying to muscle his way past Charlotte was fresh in Maple's memory. So was her official warning from the sheriff's deputy. She grimaced.

"I thought Harry was the only reporter for the *Tribune*."

Ella smiled, and for the first time Maple detected a trace of nervousness. "Oh, Mr. Needles was the only one for a long time, but circulation is growing after the war, and the editors want to expand the reporting to include more feel-good feature pieces, particularly to appeal to our increasing number of female readers." It sounded as if she were cheerfully reciting a script. "So, here I am. You—you *are* Maple Bishop, right?"

Maple frowned. "I don't understand what any of this has to do with me."

Ella brightened. "Oh, you're a big story, Mrs. Bishop! Everyone's curious about you."

Alarm surged through Maple's body. Was she going to be forever punished by other people's attention simply because she'd been in the wrong place at the wrong time? Because she'd had the bad luck of being the one to discover a man's dead body?

"I'm not interested in talking to you. Ask Harry Needles how eager I was to speak with him. I have nothing to say about Elijah Wallace's death."

Ella arched an eyebrow. "Oh, Mr. Needles told me all about that."

Was there anyone left in Elderberry who didn't know all about it? Maple supposed this was what happened when you picked a fight with a reporter.

Ella cleared her throat. "But you don't understand what I—"

"I said no."

Maple tried to steer the wheelbarrow around the young woman, but Ella Henderson was quick on her feet and shadowed her movements.

"Oh, please, Mrs. Bishop," the young woman said, "It's not about that. Please just give me a minute of your time. Oh, I'll be in such trouble . . ." She wrung her hands.

Maple studied Ella Henderson more closely. The reporter stood at maybe five foot two and probably didn't even weigh a hundred pounds soaking wet. Not exactly intimidating. And, besides, she looked to be on the verge of tears. Maybe because she'd turned down Kenny's earnest request for help, maybe because she'd seen the disappointment in Ben's eyes, or maybe because she'd discovered she had a secret fan club based around her aiming a rifle at Harry, Maple decided to hear the young reporter out.

She sighed. "I'll give you one minute. Explain yourself."

Ella's relief was obvious in the smile she flashed. "Well, ma'am, I heard about your new business, making and selling dollhouses here at the hardware store, and I'd love to write a story about it. It's a real human-interest piece—you know: 'Local widow reinvents herself after the war' and whatnot—and I'll bet it'd drum up some business for you too."

It took a moment for this to sink in: Ella wasn't interested in Maple's role in discovering Wallace's body.

"How is there . . . public interest in my business already? I just started it."

"It's a small town, Mrs. Bishop. Word travels fast," Ella said, a note of hope creeping into her voice.

"Does Harry Needles know you're here?" Maple asked.

Ella suddenly seemed to find her own shoes extremely interesting. "Not exactly."

Maple considered the benefits of a "human-interest piece," as Ella had called it, and how it could translate into more sales and more money. She had justified saying no to Kenny's proposition so she could focus on building her dollhouse business; here was a chance for free publicity. But, as a deeply private person by nature, could Maple convince herself to be comfortable with the idea that, in order to publicize her business, she'd have to publicize *herself* as well? And how would the residents of Elderberry, most of whom hadn't exactly welcomed her with open arms, feel about it?

Then again, could she really pass up an opportunity to stick it to Harry?

"I'll think about it. Can you come by the store in the morning? I'll have a decision for you by then."

Ella nodded, thanked her more profusely than the situation warranted, and scampered off.

CHAPTER 18

Later that afternoon, Maple dropped the wheelbarrow off at her house, changed into her sturdiest shoes, and headed for her favorite trail. No one had been more surprised than Maple herself when she'd discovered a passion for hiking. Back in Boston, she'd always enjoyed long, solitary walks through the city. She could lose herself in the crowds, among the mishmash of history and progress that was her city. There was so much to look at and think about. There were so many dreams and possibilities coexisting right alongside poverty and filth.

One of the first things she'd thought when she'd seen Elderberry for the first time was how much she'd miss those city walks. Her heart had sunk in inverse proportion to Bill's joy as they drove down Main Street for the first time, Bill excitedly extolling the charm of small-town life while Maple tried to hide her dismay at how . . . well, how *small* it seemed. She told herself not to be disappointed. After all, she'd dreamed of escaping the city for as long as she could remember. It would just take some time to adjust.

While Bill saw patients, Maple explored her new hometown. Soon she discovered that hiking the trails near their house brought her a different kind of joy than walking in the city had. Maple grew to appreciate the quiet of the woods. As she walked among the trees and ponds, she felt a sense of peace settle over her—plus, when she blew her nose at the end of a day in Elderberry, her handkerchief didn't turn black with soot the way it had in Boston.

Today, she chose the longest path, knowing she'd need more time and effort to clear her head. The peak of foliage season had passed, and her feet crunched through dried leaves on the path. But a few leaves still clung stubbornly to branches, as though deep down they knew winter was coming but refused to give in to it.

Maple understood how they felt. As her feet moved, her heart rate increased and her breathing got faster. She liked how alive it made her feel. Walking through the woods like this was the only time her orderly brain allowed itself to wander. Maple knew that she needed that today as much as she needed the physical exercise.

She turned a corner onto the first of several switchbacks on this trail, lowering her shoulders and shortening her stride to mount the incline. With each consecutive switchback, her muscles pushed and her breathing became more rapid. She stopped abruptly at the top of the trail and looked down on the town where she'd come to start over. She shivered. Here in Elderberry, she'd thought she could move past her mother's and brother's deaths and transcend her rough childhood. She'd expected to have it all: a good marriage and a career that challenged and fulfilled her.

Things hadn't exactly worked out according to plan.

She breathed in the mountain air deeply and then exhaled, enjoying the way it filled her lungs and cleansed her spirit. Standing up here with this bird's-eye perspective was oddly comforting. She could see everything, but from a safe distance. She found her own house, nestled in a neighborhood almost directly below her.

From up here, she didn't have to worry about what Ginger Comstock was saying about her or whether the ladies from the knitting circle were offended that the uppity big-city doctor's wife had chosen, yet again, not to join their weekly meeting.

From up here, her financial woes seemed far away.

From up here, everything—houses, cars, trees—looked miniature.

Manageable.

Unbidden, her gaze traveled to the Wallaces' farm. An image of the tire tracks she'd seen both outside and inside the barn crystallized in her mind. Had they been made by Elijah's truck, or someone else's? Maple yearned to compare the tread on the Wallaces' truck to the pattern of the mud—and in that moment, gazing down on the scene from way up on the hill, Maple knew, deep down, that she wasn't finished with Elijah Wallace just yet.

Or maybe, she thought, wrapping Jamie's coat more tightly around herself, Elijah Wallace wasn't done with *her* just yet. Maple realized she wouldn't be able to rest, or even to fully move on with her own life, until she examined every loose end, chased down every lead, and put the messy details of Elijah Wallace's death into as much order as was possible in such a situation.

Her eyes traveled across the landscape to a local cemetery, and she thought of the rubbings she'd taken of her mother's and brother's headstones when she'd wanted a tangible memory of their final resting places to travel with her to her new home in Vermont. Maple thought of how lonely Angela Wallace must feel. How isolated. Maple, of all people, knew what that felt like.

Suddenly, she also realized there was something she could do about it. Her conscience pricked; she knew full well that her idea was a double-edged sword, allowing her to provide comfort to a fellow grieving widow while also satisfying her own curiosity about details of her husband's death. Then, an idea stopped her in her tracks: Was she no better than Ginger Comstock, who brought cookies as a thinly veiled excuse to seek gossip?

No, Maple decided as she turned and began the hike back down the mountain, she was most definitely not the same as Ginger. And when she got home, she was too busy working on her new project to probe that question any further.

CHAPTER 19

Though she worked late into the night, Maple awoke energized on Tuesday morning. After her morning ritual of tea and toast, she stood back and examined her work from the previous evening. The repaired dollhouse closely resembled its pre-accident self. She'd removed the cracked back wall and replaced it with a new piece of plywood. Then she'd restored all the interior walls to their previous condition, painting most of them and repairing the rose-patterned wallpaper in the living room. She'd also made a new brunette doll. She wasn't sure why, but she felt a deep attachment to the one she'd left propped on Bill's desk. That doll had seen her through the night after she'd found Elijah's body, and Maple had decided to allow herself to indulge this emotional attachment and keep the doll. Angela would never know the difference.

She loaded the newly repaired dollhouse into the wheelbarrow and set off, walking even more quickly than normal as she retraced her steps from Friday evening. This time, when she walked by the Mooreland place, her heart leaped into her throat: Russell Mooreland himself was in his yard, moving hay with a pitchfork just outside his barn. He stopped when he saw her, and

Maple, through no conscious decision of her own, stopped too, her feet suddenly cemented to the ground. It hit her suddenly that he was a real person, not some caricature. It was a big deal to wonder—aloud, to the sheriff—whether someone had committed murder.

Mooreland moved toward her, still carrying the pitchfork. As he came closer, she was very aware of his burliness and his cold eyes. His frown lines were so deep they looked like they'd been permanently carved into his weather-beaten face. She briefly considered fleeing, but before her brain and her feet could agree on a plan, he was right in front of her. She tried to keep her eyes on his face rather than on the sharp tool he carried.

"Can I help you?"

He stabbed his pitchfork into the cold ground; Maple could feel, even through the soles of her shoes, how hard the earth was, and noted the effortlessness with which he had pierced it. Russell Mooreland was a strong man—one who Maple couldn't help but think was more than physically capable of forcing Elijah Wallace up into the hayloft against his will.

This close, she saw that his face and forearms were covered in horrible red welts. Those, she was sure, had not been there when she'd witnessed the fight last Wednesday. Maple's heart beat faster.

"Can I help you?" he asked again, but his tone had a hard edge to it as he crossed his arms and fixed her with a stare. "We don't get too many lost folks wandering around up this way."

Maple could tell he didn't recognize her from outside the grocer's. She located her voice. "Oh, I'm not lost. I'm just delivering this to Mrs. Wallace," she said, pointing unnecessarily to the Wallaces' farmhouse.

A dark storm cloud settled over Mooreland's face, making the red welts stand out even more.

"I'll just be on my way, then," Maple said.

Every nerve in her body screamed at her to escape quickly, but she forced herself to move at a normal pace when she picked up her wheelbarrow handles again. She fought the urge to look back over her shoulder, but she felt Mooreland's eyes burning into her back as she put distance between herself and the farmer.

This time, when she paused at the top of the Wallaces' driveway, several things were different from how they'd been on Friday: smoke curled out of the chimney, and Wallace's truck was parked in the driveway.

Perfect.

The goats appeared at the edge of their fence and bleated insistently, just as they had Friday night. She glanced at the house but saw no sign of movement within. Her heart rate picking up, she moved toward the truck and crouched down behind it, on the far side so she'd be blocked from view should Mrs. Wallace emerge suddenly from the house. She placed the dollhouse on the ground and examined the rear driver's side tire, noting the interlocking pattern imprinted on the rubber and the location of the wear on the treads.

Quickly, she moved closer to the barn to look at the tracks on the ground. She studied them carefully, working to separate the ones that had been there before she discovered the body from the ones on the police car that had driven over them. The bottom set was distinctly wider than the tires of the sheriff's car, and there was evidence it had skidded to a halt. The tracks curved and the imprint became smudged as though the car had made a sudden turn just before stopping.

Crouching, Maple followed the tracks and realized they continued right into the barn. Peering through the light covering of hay at the threshold, she could see evidence of muddy tire tracks on the cement floor. She knew that neither Sheriff Scott's nor Kenny's cars had come in this far. And after a minute's examination, she was certain: Elijah Wallace's truck had not left those imprints. Based on the pattern she could see more clearly now, a different vehicle had made those tracks, and based on the tire width, she was willing to bet it had been a truck.

Just not the one that belonged to the dead man.

So, what had another truck been doing parked partly inside the Wallaces' barn? Moments ago, she'd seen Russell Mooreland's truck parked in front of his own barn next door, and it was a bigger than average model with a bumper that was higher up than that on most vehicles. Maple figured it was definitely a contender for the truck that had left the gash in the Wallaces' barn doorframe.

Maple pulled a pencil and paper out of Jamie's jacket pocket and set to work. She placed the paper over a clear section of the track and swiftly moved the pencil over it, capturing the shape and scope of the tracks just as she'd done on her brother and mother's headstones. Heart in her throat, she tucked her supplies back into her pocket. If she ever got a chance to take a close look at Russell Mooreland's truck, now she'd have something to compare it with.

A shiver ran down Maple's spine as she straightened up. Another furtive glance at the house told her Angela Wallace was not coming out. Maple decided to chance one more look at the gash.

She realized the doors were ajar in nearly the same way they'd been when she'd found Elijah's body on Friday. Eyeing the tracks again, she could see that the truck would have been very close to this side of the door. She cocked her head and did some mental calculations. It looked to her like the gash was at just about the exact height where a truck's bumper would be. She stood next to the gash and leaned her back against the edge of the doorframe, remembering when her mother used to mark her height on the kitchen wall when she was a child. She took mental note of exactly how far up her leg the gash measured and stepped away again.

Before she could stop herself, she tried to push the door closed. It wouldn't latch, and she realized the gash was sticking out just enough to prevent the doors from closing fully. As she studied the latch, she became aware of a buzzing above her.

Three yellowjackets dive-bombed her from just above the doors. Startled, Maple stepped back and nearly knocked over the dollhouse. When they had dispersed, she peered up and saw a paper nest clinging to the rafters just out of sight. It had been late enough the last time she'd been here that the wasps must've been asleep.

She was relieved to have avoided being stung. She hated the sharp, burning sensation and the inevitable red welts—about to bend down and retrieve the dollhouse, she paused as she recalled the angry red welts on Mooreland's body. Her skin tingled.

She picked up the dollhouse, made her way to the front door, and knocked. Angela Wallace stuck her head out, through the threshold between the kitchen and mudroom, with a quizzical look. Upon recognizing Maple, she came to the front door and unlatched it. Maple noticed the other woman was wearing an overcoat, which seemed odd since she was in the house.

"Mrs. Wallace," Maple said, "I'm so sorry for your loss."

"Thank you," Angela said. "I heard you were the one who found him. I'm sorry you had to go through that. I was away visiting my sister when he—when it happened."

They stood awkwardly for a moment, and Maple realized it was her turn to speak again.

"Oh," she said, feeling her cheeks redden, "Yes, well—thanks. And . . . you're welcome."

Maple's tongue felt too big for her mouth. She thrust the dollhouse at Angela. "It was damaged, but I managed to fix it up and thought you might like to have it."

Angela's pale blue eyes lit up with childlike delight. "Look at the rose wallpaper! It's so pretty!"

Maple's awkwardness lessened. "I'm glad you like it."

"Oh, thank you. I just can't tell you how much this . . ." Angela trailed off and started again. "I didn't exactly have a very happy childhood, and my old dollhouse was an escape for me. My sister and I could play with our dolls and lose ourselves in their pretend world and—well, anyway, you have no idea how much this means."

The other woman gazed lovingly at the house. When Angela looked up at Maple again, it was with regret.

"I'd invite you in, but I'm about to go to town for an appointment."

She spoke shyly, and Maple realized that she wasn't accustomed to having visitors.

"Oh, please don't worry. I need to get back to work anyway."

"What's it like?" Angela asked, her eyes wide.

Maple arched an eyebrow. "What's *what* like?"

"Having a career. Supporting yourself."

The other woman's voice was filled with awe. Maple blinked. She'd been too busy figuring out where her next meal was coming from to consider what supporting herself was like. And besides, making dollhouses wasn't a *career*, not the way being a doctor or lawyer was a career.

Was it?

"Oh," Maple said. "Well . . ." but she couldn't think of anything to say.

"Never mind. I didn't mean to put you on the spot. I'm just impressed with what you're doing. Your husband died in the war, right?"

Maple nodded.

"I'm sorry. Now you and I are both women alone, but I'm not sure I'm going to be able to stand on my own two feet like you." She averted her eyes. Maple's neck prickled uncomfortably. "Anyway. Let me go put this down, and then I can give you a ride back to town," Angela said. "Oh! And what do I owe you?"

"Oh—"

Maple felt foolish for not having considered that this issue might come up. Before she could reply, Angela spoke again.

"A dollar fifty. I remember. Hold on a minute."

Angela disappeared into the kitchen and returned a minute later without the dollhouse, but with a neatly folded dollar and two quarters, which she handed to Maple.

"Oh, I don't feel right—" Maple started.

Angela waved her concern away and picked up the truck keys from a nail near the mudroom door.

"I insist on paying you for your work. It's the least I can do after how Elijah treated you that day in the store. And after you . . ."

She trailed off and looked over Maple's shoulder out to the barn. Angela Wallace was still a young woman—much younger than her husband, who Maple guessed had to have been in his late forties at the time of his death. She was probably younger than Maple herself. Presumably, Angela had a lot of life ahead of her. Maple wondered fleetingly whether she'd ever be able to truly escape the years she'd spent as Elijah Wallace's wife.

Would Maple herself be able to escape the worst things in *her* past?

"Anyway," Angela said, "please take the money."

Maple gathered herself back to the present moment and frowned. "Are you sure you have enough?"

"Yes," Angela said. "Don't worry about me."

Maple could see it was a matter of pride that Angela needed to pay her in order to avoid feeling like she was receiving charity. She decided not to argue; after all, the poor woman seemed to have little enough pride as it was.

"Well, thank you." She tucked the money away and felt her heart rate pick up. "There's something I wanted to ask you."

Angela cocked her head.

"Uh, well, I heard that the coroner ruled your husband's death accidental, and I was confused. That's not what I, well . . ."

Angela nodded, closed her eyes for a moment, and exhaled.

"It's embarrassing, really, but Elijah was . . . well, he was hot-tempered. And rash. And often unkind. When he got angry with me, which was a lot—"

She paused here, and tears glistened in her eyes. Maple, feeling a pang of guilt, pulled a fresh handkerchief from her purse. Angela accepted it gratefully and then continued.

"Sometimes, he would threaten to kill me. Other times, he'd threaten to kill himself. More than once, he tied a noose and showed it to me. A few weeks ago, he called me out to the barn and was standing in the hayloft with it around his neck."

A shudder ran through Angela's small body, and Maple felt one go through her as well.

"And then on Friday, before I left for my sister's, he was angry. Didn't want me spending so much time over there. He said I was ungrateful and he'd show me—that if he was gone, I'd have nothing. *Be* nothing."

She took a deep, shaky breath. "But my sister needed me. She'd just had her baby—my first nephew—and I was determined to go. I got so tired of his . . . well, anyway, I got the keys to the truck and I went out to the car. He called out to me from the barn. I went in and he was standing in the hayloft, wearing the noose. He said, 'If you go, you're just gonna find a dead body when you get back.'"

Angela sobbed into the handkerchief. Maple patted her shoulder awkwardly, her mind working busily. Angela's explanation was the only one that made sense, and it wasn't a scenario Maple had considered before.

Angela looked up, eyes blazing.

"But here's the thing, Mrs. Bishop, the thing I finally realized—he wasn't suicidal. No way. These times when he'd pretend he was going to do it? They were just a way to try and manipulate me. Control me. In the past, when he did this, I'd try to reason with him. I'd beg him to stop, to not hurt himself, agree with him that I'd be nothing without him—anything to placate him, to get him to stop saying he'd hurt himself. And eventually, he'd come down. But you know what? That's exactly what he wanted, and I was sick of it. Sick of *him*. So I left. And then he must've—I don't know, he must've slipped or something, and now—"

Maple nodded and patted her shoulder again. In the context of Angela's story, the ruling of accidental death made sense. Presumably, the sheriff and coroner had been made aware of the same details Angela had just shared with Maple. Dully, Maple realized she had jumped to a judgment on the situation without knowing all the details—a rookie mistake.

But then why was Kenny so keen to pursue an alternate investigation?

After a minute, Angela had collected herself enough to move on. Maple told her she could keep the handkerchief. The two women left the house. A light rain had started to fall. Angela helped Maple load the wheelbarrow into the truck bed, and then they settled into the cab. Angela backed the big truck down the driveway with surprising ease for such a tiny lady.

Maple's mind spun as they headed down the road that led to town. What about the tire tracks? The gash in the doorframe? The marks on Elijah's wrists and side? She cleared her throat, not wanting to upset the woman further, but also burning to know.

"Does Russell Mooreland come over often?" she asked.

Angela raised her eyebrows. "Russell? No. He and Elijah— well, let's just say they weren't exactly the best of fr—"

"I saw some tire tracks when I arrived to make the delivery on Friday and I noticed there's a gash in the barn doorframe, like somebody hit it with their bumper when they were trying to back out."

She was talking too fast. *"Stepping on other people's words"* was what her mother used to call it when Maple would begin speaking before the person she was talking to was finished. She had gotten better control over this bad habit as she aged, but it still crept back in when she was especially agitated.

Angela hiked her shoulders. "Elijah had customers in and out all the time."

Maple's ears pricked up. "Customers?"

"Yes. He sold squash and gourds from the farm and soap made from our goats' milk. And other small things. We used to have cows and much bigger fields, but after Elijah's accident a few years ago, he hasn't been able to do as much."

With significant effort, Maple held her tongue until she was sure Angela was done with her sentence.

"And did he—well, I hate to ask, but did he ever tie his own wrists? Maybe when he was threatening suicide?"

Angela threw her a surprised sideways glance, and Maple realized she'd gone too far.

She hurried to elaborate: "I ask because when I found him, his wrists had these pink marks on them, like a rope burn. And so I was wondering . . ."

"I don't remember," Angela said shortly, returning her eyes to the road. "And I'd rather not talk about it anymore."

Maple flushed, a little surprised at the authority in Angela's voice. The interrogation, such as it had been, was over.

"Certainly. How was your visit with your sister?"

This brought a small smile to Angela's face, and for the remainder of the ride, Angela chattered about her sister's son, her six-week-old nephew, whom she clearly adored. In fact, Angela told Maple she was planning to spend the next week at her sister's house.

All the while, Maple churned over everything she'd learned. She'd never found babies particularly interesting, and this one was no exception. Maple couldn't have cared less how much the baby slept and which lullabies he liked best, but Angela Wallace and Russell Mooreland had both given her a lot to think about. When Angela pulled onto Main Street, Maple was surprised they were already back on Main Street. Out the window, Maple saw Harry Needles smoking a cigarette on the sidewalk outside the newspaper office. When he saw her through the window, his eyes widened and he hurried inside. Maple allowed herself a small smile as Angela continued down the street and pulled to a stop in front of the hardware store.

The two women got out of the truck and, together, hoisted the wheelbarrow out of the bed. Maple brushed a stray lock of hair from her face and thanked Angela for the ride. Angela in turn thanked Maple for the dollhouse. Maple was struck by the change in tone. Whereas mere minutes ago, Angela had been sobbing confessions about her manipulative husband, now she and Maple were stiff and formal with their interactions.

People were exhausting. It occurred to Maple that she had engaged in more interpersonal relations in the past week than she typically did in a month, and she longed for the solitude of her house, where her only company was the stray cat who required only food and the occasional pat.

Bless him, she thought, *for his straightforwardness and emotional transparency.*

She said goodbye to Angela and stood next to the now-empty wheelbarrow out on the sidewalk. Angela headed off on foot toward the center of town. Maple watched her for a long moment, noticing how the other woman's shoulders still hunched forward, as if anticipating a blow—whether physical, verbal, or both— from a husband who was no longer there.

Then she looked in the window of the shop and made a decision.

She went inside and asked Ben if she could use his telephone.

"Well, good morning to you too." Looking amused, he gestured for her to go ahead.

Maple grunted in reply, then brushed past him, picked up the receiver, and asked the operator to put her through to the sheriff's office. When the secretary answered, Maple coughed and spoke in a voice much deeper than her usual.

"Hello, that nice young officer helped me out the other day, and I wanted to thank him in person. Is he available?"

"Isn't Kenny just the sweetest?" the secretary gushed. "I'm glad he was able to help you. What did he do, if you don't mind my asking?"

"Rescued my cat from a tree," Maple invented.

Ben arched an eyebrow. Maple turned her back to him while the woman on the other end of the line cooed her approval, finally coming around to the whole point of Maple's call: "I'm sorry, ma'am, this is actually Kenny's day off, but you can be sure I'll give him the message. What's your na—"

Maple hung up, having attained the information she needed. She informed a bemused Ben that she might or might not be back later, grabbed her nutshell from its spot under the table, and returned to the sidewalk. Then, she took hold of the wheelbarrow's handles and pushed it down the street in the direction of an address she'd looked up in the phone book the night before, just in case.

It took her twenty minutes to walk to the Quirks' house, which turned out to be a small Cape Cod on a quiet side street. The neighborhood was a modest one, peppered with tire swings, mowed lawns, and trimmed hedges. Maple parked her wheelbarrow in the Quirks' driveway, picked up her nutshell, and rang the doorbell.

Kenny opened the door and immediately frowned. Maple's stomach sank as Kenny moved into the doorframe, blocking the entryway. A wave of nervousness shot through her. Maybe she was too late. Maybe he'd changed his mind. She hadn't let herself realize fully until this moment, standing on his front step and looking him in the eye, how much this meant to her—both getting her nutshell back and working in partnership with Kenny.

"Why are you here?" His voice was wary.

She swallowed past the lump in her throat. "If your offer still stands, I'd like to say yes."

After a long pause, Kenny said, "It still stands."

Maple smiled. "Then, let's get to work."

CHAPTER 20

He moved aside so she could enter, and she found herself in a small, comfortably furnished living room, looking at an older couple. The man sat in a worn recliner. His eyes stared vacantly at the wall as his upper body rocked in small, repetitive motions, forward and back. The woman sat on the end of the couch closest to the man and smiled up at them.

"Mom, Dad, this is Mrs. Bishop. She's here about a case. Mrs. Bishop, my parents: Ken Senior and Mary." Kenny gestured from Maple to his parents and back again.

Mrs. Quirk was a small woman, but there was a steeliness about her. She stood up, her shoulders in the posture of a proud soldier. Her graying hair was done up neatly in tight curls, and sharp blue eyes shone out from behind round glasses.

"Pleased to meet you." Mrs. Quirk took Maple's hand in both of her own. "Your husband treated me for strep throat last year. A lovely man. I'm so sorry for your loss."

A lump formed in Maple's own throat at the compliment. "Thank you."

Mr. Quirk closed his eyes and moaned softly, and his wife dropped Maple's hand and crouched at her husband's side.

"It's all right, Ken," she said softly. "You're home. We're all here."

Kenny cleared his throat. "Let's go into the kitchen."

Maple followed Kenny into the hall. After a few steps, he paused, so Maple did too.

"My dad is . . . not well," he said.

"I'm sorry." She felt a surge of pity as his shoulders slumped.

"Yeah . . ." The tips of Kenny's ears burned bright red. "Thanks. He hasn't been the same since he came back from . . . over there." He paused, then explained in a rush, "It's not always this bad. Sometimes he has hours—even whole days—where he can carry on conversations and work on projects. He was a carpenter before. He built this house." A note of pride was evident in his voice. "Anyway, here's the kitchen."

Maple closed her eyes briefly, wondering what horrors Mr. Quirk had seen at war. Then, she followed Kenny a few more steps to the end of the hall and stepped into a small, tidy kitchen. Four well-worn chairs sat around a circular table that was scuffed and scratched, but clean. Kenny pulled out one and gestured for her to sit. She carefully placed the nutshell on the table and took her seat.

"Mrs. Bishop, I'm really glad you—well, I'm looking forward to—I mean, thanks for—"

Maple held up a hand. "Thanks for inspiring me. You were right, you know. What you said about truth and justice. What sets us apart from them." She thought of the Nazis hanged at Nuremburg and felt a tug deep in her belly.

Kenny cleared his throat. "So, whaddaya got? Anything new?"

Maple summarized her encounters with Russell Mooreland and Angela Wallace. Kenny listened with rapt attention.

"Very interesting." Kenny tipped onto the back legs of his chair and clasped his hands behind his head. "Do you believe her about the past suicide threats? And what she said about him not meaning it?"

Maple eyed him, nervous that he'd fall backward. "I do."

"But . . ." Kenny prompted.

"But I'm also not at all convinced he died by accident while threatening suicide. Let's walk through it." Maple took the doll version of Elijah out of the noose. "So, in the accident scenario, Elijah climbs up into the hayloft."

She made the doll climb up the ladder.

"He stands here and puts the noose on, but probably loosely." She put the rope back around the doll's neck and wiggled it open a little further than it had been. "And calls for his wife."

To Maple's relief, the front legs of Kenny's chair clattered onto the floor. Kenny formed his pointer and middle fingers into an upside down V, resting the pads of his fingers against the table, and looked at her expectantly. She raised an eyebrow at him.

"I'm being Angela." His tone suggested that this should be obvious. He wiggled his fingers around as if making "Angela" walk.

Maple pressed her lips together and tried not to laugh.

"They have words," she went on. "Elijah threatens to kill himself. Angela leaves anyway."

Kenny walked his fingers away from the barn door.

Maple frowned. "And then he slips or something and"—she let go of the doll, which swung off the hayloft and hung suspended by its neck over the main section of the barn—"I find him a few hours later."

Kenny nodded thoughtfully and drummed the fingers that had been Angela's legs against the tabletop. "That explains how he came to be hanging there but doesn't account for the gash, the tire tracks, or the rope burns on his wrists."

Maple nodded her agreement. She wished she had a cup of tea to settle her nerves and help her think.

"There's something else," she said. "According to the medical literature I read, accidental deaths by hanging are very rare. Assuming that what Mrs. Wallace told us is true, Elijah most likely thought standing up in the loft and threatening to jump would be a more dramatic visual than simply standing on a chair. But, actually, in the end, he didn't jump. This scenario doesn't work."

Kenny gaped at her.

"I . . . used to study law, and my husband was a doctor. I have a lot of textbooks at home."

Kenny still looked wary, but he leaned forward. "How do you know he didn't jump?"

"Well, this is what I was going to tell your uncle before he unceremoniously kicked me out of his office. Remember the bruise on Elijah's side?"

Kenny nodded. Maple pointed to the area on the doll version of Elijah. "It's not actually a bruise. Something called lividity happens after death. The dead person's blood settles into the lowest gravitational place in the body, creating a bruise-like appearance."

She pulled Elijah out of the noose and placed him, bruised-side down, on the floor of the barn.

Kenny watched. "So, he would've had to be lying on that side for a while in order for the blood to settle . . . and that must've happened before he swung from the rafters."

Maple nodded, pleased that he was following her train of thought. "He was already dead when someone put that noose around his neck and pushed him."

She put his neck through the noose again and let go. They both watched the tiny Elijah swing back and forth, and Maple wondered, again, how he'd ended up hanging from his own hay hoist.

"Let's try another scenario." She reset the scene, pulling Elijah out of the noose and hooking the rope around the ladder again.

"Wait," said Kenny. "Did he just keep a noose tied like that in his barn all the time, ready to go? That'd be odd, wouldn't it? Even if the wife is telling the truth about how he'd threaten suicide regularly?"

It was a keen observation, and Maple agreed with his logic. She untied the noose so that it was just a rope.

"Now, that's more likely what you'd find in a hayloft," Kenny said. "A rope like that attached to a winch would've been used to lift bales of hay up there for storage."

Maple nodded.

"Good point."

Kenny sat up a little straighter, clearly proud to have received her praise.

Maple indicated the doll in Kenny's hand by inclining her chin toward it again. "You get to be the bad guy this time."

A devilish smile flashed across Kenny's face. "Okay, but don't threaten me with a rifle."

Maple pursed her lips, wondering whether she ought to be amused or annoyed. It seemed everyone in town knew about her method of ridding herself of Harry Needles.

Kenny cleared his throat and refocused on the task at hand. He clutched the doll tighter and nodded once. Maple cut a small section of twine from the same roll she'd used to fashion the noose and handed it to Kenny.

"Let's assume Elijah was down on the floor of the barn, and not up in the hayloft, when the attack happened," Maple said, placing her doll in the center of the barn's main floor. "Russell Mooreland enters—"

Kenny walked his doll in the main entrance.

"—and subdues Elijah."

They stopped and looked at each other. Kenny voiced what they were both thinking.

"How?"

Maple sighed. "How, indeed? There was no evidence that he was bashed in the head. He certainly wasn't shot. But Wallace was a large man. Even with his missing leg, he'd have been hard to subdue, even for an attacker who was also a strong man . . . but the rope burns on his wrists indicate he must've struggled," she said.

They both sat in quiet contemplation. Finally, Maple placed Elijah facedown. "For now, I'm just going to put him on the floor. Tie him up."

Kenny fastened the small amount of rope around the doll's wrists, but then frowned. "Maybe it makes more sense that the attack happened when they were already up in the hayloft. Think about it: How does the attacker get him up into the loft if he's already unconscious? That's a lot of dead weight to haul up a pretty rickety ladder."

Kenny untied Elijah. Maple picked up the doll and positioned him facedown on the hayloft's floor. Kenny made his doll climb the ladder and then retied the ropes around his wrists.

Maple turned the doll slightly onto its left side.

"He must've been in this position for a little while, at least, because of the lividity," she said. "Maybe while the attacker fashioned the noose."

Kenny put his doll down for a moment and tied the appropriate knot.

Maple sucked her teeth. "That's not enough time for the lividity to set in. He must've done something else while Elijah was unconscious . . . but what?"

"Maybe just hauling the body over and putting the noose around his neck took a while," Kenny said, shrugging.

Perhaps, but Maple didn't think so.

"The bee stings, the fight, and the big truck all point to Mooreland as the killer," Maple said, holding up a new finger as she recited each piece of evidence.

"Not to mention the ongoing feud. From all accounts I've heard, they despised each other. But how do we prove it?" Kenny spread his palms in the air. "My uncle's not going to take your word for it over the coroner's ruling. He'll never agree to reopen the case unless we've got something so ironclad he can't ignore it."

Maple knew he was right. Kenny's eyes met hers over the nutshell. "I'll talk to Dr. Murphy."

Kenny shook his head. "He won't be able to talk to you about it, Mrs. Bishop. Autopsy results are confidential unless the sheriff decides to release them publicly, which almost never happens."

Maple flushed. She, a trained lawyer, shouldn't have needed a rookie kid to tell her this—but because she had no official role in this investigation, she had no legal right to such confidential information. Were her training and skills fading before she could even put them to use, just as muscles atrophied if they weren't exercised? Kenny's words were a wake-up call; though she'd started feeling like an insider as they hashed out possibilities and discussed discrepancies, she still remained an outsider.

She cleared her throat, wanting to move past her embarrassment. "So, we'll meet at the hardware shop tomorrow afternoon?"

Kenny agreed.

Knowing he wouldn't like what she had to say next, Maple used an intentionally casual tone. "You know what'd be helpful? Comparing the tire tracks from the barn to the tires on Mooreland's truck."

"Not possible."

Saying those words to Maple was like waving a red flag in front of a bull. "Anything's possible."

Kenny's expression became stern. "Mrs. Bishop, don't go doing anything crazy. Don't go out to his farm alone or anything like that. Promise me."

"I wouldn't dream of it," she said airily, though she'd been thinking of doing that exact thing.

CHAPTER 21

All Maple could think about was her new investigation, but the next morning she had to work on her next commissioned project. Except for Frank, whose tail started thumping as soon as Maple pushed open the door, Ben was alone in the hardware shop. She placed the nutshell carefully on her table and then took a step back into the entryway to remove Jamie's coat. Frank waddled over, and Maple held out the piece of toast she'd saved for him, as had become their daily ritual. He wagged harder and gulped it down in one bite.

"Hi," she said.

"Hi," Ben said.

They stopped and smiled. Even though she was in the doorway and he was all the way across the room behind the counter, Maple could see his smile reach his eyes. She noticed how they crinkled around the edges.

She was surprised to feel heat rise to her cheeks, and busied herself by stowing her umbrella by the side of the door and putting her work apron on.

"How's the dollhouse business?" Ben asked.

Maple sighed before she could stop herself. "It's fine, thanks. Actually, that reporter's stopping by soon to do a story on me for the *Elderberry Tribune*."

Ben exclaimed that this was exciting news, and set about straightening the end caps and sweeping the floors.

"We need to make a good impression," he explained earnestly.

Despite Maple's doubts about agreeing to the article, a tiny firework of pride flickered in her chest, and she flashed him a quick smile before setting about her work. She set the sample house she'd brought in from home up next to her current work in progress, thinking it'd be nice to show a final product as well as one still under construction. When Ella Henderson turned up fifteen minutes later, she oohed and aahed over the tiny people in their tiny house.

The reporter wanted to know how Maple had become interested in making dolls and their houses, where she got her materials—things like that. Maple answered all of her questions easily as Ben hovered nearby, beaming. Ella snapped several photographs with the camera she'd brought along.

Finally, Ella stuck out her hand and said, "I've already got the headline: 'Maple's Miniatures: War Widow Turns Entrepreneur.'"

Maple shook the offered hand as a queasy feeling settled in her stomach. As much as she'd been flattered by the reporter's interest and excited at the prospect that it would lead to more sales, she still felt . . . cheap, somehow. Would others in town feel, like Ella did—and, Maple realized, like Angela Wallace did—that Maple's endeavor was inspiring, or would they think it was beneath a respected doctor's widow to sell arts and crafts? It wouldn't be the first time she had faced harsh judgment from her adopted home-town, but somehow the unsettled feeling never really got much better.

The reporter leaned in and said conspiratorially, "Between you and me, this is the most interesting thing I've gotten to cover. Harry's the senior reporter, and I only just started at the paper. Usually I'm just typing up lists of who was born, died, or won an award." She shrugged good-naturedly. "Comes with the terri-tory. That's what our readers want from me: the girl reporter with the soft, feminine touch."

A hint of resentment slipped into her voice, and Maple found herself feeling empathy for the young reporter. She certainly knew how it felt to be judged because of your gender, and not your professional qualifications, to be seen as the person who should be fetching coffee for the men rather than doing the job yourself. Even so, she wasn't sure what to say. She figured that she ought to give the younger woman some words of encouragement, but her tongue seemed stuck in her mouth—perhaps, in no small part, because Maple also recognized herself in the reporter's bitter description of a *soft, feminine touch*. After all, wasn't that what peo-ple wanted from Maple too? The sheriff's secretary had referred to her as "the dollhouse lady." Was that what Maple wanted for herself? Angela Wallace had been impressed with Maple's initia-tive, and so it seemed was the young reporter. But by leaning into her dollhouse making, was Maple truly making a name for herself as an independent business woman? Or was she settling for what society expected and allowed for her?

The thought was disconcerting, and she found herself feeling impatient for the evening, when she and Kenny would meet again to plan their next moves. Even if no one else could know about the clandestine investigation, Maple herself took some solace in the fact that she was doing something besides crafting cheerful dollhouses.

After thanking her one more time, Ella handed Maple a business card, picked up her camera, and left the store. Maple studied the business card for a long moment: *Ella Henderson, junior reporter.* Then, she slid it into her coat pocket.

It was a slow morning in the store; in fact, no customers had come in yet that day. She glanced down at her apron pocket and thought of the money she had, the amount she still needed to pay the mortgage, and the discrepancy between the two. Ella's interest was nice and all, yet Maple still doubted she'd be able to make her next mortgage payment—let alone all the ones that would come after it—by crafting dollhouses.

There was no sense dwelling on it. She just needed to push through. She measured, cut, and sanded boards while Ben filled out paperwork and restocked shelves. She felt her tension diminish as she worked with her hands, concentrating on the details of this house and thinking about what furniture it would still need.

By lunchtime, Maple felt good about the amount of work she'd accomplished. A glance out the window revealed that the rain had stopped. She headed out to meet Charlotte at the diner. A warm rush filled her chest as she got close to the entrance. Maple could smell grilled chicken and . . . she closed her eyes and breathed in. Was that French onion soup? Her favorite.

Charlotte guided Maple to a table by the window and sat across from her, baby Tommy clinging to her chest. Before she could say anything, though, the door burst open, and Charlotte's twin boys, Matthew and Michael, burst in like a pair of blond tornadoes. Laughing and wrestling, they bumped into a table and nearly knocked over the vase perched on it.

"Boys!" Charlotte stood, chastised them to be more careful, and kissed them each on the head. "Dad's got your lunch ready."

She watched her sons with fondness as they raced through the swinging kitchen doors. In the brief moment the doors were open, Maple caught a glimpse of Hank, who grinned and waved at her.

Charlotte sighed and addressed the baby in her arms. "You, my sweet baby, will be joining your brothers in no time, running around causing all kinds of trouble and giving your mother gray hairs."

Maple smiled at her friend's obvious affection. Despite her halfhearted complaints, Maple knew Charlotte adored being the mother of three boys.

She planted a kiss on the baby's cheek. "Let's get you down for a nap."

Charlotte disappeared upstairs with Tommy, and the twins returned with plates piled high with chicken, potatoes, and green beans. They plunked themselves down a few tables away from Maple and immediately began an intense conversation as they shoveled food into their mouths. Maple marveled at young boys' ability to eat and talk simultaneously. Their energy reminded her of her brother, and a familiar ache followed. Amid all the losses Maple had experienced in her life, losing her only sibling had hit especially hard. There was something special about a person with whom you'd shared your childhood. Maple considered whether Charlotte had been correct after all—was her obsession with the details surrounding Elijah Wallace's death driven by her sense of helplessness over Jamie's untimely demise?

Charlotte returned and sat with Maple, refusing to let her go until she'd finished her tea and two bowls of French onion soup. Maple told her about the upcoming article, over which Charlotte exclaimed, and did not tell her about the clandestine investigation, which made Maple feel guilty; she didn't like keeping secrets from her friend. When she finally gathered her things to leave, chaos had erupted at the diner. The lunch rush was fully underway, and Charlotte was attempting to wrangle her unruly twins into returning to school for the afternoon.

Maple skirted around the boys and, her head down, bumped into Dr. Murphy as he entered the diner.

"Oh! Hello, Maple." He adjusted his glasses.

"I'm so sorry!" she said, getting her feet under her and standing up straight again.

They stood in the doorway, exchanging brief pleasantries. Maple practically had to physically restrain herself from asking him about the autopsy findings. It was awkward to dance around the topic she truly wanted to discuss with her mentor, with whom there were usually no barriers to what they could discuss. An invisible wall seemed to have sprung up between them.

Maple sighed as she stepped outside a minute later. It had been nice for a brief time to escape her brooding thoughts about death, secrets, and mortgages. She turned her face up to the sky, happy to feel the sun—weak as it was—on her cheeks.

As Maple approached the hardware store on the sidewalk, a truck passed and parked about a block ahead of her. She stopped in her tracks and inhaled sharply when the driver climbed out and slammed the door. It was Russell Mooreland.

He walked away from his truck in the opposite direction from where Maple herself stood. Kenny had told her not to go out to his farm by herself to compare the tire tracks, but he hadn't said anything about what she should or shouldn't do if Russell Mooreland offered up his truck to her on a more or less deserted public street as though on a silver platter. The only other people were several hundred yards farther down on the opposite side of the street, and they were engaged in conversation in front of a shop window and seemingly paying no attention to a lone pickup truck a few blocks away. Maple made her decision in under a second, ducking quickly into the hardware shop to grab a pencil and piece of paper from her desk.

"Welcome . . . back?" She heard the confusion in Ben's voice as she darted back out mere moments after she'd entered.

A quick visual sweep revealed the same small group congregated in front of the same storefront. There was no sign of Mooreland. She narrowed her eyes, half expecting Ginger to leap out from behind a bush at any moment and start peppering her with questions.

Before she could reconsider what she was doing, she strode over to the front of the truck and positioned herself strategically, placing the vehicle between herself and the people. She glanced up and down her side of the street once more. Seeing no one, she crouched down and examined the front driver's side tire, and her heart jumped into her throat. The tread certainly looked similar to the patterns that had been left behind in the mud in front of the Wallaces' barn. With her hands shaking just a little, she placed the paper over the tread and began rubbing across it with the pencil. Despite the chill in the air, a bead of sweat ran down Maple's back as she prayed Mooreland wouldn't come back to the truck before she was finished.

There. She had what she needed. She dashed back to the hardware store, only realizing when she caught sight of her own reflection in the window that she was still in a semi-crouched position. She straightened up and opened the door. Ben gaped at her from behind the cash register. She ignored him, her heart pounding as she fumbled in her bag until she found what she was looking for. She placed the two rubbings side by side and looked rapidly from one to the other.

They were a match. Russell Mooreland had been at the Wallaces' barn.

Chapter 22

"No, it *looks* as though his *truck* might've been there," Kenny said several hours later when she told him the news. He shot her an exasperated look. "Assuming your, uh, decidedly unscientific grave rubbing–type comparison is accurate—which is a pretty big assumption, no offense—how do you know who was driving the truck?"

Maple crossed her arms and leaned back in her chair, glaring across the table at her new partner. His reaction to her discovery was disappointing, to say the least. The sun had just about disappeared below the horizon, and Maple's patience with Kenny was vanishing right along with it.

"Are you sulking now?" Kenny pursed his lips. "You're sulking, aren't you?"

"I don't think you understand the significance here, Kenny," Maple fumed, "and I don't appreciate your flippant tone. Come on, does Russell Mooreland really strike you as the kind of guy who'd let someone else drive his truck? You know it was him!"

She smacked her palms down hard on the table. Kenny jolted in his seat and opened his mouth to respond, but Maple continued before he could speak. "Furthermore, we know the tracks were left that day because it had rained that morning for the first time in weeks, and then the ground froze in the late afternoon because we had that drastic temperature drop. The tracks must have been left after the rain started and before the deep freeze set in."

Kenny sighed. "I'm still not convinced we need to go to the barn tonight."

Maple was encouraged by his resigned tone. It told her she was wearing him down. She leaned forward and gazed steadily into his eyes.

"Kenny, now that we have this piece of evidence, who's to say what else is just lying around up there waiting to be discovered? The sheriff didn't exactly exert himself looking for clues, particularly after Dr. Murphy ruled the death accidental. But you and I agree there's an excellent chance they're both wrong. That's why we're here, isn't it?"

Kenny closed his eyes and then opened them, and that was the moment Maple knew she'd convinced him.

"Okay," he said, shaking his head. "Let's go."

Maple stood so quickly she knocked over her chair. She righted it, threw on Jamie's coat, and was out the front door before Kenny had even risen from his seat. She waited impatiently for him to catch up, and then they climbed into Kenny's car and set off.

They were both quiet for the first few minutes of the drive, Maple silently gloating that she'd persuaded him.

After several minutes, Kenny spoke again, but this time his voice was tentative. "Can I ask you a favor, Mrs. Bishop? It doesn't have to do with the case."

She looked at him in surprise. "Of course. What is it?"

"Well, the thing is, my father isn't the same since the war, as you saw . . ." He trailed off and scratched his nose. Maple waited him out.

"And, see, my mother keeps saying how nice you seem ever since you stopped by. We don't get a lot of visitors anymore. My parents' friends from before the war—well, it's like they don't know what to say or how to act now that he's different."

Kenny gulped. Maple placed a hand on his arm.

He took a deep breath and continued, "I made an appointment with the insurance agency tomorrow because I think my dad's entitled to some money because of his disability, but my mom's nervous about the whole thing, and . . . well, my father was always the one who handled the business, you know? And he can't really do that anymore. He can't work, and she has to take care of him all the time. Money's real tight."

He swallowed hard, and Maple felt an awkward surge of sympathy. It had to be hard to say all this.

"And anyway, I know you're trained as a lawyer and all, so you could help make sure everything is on the up and up, plus I think my mom'd be more comfortable having another woman there, and I was just wondering—"

"Of course I'll go."

His shoulders sagged with relief, and Maple felt an affection for the earnest young man beside her.

"Oh, thank you, Mrs. Bishop."

The relief and gratitude were palpable in Kenny's voice. He told her the particulars, saying he would pick her up at nine the next morning. Maple gazed out the window. Her emotions were jumbled—pity for the Quirk family, satisfaction that her legal skills might be able to help someone, and nervous anticipation at visiting the Wallaces' barn.

They passed Russell Mooreland's property, which was buttoned up for the night. Maple saw no lights on. His truck was parked right outside his barn. When they arrived at the Wallaces' a moment later, there was no sign of their truck, and the house lights were off. Otherwise, it looked the same as it had when Maple had left with Angela earlier that evening.

Kenny parked in front of the barn and pulled a flashlight from the glove box. He clicked it on and raised his eyebrows at Maple as they both stepped out of the car. "Ready?"

Maple didn't think Kenny looked ready. He looked terrified, yet there was a steely resolve in his eyes that Maple liked. "Let's go."

They moved toward the door. The crunch of their feet on the gravel was almost unbearably loud, and Maple was relieved when they stepped onto the hardened mud just before the barn door entrance. Before they opened the doors, they could hear the goats begin to bleat their greeting. Or was it a warning? Maple recalled her observation from earlier that the goats gave off an air of guarding the property.

Kenny paused at the barn door.

"Uh, normally, I'd hold the door for a lady," he said, and Maple could sense, rather than see, his ears going red. "But I think as a law enforcement officer I should enter before you."

His voice was deep and serious. Maple couldn't suppress her smile. She tried to keep her tone neutral so he wouldn't think she was laughing at him.

"That's fine," she said. "And I don't think we need to worry about the bees this late at night. They'll all be asleep."

She pointed up into the rafters, and Kenny trained his light on the nest.

"Why hasn't anyone taken that thing down?" he wondered.

Maple hiked her shoulders. "I imagine ladders were tough for Mr. Wallace, given his leg. Mrs. Wallace is pretty small and frail, so it wouldn't shock me if she wasn't up to it. And I don't get the sense they had many friends or neighbors dropping by to help with household chores. She made it sound like the only visitors they got were customers."

Kenny cocked his head. Maple explained what Mrs. Wallace had said about the gourds and soap, and he looked thoughtful.

"What?" she asked.

"Well, it just seems odd that I didn't know they were doing that. You'd think in a town this small, everyone would know about a place to buy soap and vegetables. I wonder why the Wallaces didn't advertise in town or even set up a little shop, like you did with the dollhouses in the hardware store."

It was a good point. Their house being positioned so far out of the town center, the Wallaces certainly could've expected to increase their sales by doing either of the things Kenny had just proposed.

"Maybe they value their privacy over their revenue?" she suggested. "Come on."

And so they entered the barn, first Kenny and then Maple, who pulled the door closed behind them. Kenny swung the flashlight beam around the space slowly, panning from left to right and training it up and down the walls. Outside, the goats stopped their bleating.

"Where should we start?" he asked once they'd scanned the entire interior.

"Let's do a slow lap down here first," Maple replied, "and then check out the hayloft."

They started on the left side of the barn, where a few neat shelves held basic farm supplies: seeds, buckets, and small garden tools. Without touching anything, Kenny and Maple scrutinized everything by the beam of the flashlight. Nothing seemed amiss. They continued on, circling slowly around the barn's perimeter. Maple's initial jumpiness began to subside, replaced by frustration. They were taking a big risk here, and it was beginning to look like it was all for nothing.

But then, when Kenny's beam swung over the last corner of the barn, she spotted the rope. Coiled, innocuous, in a pile, it was dirty and well-worn; perhaps Elijah had used it to wrangle the goats or even cows back when he used to have them. It wasn't the rope's practical farm-related uses that piqued Maple's interest, though.

"Kenny," she said, pointing, "put the light on that rope again."

Kenny, whose eyes kept darting back and forth as though he expected someone to jump out at them any second, swung the beam back to the corner. Maple noticed the beam flickered and realized Kenny's hand was shaking.

"What about it?" he whispered.

They moved closer and Maple studied it. Then, she asked Kenny to shine the light on the length of rope that remained suspended from the hayloft, which was much shinier and thinner with a markedly different texture than the one in the corner.

"Oh!" he exclaimed, nearly dropping the flashlight. "It's not the same."

"No, it's not," Maple agreed. "The rope the noose was made from is much newer."

"What do you think it means?" Kenny breathed.

He sounded like a child afraid of campfire ghost stories. Maple wouldn't have been surprised if he'd grabbed her hand.

"Maybe nothing," Maple said, but an idea was already forming.

She told him to aim the light at the center of the barn and stepped into the beam. The sheriff had left the noose itself attached to Elijah's neck after cutting him down, but Maple thought she remembered . . . there! A small segment of the rope, maybe four inches long, lay on the ground, having been discarded in the haste to remove the farmer's body. She pocketed it.

"It's interesting that the only rope of this type is attached to the hay hoist," she said. "There's no leftovers, no coil of extra rope anywhere. How often do you suppose someone buys *exactly* the length of rope they need? And Elijah doesn't seem the type to waste anything, so I'd be surprised if he threw away the remainder. I think the killer brought this rope with him. Let's go up into the loft."

Kenny climbed up the rickety ladder first and then shone the light back down over the rungs while Maple made her way up. Both were out of breath by the time they reached the top.

"Well," Maple said, "I'll tell you what. I'm reasonably certain now that no one—not even a strong farmer like Mooreland—carried Elijah up this ladder against his will."

Kenny nodded his agreement. "Or dragged his unconscious body up it."

For a moment, they stood there catching their breath. Then, Kenny began to shine the light around the hayloft.

"Then how did the killer persuade Elijah to come up here?" Maple whispered.

Her eyes followed the flashlight's beam. There was very little hay in the hayloft. Two bales were haphazardly stacked in the corner farthest from them, and stray pieces were scattered across the wood beam floor, but Maple doubted the meager supply up here would go very far, even for the two scrawny creatures out-side. How much hay did goats need?

The ceiling was very low, and they had to stay in a semi-crouched position until they made their way to the center, where the ceiling was tallest. They stood there for a moment and looked down. Maple's eyes latched onto the rope hanging down in the center of the barn. Had this been Elijah Wallace's final view before he was pushed? It had certainly been his murderer's. She felt bile rise up in her throat.

Kenny shone the light on the far section of the loft, near the two hay bales. Maple spotted a scrap of brown paper, a triangle maybe an inch in diameter that had been torn off a larger wrapper of some sort. The letters *om* were printed on it. It looked familiar somehow, but she couldn't place it. She held it up to show Kenny, who shrugged. She put it in her pocket along with the segment of rope. They ducked to avoid the low ceiling on this side of the loft and continued looking.

"Mrs. Bishop," Kenny whispered, "this is weird."

She looked over his shoulder and saw he was pointing to a small, scattered pile of white granules behind the hayloft.

"It looks like . . . salt?" she said, squinting. She remembered seeing the white cubes lashed to the fence. "Could it be from those salt licks they have for the goats?"

Kenny's face fell at this very mundane explanation. Maple smiled crookedly at him, amused at his obvious disappointment.

"We'll take a few with us, just in case," she said.

Mostly to placate Kenny, she squatted and pinched up some of the granules and tucked them, too, into her pocket.

Maple considered whether she ought to compliment Kenny for his observation, even though it probably wouldn't amount to much in the way of a clue. Before she could, though, from outside came the unmistakable sound of a car's tires crunching on the gravel driveway.

The goats promptly resumed their bleating. Kenny's eyes widened to the size of dinner plates. Maple stood up and promptly banged her head on the low roof. For the first time in her life, she understood the expression "seeing stars."

Various scenarios raced through Maple's mind. Had Mrs. Wallace changed her mind about staying at her sister's? Was this the killer (Mooreland?) returning to the scene of the crime? Maple's first instinct was to hide, but she quickly realized the sheriff department's car was parked right in front of the barn, out in the open, so that wouldn't work. Whoever had just pulled in had certainly already seen it.

They were sitting ducks.

She looked at Kenny's face, which was wild with panic. For once, he had not gone red; in fact, his face was so white that Maple thought he might be on the verge of passing out.

Outside, a car door slammed shut.

"Kill the light," Maple whispered. At the very least, the absence of the flashlight might give them a few seconds' advantage over whoever this was.

Kenny turned the light off, and Maple heard him fumbling with something in the sudden darkness. She grabbed his arm and pulled him over into the corner behind the hay bales.

There was a click. Then the barn door creaked open.

CHAPTER 23

They heard someone step into the barn. A flashlight beam swept the interior, lower level first and then the hayloft. Maple and Kenny held their breath.

"Kenny," came a voice hovering between exasperation and annoyance, "what in the hell do you think you're doing? And *you*." Maple flinched as the light shone directly in her eyes. "Both of you come out now."

It was the sheriff.

Maple dropped Kenny's elbow, which she hadn't even realized she'd still been clutching. Kenny fumbled for a moment, and then his flashlight switched on. Instantly, the sheriff's beam swung their way, each man's light illuminating the other.

"Put the gun down, boy," the sheriff said, narrowing his eyes.

Surprised, Maple glanced over and saw that Kenny, indeed, held a quivering gun pointed at his uncle. At the sheriff's command, he holstered the weapon. The sheriff pulled a string attached to a lightbulb, and a harsh glow illuminated the barn.

Kenny and Maple then scuttled back across the hayloft and scrambled down the ladder. They stood in front of the sheriff like chastened schoolchildren. Sheriff Scott, having killed and holstered his own flashlight, made the now-familiar move of hiking up his belt. Maple watched it settle again seconds later.

"How did you know we were here?" Maple blurted.

"Russell Mooreland called in saying there were trespassers on his neighbor's farm— Wait a minute, I'm asking the questions!" the sheriff snapped. "What are you two doing?"

Maple glanced at Kenny, who was still as white as a sheet. She could hear his teeth chattering. Her mind raced. Kenny might regain control of his faculties at any moment and spill exactly what they'd been doing. Maple couldn't let that happen, for the sake of protecting both his career and their fledgling investigation. Her thumb went automatically to touch the back of her wedding ring, giving her a very un-Maple-like idea.

She lied.

"I realized I lost my wedding ring," she said, meeting the sheriff's gaze with her own.

Kenny made a squawking noise in his throat. Maple stepped on his right foot gently but firmly, hoping he understood the message as she intended it: *"Stay quiet. Let me handle this."* She hoped she was conveying more confidence than she felt.

To her mild surprise, the sheriff hadn't yet responded by arresting her for trespassing, telling Kenny he was fired, or holding them both at gunpoint. Her eyes burned with a desire to blink rapidly, but she didn't let herself. Somehow she knew she had to keep her outward appearance calm, even as her insides roiled. She wanted to protect Kenny from getting into trouble, but also, she realized, she needed to protect this mission. If the sheriff shut them down, they'd never know what had happened to Elijah Wallace. Maple couldn't bear that thought.

She kept her voice steady. "I was very upset. Your deputy was in the hardware store when I realized it. The last time I remembered having it was here, the night I found Mr. Wallace's body and called you."

She maintained eye contact, willing herself not to blink.

The sheriff narrowed his eyes but said nothing. Maple realized he was playing the waiting game, banking on her need to fill the silence and hoping she'd say something that he could use to trip her up. But Maple wasn't one to clutter up any situation with extra words, so she only used three. Holding his gaze, she held up her left hand and pointed to the ring on her finger.

"We found it."

Kenny exhaled nervously, and Maple took her foot off his.

"You found it," the sheriff repeated incredulously.

Maple arranged her face into what she hoped was a look of innocence and nodded.

The sheriff glowered. "You've been missing your wedding ring since Friday, and you only just now realized it was gone?"

"Correct," she said, keeping her eyes wide and innocent.

He gave her a skeptical frown. "And you"—he leveled his penetrating gaze at his nephew—"you just happened to be at the hardware store when she had this sudden realization?"

"Yes."

Maple kept her mouth shut, waiting until the sheriff asked her a direct question. He turned back to her, raising his eyebrows. "Why were you up in the hayloft? Thought your ring might've grown arms and legs and climbed the ladder, did you?"

"We thought we heard something up there," Maple invented, "but it turned out to be a mouse. Then your car pulled in just as we were about to climb back down."

She thought his eyebrows might shoot off his forehead at this admittedly thin reasoning. She felt her armpits grow damp from the stress of all this lying. Her brain was about to burst.

"So," he said slowly, looking back and forth between the two of them, "this is about a wedding ring. It has nothing to do with the two of you conducting an unauthorized investigation into a closed case."

Maple's eyes darted to the sheriff's weapon, which remained holstered at his hip.

"Goodness." Maple widened her eyes even more. "No."

The items she'd collected from the barn that evening burned in her pocket. She willed herself not to touch them.

"Because that," the sheriff said, swinging his gaze back to his nephew, "would be grounds for firing a deputy."

Kenny gulped. Maple swallowed hard.

Keeping his eyes trained on his nephew, Sheriff Scott swiftly changed subjects. "Why were you in the hardware store today?"

He fired the question at him like a bullet.

"I, uh—" Kenny stammered.

"Your granddaughter's birthday," Maple cut in. "He was arranging for me to make his, uh, cousin a dollhouse."

Where was this sudden ability to lie coming from? Maple barely recognized herself. She sent a silent thanks to the sheriff's secretary for putting this idea in her head.

The sheriff shot her a skeptical sideways look and then turned his gaze back to Kenny. "Is that true?"

Kenny found his voice. "Yes, sir."

Please believe us.

Maple hadn't fully realized until this moment how much she needed all of this—the investigation itself and her partnership with Kenny. She found herself clinging to the hope that they would somehow claw their way out of this situation. She was absolutely desperate for the sheriff to let them go. She'd lost everyone closest to her, and the career she'd trained for. Making dollhouses might help her earn some money, but it didn't fulfill the fire in her soul the way this did.

The sheriff turned to Maple. "So, your ring, just, what—flew off your finger while you were here Friday?" he said, changing subjects again.

"Must've," she said, forcing herself not to look away.

"Where'd you find it?"

"Just inside the door there." She gestured vaguely at the barn entrance. "It was cold that night. My finger must've shrunk. Maybe it fell off while I was rushing outside to vomit."

Please, please, please.

Maple wondered whether he believed them at all—or whether he even wanted to. She'd said all she intended to say. It was the sheriff's play now. He would decide how to move forward with the version of events Maple and Kenny had laid out.

Well, mostly Maple. She snuck a glance at Kenny, whose face was still white but whose ears had gone beet-red at the tips.

The sheriff exhaled loudly, reminding Maple of a bull about to charge. He then went through his ritual of hitching up his belt. Maple watched it settle, inevitably, below his ample waist again as he rubbed his forehead.

"*You* come with me," he said, pointing at Maple. "I'll drive you home." Then, he turned to his nephew. "And I'll deal with *you* tomorrow."

CHAPTER 24

With a heavy heart, Maple watched Kenny climb into his deputy's car and drive away alone before she got into the passenger seat of Sheriff Scott's slightly bigger and newer vehicle.

The ride was silent. Maple didn't want to offer any unnecessary fictional details that might cause her whole story to unravel. *"Loose lips sink ships,"* and all that. She wasn't ready to share what she'd discovered about the tire tracks yet either—partly because she didn't want to cause any further trouble for Kenny, and partly because she was sure the sheriff would rebuff her, just as he had when she'd raised concerns at the scene and when she'd brought in the nutshell.

The sheriff, who seemed disinclined to chat even under normal circumstances, brooded as he drove. By the time they arrived at Maple's house, it was well past midnight. When he parked the car, the sheriff gazed out the windshield, not looking at her, but Maple could tell he had something to say.

Finally, Sheriff Scott broke the silence. "Whatever you're doing, stop. And above all, leave my nephew out of it."

Her heartbeat thudded in her ears, and she considered denying she was doing anything, but something made her hold her tongue. The sheriff's arms were extended in front of him, his wrists draped over the steering wheel. His voice was soft.

He continued, "Kenny's father came back from war . . . different. He sits and stares all day. Doesn't sleep. Jumps out of his skin at the slightest noise. And Kenny's been on some sort of mission ever since, like he needs to personally right every wrong. And that's admirable, but he's also an impressionable kid easily influenced by a strong personality."

His eyes darted to her and then back to the windshield. With a jolt, she realized the strong personality he was talking about was *hers*. She was indignant; after all, it had been Kenny who'd approached *her* about teaming up on a clandestine investigation, not the other way around. Obviously, she couldn't say this to the sheriff, though.

He continued, "The case is closed. If Kenny's breaking protocol, I'll have to fire him. If I have to fire him, it'll destroy my sister. But make no mistake—if I have to do it, I will. I took an oath to uphold law and order, and nothing is more sacred than that. Not even family."

Maple studied his profile in the dark car. She could only make out the soft edges of him, but somehow she felt as though she was truly seeing him for the first time—and that she might have seriously misjudged him. Beneath the gruff, impatient exterior, Sheriff Scott was dedicated both to his family and to the pursuit of truth and justice.

Or so it seemed. Maple recalled all too well the man's callousness at Elijah Wallace's death scene and the finality with which he'd dismissed her concerns after the fact. Which version of the sheriff was the most authentic?

Equally important, what would Maple's next move be? The sheriff's assertion that she was leading Kenny down a destructive path didn't sit well with her.

"Good night," he said.

"Good night," she replied as she climbed out of his car, "and . . . thank you."

She watched him drive away until his taillights disappeared. Then, she went into her dark, quiet house. She stowed Jamie's coat in the closet and kicked off her shoes. Padding into the kitchen, she flicked on the light, noticing the lack of meowing from the back steps; Mack must've found dinner elsewhere tonight. She tried to ignore her sadness when she realized that he wasn't there.

Her eyes were drawn to the kitchen table, where the chairs were askew, having been pushed back in a hurry. Maple rubbed her forehead. Had it been only a few hours ago that she and Kenny had sat here making plans for their investigation? It seemed like days, weeks, a lifetime had passed since they'd been in such a hurry to get going.

Maple pushed Kenny's chair back in and dropped into the other one. The sheriff's words weighed on her, and she didn't know what to do. They'd found potential evidence at the barn that evening—the rope, the paper, and even maybe the salt crystals were potential leads that should be chased down. However, Maple believed the sheriff when he said he'd fire Kenny if he continued to be involved. The memory of Mrs. Quirk's sad eyes and Mr. Quirk's incessant rocking were strong. Kenny's job might be the only thing keeping that family afloat.

Maple sighed. Charlotte always said Maple was the most principled person she knew, but in reality Maple thrived in situations where the morals were black and white—where it was easy to know the right thing to do. This was far messier. If they gave up, Kenny's job would be safe, but the truth about Elijah Wallace's death would remain hidden. If they continued, they might bring truth to light about the death, but it would come at a devastating cost for Kenny . . . and *was* there even more truth to uncover about Wallace's death? She trusted Dr. Murphy implicitly, and this evening the sheriff had revealed himself to have a higher moral code than she'd expected. Maple was forced to consider the idea that she'd been wrong. Maybe Elijah Wallace had indeed hung himself by accident.

Immediately, counterpoints popped into her head. Her legal training had irreversibly sharpened her natural inclination to play devil's advocate, even if she hadn't gotten to put it to use professionally: What about Mooreland's truck? What about the brand-new rope? What about the marks on Wallace's wrists and the lividity present on his side?

Maple pulled the rope, the paper, and the crystals out of her pocket and placed them on the table. She studied them for several moments, recalling why she and Kenny had collected each of them. Why did the paper and its partial letters look so darn familiar? She frowned. There were too many unexplained details to let this go.

Then, she saw a flaw in her reasoning. She'd been thinking of herself and Kenny as a single unit, as though they had to operate in tandem, but that wasn't necessarily the case. There was another option: she could protect Kenny by shutting him out of the investigation and continuing on her own.

After all, she thought, gazing around her empty house, what did *she* have to lose? Not even a stray cat.

She got up and pulled a box of Kraft macaroni and cheese off the shelf. Having never been much of a cook, she'd liked it for the convenience. Now, the fact that she could buy an entire box for nineteen cents and squeeze at least three meals out of it was the driving factor. It also reminded her of the night she'd met Charlotte. She set a pot of water to boil and tore open the box, pulling the sealed envelope of the crumbly cheese–like substance out and placing it on the counter. Her stomach rumbled, but Maple had no appetite as she contemplated her next move.

Tomorrow, when she accompanied Mrs. Quirk to her appointment at the insurance company, she'd cut Kenny loose. She told herself it was the right thing to do, but the ache in her heart was hard to ignore.

CHAPTER 25

Maple arrived at the store before Ben the next morning and immediately made her way toward the back. It only took her a few moments to find the aisle that contained rope. She pulled the piece out of her pocket and held it up next to each one that Ben had on the shelves. The third one was a match. Her heart thudding, she picked it up and carried it back to her workstation. Movement outside the window caught her eye. She glanced out to see Deputy Rawlings hurrying past. Instinctively, she slid the rope behind her, out of his view, and almost immediately realized that was just the sort of thing someone who had something to hide would do. It didn't matter anyway, because Rawlings never looked in her direction. She tapped her feet, waiting impatiently for Ben to arrive, and accosted him the moment he came through the front door.

"I don't know how you're going to feel about this," she started, "and I don't think I should tell you exactly why I want to know, but can you find out everyone you've sold this rope to? Going back a few months?"

Ben raised his eyebrows. "Well, good morning to you too."

Heat rose in Maple's cheeks. "Sorry."

Frank waddled over and gazed hopefully up at her. She fed him the piece of toast she'd brought, and he munched happily.

She scraped a toe along the floor. "Only if you have time," she added lamely.

"That's kind of an odd request."

Ben stowed his bag behind the counter. He shot her a quizzical look, clearly waiting for her to elaborate. When she didn't, he sighed.

"Here's the thing—I can cross-check my inventory and receipts and will be able to see on which days I sold that particular rope. The records won't show me who the customer was, though."

Maple's heart sank. That sounded time-consuming and not as potentially helpful as she'd thought it might be.

"I'll give it a shot. I don't mind." Ben smiled crookedly.

She smiled gratefully at him, finished shrugging Jamie's coat on, and started to turn toward the door.

"I've never been involved in a murder investigation," Ben offered. "It's kind of exciting."

Maple froze. "Uh—"

The corners of Ben's eyes crinkled. "I know, I know. *What* murder investigation?"

He plastered a look of such extreme innocence on his face that Maple laughed, immediately wondering when she'd last laughed like that, so spontaneous and genuine. It felt good.

Then, she thought of Bill, and a stab of guilt punctured her levity. She twirled her wedding ring with her thumb and considered the fact that she'd used it as an excuse for her unauthorized presence at a crime scene. The sudden ache in her chest stopped her in her tracks. Her memory of Bill's face was no longer crisp and exact. It was starting to go soft and hazy around the edges.

How could she—*she*, of all people, with her photographic memory—start forgetting what her dead husband had looked like? What kind of woman did that? She had a sudden urge to race home and study his photograph, to burn his image into her mind.

Out of the corner of her eye, Maple saw Kenny's car pull up and park in front of the shop window. She was relieved to see he was driving the official sheriff's vehicle and wearing his uniform, which meant his uncle had decided not to fire him for the time being. He also looked like he had aged about ten years in the few hours since she'd last seen him. Kenny climbed out the driver's side while Mrs. Quirk stayed seated in the passenger side. Maple's heart squeezed at the memory of the older woman caring so tenderly for her husband.

"I'm headed out for an appointment," she told Ben, rummaging around in her pockets for her gloves. She found one and put it on. "I'm not sure what time I'll be back."

He assured her he'd have any prospective dollhouse customers leave a note. She thanked him and remembered she'd lost her other glove, so she could stop looking for it in her pocket. Flustered, she took off the one she'd put on, and shoved it back into the pocket it'd come out of. Then, she turned and just about ran out the door, nearly crashing into Kenny, who'd been about to enter, on the sidewalk.

"Ma'am, I owe you an apology."

Maple blinked. "You don't—"

"No, let me finish," he said. "I shouldn't have encouraged you when I gave back your nutshell. That was against protocol."

She waited a beat, but he didn't say anything else. He continued to stare steadily above her head, his Adam's apple bobbing up and down.

"Kenny," she said, "if anyone should be apologizing, it's me. I'm the adult here. I—"

His eyes snapped onto hers so quickly that Maple stumbled back. "I'm *not* a child," he said, his facial features twisting.

Maple held up her hands, palms toward him, in a placating gesture. "That's not what I meant. I—"

"I support my family." His voice cracked. "I'm an officer of the *law*, but everyone underestimates me. My mother, my uncle. I thought *you* were different."

A rock formed in Maple's stomach. "Kenny, please—I misspoke. I'm sorry. I don't think you're a child. I'm very impressed with you, actually."

The look he gave her reminded her of a wounded puppy seeking praise. Over his shoulder, she saw his mother looking at them, her eyes blinking behind her round spectacles.

Maple smiled sadly and moved her gaze back to Kenny's face. "In fact, I find you quite inspiring. Your level of dedication to truth and justice is all too rare, and you've helped me realize some important things in the last day or so."

He brightened a little. She considered whether to tell him then about her brother, to help explain her own continued dedication to the case, but something held her back. She'd already shared more personal details than she was technically comfortable with. Kenny, she decided, didn't need to know about all of that.

"You shouldn't be involved anymore," she said tentatively, still in awe of the unprecedented forcefulness he'd just displayed. "Your uncle's right about the unsanctioned investigation. You have your whole career ahead of you. Imagine the good you'll be able to do. I can . . . continue investigating alone. I asked Ben about the rope we found," she added, trying to hide the loss she was feeling as she pushed him away. "He's going to look into it. And that's the last update I'll give you."

She shook a finger at him in mock sternness. This wasn't how she'd imagined their interaction, how she'd rehearsed it on her walk in this morning. In her mind, it had been swift and clean—a quick, complete break. But people and their emotions were rarely as straightforward in real life as they were in Maple's mind. She watched Kenny's face for a reaction. He nodded almost imperceptibly.

And just like that, Maple was alone again. She realized in that instant that it wasn't just Kenny's investigative skills she'd miss. However brief their time together had been, she'd liked having him as a confidante, someone to share the mission with, to bounce ideas off of. A partner. A friend.

She gathered herself, determined not to let her sadness show. "Okay, then. Let's get your mother to this meeting."

CHAPTER 26

Maple and Mary Quirk greeted each other, but before they could get past opening pleasantries—and before Maple could get into the car—the radio squawked. Kenny reached through the open driver's side window, picked it up, and listened for a moment. Maple could hear Deputy Rawlings's garbled voice, interspersed with loud crackles. Kenny spoke into his own radio and looked at the women with a grim expression.

"I have to go on a call," he said, his expression tense and apologetic.

Maple was tempted to ask him what had happened, but she restrained herself. She looked from Kenny to his mother.

"Mary," she said, "would you feel comfortable if you and I went to the appointment together, just the two of us?"

Mary Quirk looked into Maple's eyes for a long moment and seemed to come to a decision. She nodded once and turned to Kenny.

"Do what you need to do. We'll be fine."

Maple found that she believed her. She didn't know why or how, but somehow she was sure of it: if this tiny woman carrying the weight of the world on her shoulders said they would be fine, then they would. Mary Quirk climbed out of the passenger seat, and they set off down the sidewalk together for the short walk to the insurance office. Behind them, Maple heard the screech of tires as Kenny pulled out of the spot. A moment later, she was surprised to hear the siren wail. She looked over her shoulder, wondering what had happened to send him off in such a hurry.

Despite feeling unsettled about Kenny's abrupt departure, Maple found that Mary made for a companionable walking partner, easily matching Maple's notoriously brisk stride despite her short stature. For the first few minutes, neither woman really said much. Somewhat to her own surprise, Maple broke the silence.

"Kenny's doing a very good job," she said.

Immediately, she winced at the awkwardness of the compliment. Was a grown woman supposed to compliment another grown woman's grown son? And who was she to comment on Kenny's job—she, who'd enticed Kenny to conduct a clandestine investigation that threatened his career? Not for the first time, Maple reflected that situations like this were why she had only one friend.

Or maybe two? She supposed Ben was her friend now too. Charlotte certainly seemed to think so, anyway. Didn't she?

People were so exhausting.

But Mrs. Quirk's face broke into a smile.

"Thank you," she said. "He makes us very proud. He's a good boy. A hard worker."

Maple nodded once. "So," she said briskly, turning to the business at hand, "I think you ought to give me some background before we walk into this meeting. What is it you're asking for?"

Maple sensed Mrs. Quirk slow down next to her. She dropped her own pace to match that of her companion.

Mrs. Quirk gripped the shoulder strap of her pocketbook so hard her knuckles turned white, and she stopped. Maple halted a few paces ahead of her and turned to see Mary gaze off into the distance.

"Justice," Mary said.

Maple waited for her to elaborate, but she didn't. Images flickered rapid-fire through Maple's brain: Elijah Wallace's dangling feet, Jamie swinging from the rafter, her own reflection juxtaposed over the image of the Nazis in Nuremburg . . . She had posed a bigger question to her companion than she'd meant to.

Mary stopped walking, and Maple saw the other woman's knees buckle. Maple grasped her elbow and navigated them both to a nearby bench. Mary closed her eyes as she sat and gathered herself. Maple waited, watching Mary navigate an internal emotional battle.

"Justice means the country that sent him to war takes care of him now that he's back. My husband was a cheerful family man who never missed a day of work in his life. He's a very skilled carpenter." She opened her eyes and beamed with pride at this, and then frowned. "Then he went to Europe and"—she paused for a deep breath—"and he came home a shell of his former self. He barely sleeps. The nightmares are awful, Mrs. Bishop—"

"Please, call me Maple."

Mary nodded her acknowledgment and continued, "I think he's afraid to go to sleep. Sits all day and broods. No one will hire him. Nothing brings him joy, and we're out of money. I've looked for work, but—" She shrugged. "I was a housewife. I have no skills. And now all the jobs are going to the boys who came back—the ones who are physically and mentally capable of work, that is. In some ways, it feels like I said goodbye to one man and welcomed back a stranger."

Mrs. Quirk suddenly gasped and placed her palms on her cheeks. "Oh, but you must think I'm horrible! Here I am complaining when your husband didn't come back at all."

With a start, Maple realized she hadn't been thinking of Bill. She rushed to reassure Mrs. Quirk that she thought no such thing, but wasn't sure the other woman believed her. A vague cloud of guilt settled over Maple. Again, she wondered what kind of woman could forget her own husband so easily.

Mary smoothed the front of her dress. "Anyway, to get back to your original question, I need to know if Ken Senior qualifies for any help from the VA or any insurance money since he's unable to work because of his war injuries."

Maple nodded. "Well, Mr. Duncan was very helpful getting Bill's insurance money to me."

Mary looked at Maple. "I don't like this, you know. Going to this man with my hat in my hand, asking for charity."

Maple reached for her hand and gave it a squeeze. Her own throat was too choked with emotion to speak, but she hoped the gesture conveyed her feelings: *I know. I understand.*

Mary cleared her throat and stood. "No point in wallowing."

Maple agreed. They resumed their brisk pace and continued on their way, but they weren't alone. If Maple had believed in ghosts, she would've sworn there were a few trailing behind them.

As neither Maple nor Mary were the sort of woman who felt compelled to fill every silence with chatter, the rest of their walk to Main Street passed quietly, and before Maple knew it, they were at the door of the insurance agency.

The secretary took their coats and ushered them into Mr. Duncan's office.

"Good afternoon, Mrs. Quirk. Mrs. Bishop, how nice to see you again." He raised his eyebrows at Maple's presumably unexpected presence. "Please come in."

He smiled and gestured to two chairs set up in front of his desk, which, unlike the secretary's, was tidy and sparse.

"It's nice to see you again too, Mr. Duncan," Maple said. "I was telling Mrs. Quirk here how much you helped me with my insurance paperwork, and her son was unable to accompany her today, so I stepped in."

"Ah, yes," he said, clasping his hands together on his desk and nodding. Then, he sighed and said, "Well, Mrs. Quirk, I'm sorry I don't have better news for you."

Maple saw Mary's shoulders tense. "What do you mean?" the woman said in a weak voice.

"I looked over everything after our phone call last week, just as you asked. Your husband, like all returning veterans, had a ten-thousand-dollar life insurance policy paid for by the United States government. That money is payable, upon a serviceman's death, to his immediate family. I don't need to tell you, ma'am, that your husband is still alive."

He said this in a tone indicating that Mr. Quirk's living status was regrettable. Maple got a bad feeling in the pit of her stomach.

"My husband—" Mary started, then stopped. Her eyes blinked rapidly, and her lip quivered.

There was a long pause, and then Maple patted Mary's hand and looked at her, silently asking whether she wanted Maple to step in. Mary squeezed her hand, and Maple cleared her throat.

"Mr. Quirk is unable to hold a job due to his war-related disabilities. Shouldn't the GI Bill entitle him to some government assistance?"

Mary's shoulders sagged, whether from relief that Maple had said this aloud or from shame at her own current situation, Maple didn't know. Probably both. Maple recalled all too well that same mix of emotions when Mr. Duncan had handed her Bill's check.

The insurance man's gaze flashed briefly to Maple and then back to Mrs. Quirk. When he spoke, his voice was quiet and kind, but had an undertone of resignation.

"According to his records, Mr. Quirk has no physical injuries that would prevent him from holding a job."

A sob escaped from Mary. Maple scooted closer to her and hugged her with one arm around her frail, shaking shoulders. Maple made eye contact with Duncan, who quickly moved his own gaze to the file folder in front of him.

"Mr. Quirk," she said in a low voice, "cannot sleep, and on the rare occasions he does, he suffers night terrors. He is in no condition to work."

Duncan closed his eyes. "Believe me, I'm entirely sympathetic. My own father fought in the Great War and returned . . . changed. If there was anything I could do for you, I would do it, Mrs. Quirk. I'm so sorry."

Something snapped inside Maple. "How can that be? The government sent this man to war, and the war sent him back a different person."

Full-blown sobs wracked Mary Quinn's whole body now. Maple hugged her tighter and, with her other hand, reached into her pocketbook and pulled out a handkerchief.

Duncan had no reply.

"It's okay," Maple told her. "We'll figure something out. We can call the Veterans Administration directly."

"The VA has outsourced management of veteran benefits to small insurance agencies like mine all over the country because it's so swamped," Duncan said. "Save yourself the time and don't bother—I'm afraid they won't take your call."

With that, he ushered them from the room, Mrs. Quirk still crying, and shut the door firmly behind them.

With her arm still around Mary's shoulders, Maple steered her companion toward the exit. Kenny's car was parallel parked a block or so down the street. Maple saw Kenny climb out of the driver's seat, a hopeful expression on his face. But as he took in his mother's state, Kenny's expectant expression plunged into one of sadness. Maple shook her head. Kenny's shoulders sagged. He opened the passenger door for his mother.

When she was settled, Kenny returned to the side of the car, where Maple stood.

"What happened?"

"He doesn't qualify."

"For . . . anything?" Kenny asked, but Maple could tell he already knew the answer.

"I'm sorry. I tried."

A funny look came over Kenny's face. He almost looked offended, but for the life of her, Maple couldn't figure out why. She was about to ask him if everything was all right when he spoke abruptly.

"We'll bring my mom home first, and then there's something you and I need to do." He looked away when he said that, and Maple went on high alert.

"Kenny, we're not investiga—"

"I'm well aware," he snapped. "Please get in the car."

Taken aback, Maple did as she was told.

The ride to the Quirks' house was very quiet. From behind Mary, Maple watched as Kenny glanced over to check on his mother every few seconds. At one stop sign, he took her left hand with his right and held it for the rest of the drive.

Kenny parked in the driveway. The windows were all dark, save for a single pale light shining out of the last one on the left. Maple could see the silhouette of a man rocking slowly back and forth in a chair by the window. Mary turned around. Her eyes were dry. Only small traces of red remained around the rims.

"Thank you," she said, "for trying."

Words bubbled up in Maple's throat. She wanted to say, *We won't give up!* or *We'll call the VA tomorrow!* She wanted to assure the other woman that the insurance agent didn't have the last say, that hope still remained to attain justice for her husband, for their family.

But she wasn't sure any of that was actually true. The words died before they got to her lips. She watched Mary Quirk lift her head, square her shoulders, and stride up the path to her house, with Kenny trailing her. It was the bravest thing she'd seen in a long while.

CHAPTER 27

When he came back to the car, the hurt in Kenny's eyes had been replaced by steely fire. He gestured through the window that Maple should move to the front seat. She shook her head.

He narrowed his eyes, opened the driver's door, and said, "I'm not your damn chauffeur."

She was so surprised by the flatness in his voice—something she'd never heard from him before—that she obeyed. Or she tried to, but it turned out the back seat doors didn't open from the inside.

So the criminals who sit back here can't escape, she thought.

She waited for Kenny to press the button that unlocked them, and then slid, chastened, from the back and settled herself into the passenger seat.

He waited for her to fasten her seatbelt and then turned on the engine. "Ginger Comstock is missing."

Of all the things she'd expected him to say, that wasn't one of them. "Ginger . . . what?"

"That's the call I went on while you were at the insurance appointment. She's missing, and my uncle thinks you might know something about it. I'm supposed to bring you in."

Maple's head swam. "I—wait, what do you mean, 'bring me in'? Does he think I *kidnapped* her or something?"

Kenny didn't reply as he made a left turn. Maple could tell they were headed to the sheriff's office. Her heartbeat thudded in her ears.

"What is going on?" Maple could hear the shrill tone in her own voice.

"I can't tell you anything else. I've already said too much."

"Kenny, this is *me*, for goodness sake. Tell me what's happening."

He shot her a sidelong look, but she couldn't read his expression. For the rest of the drive—five minutes that felt like an eternity—Kenny remained stubbornly, infuriatingly silent.

He finally spoke after they parked. "Come on. They're waiting."

Maple followed him across the parking lot and into the office. The sky was just beginning to darken. She pulled Jamie's coat tighter around herself. This time, upon entering the office, there was no secretary to greet her. Instead of heading left into the sheriff's personal office, like last time, Kenny led Maple in the other direction. He opened a door that led down a hallway to the right. She caught a glimpse of jail cells before Kenny ushered her into a small room with a harsh white light, a chipped Formica table, and three metal chairs. The sheriff stood behind one, leaning his knuckles on the table. Deputy Rawlings was seated in a chair in the corner, holding a steaming cup of coffee.

"That doesn't look comfortable." She pointed to the sheriff's knuckles, which were white from being pressed against the tabletop. "If that pose is meant to intimidate me, you can stop. I'm sufficiently intimidated."

"You always have a witty comment, don't you." The sheriff phrased it as a statement, rather than a question.

Kenny closed the door behind them, and Maple felt the air settle around her. She immediately felt claustrophobic and supposed that was the intention. Kenny pulled out a chair for her, and she sat. He remained standing between her and the door. Deputy Rawlings reached forward and placed the coffee cup in front of her. She looked across the table at the sheriff, trying to read the expression in his eyes.

"What is this?" She gestured to the cup of coffee and then to the glowering sheriff. "Good cop, bad cop? One of you butters me up with cheap coffee while the other tries to frighten me?"

"That's not what this is," Rawlings said.

Maple kept her gaze trained on the sheriff. "Do I need a lawyer? You do know I *am* a lawyer, don't you?"

"You're a witness, not a person of interest."

"Well, that's good to know. But I'm curious: Do you interview all your *witnesses* in cramped interrogation rooms?"

The sheriff's jaw muscle twitched. Maintaining eye contact with Maple, he slowly stood up to his full height.

"When was the last time you saw Ginger Comstock?"

Maple didn't like his tone. "I'm not compelled to answer that question."

"Have you seen her since you verbally assaulted her on Monday in front of multiple witnesses?"

It took her a beat to realize he was talking about the day Ginger had swooped into the hardware store with her cronies and informed Maple that Elijah's death had been ruled an accident.

Maple glared at Sheriff Scott. "I object to that characterization of events, and I decline to answer the question."

"I've got all day."

"Well, I don't. I have things to do that don't involve being dragged into the police station for questioning." Maple's cheeks were getting hot. She tried to slow her breathing.

"I told you, you aren't—"

She waved her hand in a mock airy gesture. "Sorry, I meant *invited mandatorily into the police station as a witness.*"

"Listen," Rawlings said, holding up his palms, "no one wants to get you into trouble here, Mrs. Bishop, but I'm gonna level with you: we're concerned about Mrs. Comstock's welfare."

Maple's stomach dropped. What details led them to be this concerned? Where was Ginger?

"She went to the grocery store this morning and didn't return home. She was supposed to host a sewing circle today, but when the other ladies arrived, Mrs. Comstock was nowhere to be found. Her husband hasn't heard from her, and she didn't show up to pick up her daughter from school. She just vanished without a trace."

All three officers were studying her intently, so she fought to keep her expression and body language neutral, though her heart sank. Maple knew—as did all the officers and, really, anyone who knew Ginger—that Ginger would never voluntarily miss hosting her sewing circle. And though Maple had little regard for Ginger's character, she had a hard time believing Ginger would fail to show up for little Camille.

"Where is she?" snarled the sheriff.

She threw her hands up in the air. "How should *I* know? Probably spreading gossip somewhere. That doesn't sound like a question you'd ask a *witness*, and I can hardly be a witness when I didn't *see* anything."

"Were you interfering with an investigation after you'd been expressly forbidden to do so?"

Maple's scalp prickled. So that's what this was about. But why? Her mind whirred. There must be some connection between Elijah Wallace and Ginger Comstock. Panic rose in her as she realized that, for some reason, the police thought *she* was that connection.

She fought to keep her tone even. "You told me you closed the case of Elijah Wallace's death. How could I be interfering with something that doesn't exist?"

"You know what I mean," the sheriff spat through clenched teeth. "Are you conducting an unauthorized investigation?"

Maple fought to keep her voice steady. "Again, I feel the need to point out to you that this doesn't sound like a question for a *witness*, Sheriff. I'm concerned we're straying into territory that sounds more like I'm being questioned."

"Just answer him."

Kenny's impatient voice was so unexpected that Maple reared back a little in her chair. The sheriff, too, looked caught off guard, whether by his nephew's tone or by the words themselves, Maple wasn't sure.

She took a deep breath. "As we've already discussed, I graduated from law school. Though I don't currently work as a professional lawyer, I maintain an intellectual curiosity about legal studies and issues. That includes crime scene investigation and determinations of cause of death."

She looked at Kenny, whose expression was unreadable.

"Intellectual curiosity," the sheriff repeated skeptically.

Maple's blood boiled. "Yes, you see, intellectual curiosity is what happens when—"

"Enough," Kenny interrupted her snappish retort. "She's told us everything she knows. Send her home."

His tone was flat. Maple looked in his eyes, which were flat too.

But Kenny wasn't exactly right. She had nothing to add to their investigation of Ginger's disappearance, but what if it was linked—somehow—to Wallace's death? In that case, she could've told the sheriff about the tire tracks and the rope. For a moment, she considered doing it, but Kenny knew the same things she did, and he wasn't exactly falling all over himself to spill the beans.

With one glance at the sheriff, she remembered how quickly and completely he'd dismissed her when she'd visited him with her nutshell. And really, what had changed in the meantime? She was no closer to proving the truth about Elijah Wallace's death than she'd been back then. She'd alienated Kenny and irritated the sheriff. She had a lot of suspicions, but no proof.

And now Ginger Comstock was missing.

With a chill, Maple remembered how alone she'd felt right after gently cutting Kenny loose earlier that day. Now, she blinked under the fluorescent light. Looking from Kenny's face back to the sheriff's, she realized that feeling had been nothing compared to this one. She had no business meddling in any official business, especially not when literal life and death were involved. Maple wasn't a lawyer or a trained investigator. She was just a lady who made dollhouses. The irony that hit her then almost made her laugh aloud: if she couldn't make her mortgage payment, those were the only houses she'd have left.

They went around in verbal circles for twenty more minutes before the sheriff finally acknowledged that Kenny had been correct, and announced that Maple could go home, instructing

Kenny to drive her. Kenny left the interview room without looking at her. Maple followed him out to the parking lot. His shoulders were rigid and his stride quick and jerky. They arrived at the parked car, and he unlocked it.

"Should I sit in the front or the back?"

Her tone was sharp. Resentful. What she was *really* asking him was whether she should behave like a criminal or a guest.

"Front," he grunted.

Guest, then. Maple supposed that was a good sign, but she still felt disgruntled toward her erstwhile partner.

They climbed in, he started the engine, and they turned left out of the parking lot toward Maple's house. Maple fumed. Kenny could've given her a proper warning. He could've stuck up for her in that room beyond his cursory suggestion that the sheriff let her go, which hadn't exactly been a ringing endorsement of her innocence. And after she'd taken the entire morning to help his parents.

Her indignation was working up to a full head of steam when Kenny burst through the wall of silence: "You know, you don't always have to make it so hard for people to like you."

Maple gaped at him. He might as well have punched her in the stomach; all the air left her body.

Kenny smacked the steering wheel. "Darn it, that didn't come out right."

"How was it supposed to come out?" Her voice was calm and chilly.

Kenny winced. "What I mean is you don't have to be so suspicious all the time. And it wouldn't hurt to, you know, smile more, like other ladies do. And not get into loud arguments in public."

Maple clenched her hands together in her lap. "Oh, I see."

Kenny missed the sarcasm dripping from her voice. When he replied, his relief was palpable. "You do?"

"Sure. Because I'm a woman, I should be meek and smile and agree with everyone about everything all the time. And then you big scary police officers wouldn't think I was a kidnapper."

Kenny pulled into her driveway, slumped forward, and ran a hand through his hair. "That's not what I meant at all. I just meant my uncle wouldn't be so suspicious of you if you just . . . behaved better."

Bitterness overwhelmed her. As Maple opened her door, she paraphrased Kenny's words from earlier today, spitting them back at him over her shoulder. "Everyone misjudges me. And here I thought *you* were different."

She slammed the door behind her, putting all her fury into a satisfying *bang*—but her satisfaction was short-lived when she saw her front door. She froze.

Behind her, Kenny clambered out of the driver's side. "What the hell?"

There, hanging from a crudely fastened noose attached to her doorknob, was a doll. A note was taped above it. In large capital letters, someone had scrawled: *"THIS IS WHAT WILL HAP-PEN IF YOU DON'T MIND YOUR OWN BUSINESS."*

CHAPTER 28

Maple's hands flew automatically to her throat. A realization hit her like a ton of bricks: the doll hanging from the noose was the brown-haired one she'd kept from the Wallaces' dollhouse.

"That doll—" she started.

"What?" He moved quickly, sliding in front of her before she responded.

"It—it was in Bill's office. The person who did this was inside my house."

At this, Kenny's eyes went a shade darker.

He unholstered his gun and barked, "Stay right there."

He gestured for her to hand over her house keys, which she did. She watched him approach her house and carefully use one hand to unlock the door while keeping the gun trained in front of him with the other.

"Police!" he shouted as he entered the house.

He disappeared from view, and Maple felt each second he was gone tick by with her own heartbeat.

Finally, he poked his head out and said, "All clear. Come in."

Maple felt like a trespasser in her own home as she stepped over the threshold and followed Kenny down the hall.

"I think he came in through the office window—it was open. The desk in there is a disaster. Nothing else looked amiss in the house, but we'll do a walk-through, and you tell me."

She followed him into the office. Her hand flew over her mouth when she saw that the desk had been turned onto its side, the contents of its drawers ransacked and strewn about the floor. Books had been pulled from the shelf and thrown all around. The lock on Bill's filing cabinet was busted; all three drawers had been yanked open and left that way. A blast of cold air shot through the open window. She pulled Jamie's coat tighter around herself.

Kenny placed a steadying hand on her shoulder.

"May I close the window?" she asked, struggling to keep her voice steady.

He stepped around the debris and moved toward the window.

"Careful!" she cried. "You'll leave—"

"Fingerprints, I know," he said, pulling a handkerchief out of his pocket and wrapping it around his fingers before he shut the window.

A tour through every nook and cranny of the house revealed nothing out of place in any other rooms. Maple was relieved that her dollhouses appeared undisturbed. She followed Kenny to the kitchen, where he directed her to sit at the table. She did. Kenny filled two glasses with water and took a seat across from her, glancing at the granules and the scrap of paper that still resided on the table.

"Who do you think did it?" he asked, handing her one of the glasses.

"Oh, are we *friends* again?" Maple's tone was icy.

Kenny met her gaze. "Were we ever friends? Or were you just using me when it was convenient for you?"

A knife twisted in Maple's gut. "What?" she whispered.

"You heard me. You wanted your nutshell back. I had it. You wanted inside information. I'm your source. You needed a ride back to the scene of the crime. I have a car."

The bitterness in his voice was palpable. Was that really what he thought? That she only valued him for his *car*? Tears pricked at Maple's eyelids, but instead of allowing herself to give in to hurt and betrayal, she channeled her anger.

"Well, now *you* hear *me* when I tell you *again* that I ended our partnership to protect you!" she shouted. "And *you* were the one who came to *me* to return the nutshell! I never asked you to do that!"

They glared at each other across the table, both breathing heavily. A loud meow came from outside.

"You have a cat?" Kenny asked.

"No."

She didn't offer any further explanation, but the interruption caused some of the tension to fizzle out of the room.

"I'm sorry," Kenny said. "You're right."

Maple picked up her cup and took a long gulp of water. "I know."

Kenny cracked a smile.

In a more measured tone, she asked, "Do you really believe that I used you?"

He sighed. "No. I just . . . I don't know. I think I'm getting paranoid. Disillusioned, maybe. Being a cop isn't exactly turning out like I thought it would. I expected to be helping people. Instead, a lot of times when we show up, people are actually angry at us. A wife whose husband's been beating her suddenly turns on us when we try to arrest him and takes his side, saying she was confused when she called us and that actually everything's okay now, and we should leave, even though he just gave her a black eye. Oh, and she was seven months pregnant."

He gazed out the window, and Maple's heart twisted. She thought of Angela Wallace and how she'd cowered in the presence of Elijah. She was still annoyed at Kenny but was beginning to understand his perspective a little better.

"Or a guy yells at us when we follow up on a tip that he's been manufacturing fake ration cards and selling them." Kenny threw his hands up in disbelief. "He's the one who broke the law, but somehow it's my fault he's getting the consequence that the law specifies!"

"People are irrational," Maple agreed, but she was distracted. Something he'd just said pinged in her brain.

"It's not fair, you know?" Kenny sipped his water, and suddenly Maple's anger surged to the surface again.

"Life isn't fair," she snapped. "You know that as well as I do, and there's no sense wallowing about it. You think people are going to thank you for arresting their husbands or slapping them with a fine for breaking a law?"

Kenny sulked, then gestured to the granules and scrap of paper lying on the table between them. "Why did you even keep these? What's the point?"

Maple's eyes followed his hand, and something clicked. She peered at the granules, which—in the brighter light of the afternoon—were bigger and paler than salt crystals. She heard Kenny's words in her head: *"fake ration cards."* She studied the scrap of paper, realizing all of a sudden why she felt she'd seen it before.

Kenny said, "I'm hungry. You got anything to eat?"

Maple ignored him and licked one of her fingers and pressed it to the granules.

"What are you doing?" Kenny's tone was astonishment mixed with irritation.

Maple moved her finger to her lips. A familiar taste—one she hadn't experienced in a long time—exploded in her mouth, and she locked eyes with Kenny.

"We were wrong. This isn't salt," she said.

Kenny sputtered incomprehensibly. Maple picked up the scrap of paper and pointed to the letters, excitement and horror growing inside her simultaneously.

"I knew I'd seen these letters in this font before," she said slowly, "and I just realized . . ."

Kenny looked at her expectantly, waiting for her to finish her thought or give him a snack. Possibly both.

Instead, she started digging through her trash can. She pulled out the two cookies she'd thrown away and held them up triumphantly.

Kenny shook his head. "Listen, I don't need a snack *that* badly."

"This is it," Maple told him. "This is the connection between Elijah's death and Ginger's disappearance."

Kenny eyed her skeptically. "Cookies? That's the connection?"

"Yes!"

He rubbed his forehead. "You're gonna need to back up, like, five thousand steps to bring me up to speed here."

"This scrap of paper was torn off a Domino's package. And this isn't salt—it's sugar."

Kenny furrowed his brow. She closed her eyes. She had to say it now, damn the consequences.

"And it might be the reason Elijah is dead and Ginger is missing."

CHAPTER 29

Kenny dipped his own finger into the small pile of granules and placed them on his tongue.

"Dammit, you're right. Why on earth was there *sugar* in that hayloft?" Kenny breathed.

"What if . . ." Maple trailed off, her mind spinning. Was her idea too far-fetched for Kenny to believe it?

"What if *what*?" Kenny exclaimed. "Tell me what you're thinking!"

Maple decided she had to go for it. She looked him straight in the eyes. "What if Elijah Wallace wasn't just selling soap out of his barn? What if he was selling black market sugar too?"

Kenny narrowed his eyes. Maple's heart thudded as her excitement grew.

"Think about it," she said. "Sugar is the only thing still under major rations now that the war's over, and maple syrup's at such a premium that most people can't afford it. The soap was a cover for the sugar; customers could pretend they were there for one thing, but really they were there for the other."

Kenny pursed his lips, looking thoughtful.

"My point is this: Ginger brought me these cookies to try and wheedle information out of me after I found Elijah's body. I thought she was just after gossip, but what if it was more than that? What if she was concerned about the sugar ring being found out?" Maple shook her head. "I knew there was sugar in those cookies. I knew it, but I couldn't explain it, so I dismissed my instincts. I figured it was impossible to get sugar, so she must've used some other sweetener."

Kenny narrowed his eyes and nodded. "But it wasn't impossible—not if you knew where to buy it illegally."

Maple felt a small thrill: Kenny was back on her side. They were riding the same wave together.

"Ginger Comstock was one of Wallace's customers."

"And that kind of thing would be hard to hide from your neighbor, especially one who monitored your activity closely because he had a massive grudge against you . . . making Russell Mooreland an even more perfect suspect than he was before. Killing Wallace eliminates the feud and enables him to take over the black market sugar operation."

Kenny shook his head, and Maple's excitement drooped.

"What?" she said defensively. "You don't believe me? It makes sense!"

"I know it makes sense!" Kenny smacked his forehead but didn't elaborate.

"And if Mooreland killed Wallace and kidnapped Ginger, then he's probably the one who broke in here and left me those threats."

Kenny pressed his lips together. Maple could practically see the gears turning in his brain.

"But how the heck do we even investigate it, let alone prove it?" he finally burst out.

Maple eyed Kenny. "You have a badge."

He rubbed both hands over his face. "You want me to storm onto Mooreland's property, demanding to see his illegal sugar operation? The one we can't prove exists because our only evidence—which is highly circumstantial, by the way—was obtained illegally? The one no judge in his right mind would sign a search warrant for?"

Maple knew he was right, but it didn't stop her from glaring at him.

Kenny scratched his head. "Okay, let's assume you're right about her being a customer—and I'd like to emphasize that I consider that a big assumption, but just for the sake of argument—aside from losing her access to illegal sugar, why would she be so concerned about Wallace's death?"

"Reputation." Maple began pacing. "Ginger traffics in reputations, and gossip is her favorite form of currency. She finds out everyone's secrets, which gives her power and influence. She spreads rumors. People are afraid of her." Maple stopped and looked Kenny in the eye. "But what if her own reputation was ruined? If word got out that she was circumventing rations, people would be angry. We're supposed to all be in this war effort together. My God, her own husband fought overseas, and the whole point of rations is that we make do with less for the greater good—so the boys overseas can get what they need, so we could win this war."

Until she said those words out loud, Maple had been too busy thinking over the logistics and rearranging puzzle pieces of information around inside her brain to react to the idea of exploiting rations. Now, though, she was angry. She thought of the sacrifices she and everyone she knew had made: of Bill's car with its missing tires, of countless cups of sugarless tea—

"Why kidnap Ginger?" Kenny asked.

"My guess?" Maple arched an eyebrow. "She knew too much and was becoming a liability. Can't keep her mouth shut."

"Okaaaaaaay . . ." Kenny looked troubled. "It's just—"

"What?" Maple demanded.

He looked doubtful. "Well, it's not exactly a secret that Ginger's not your favorite person."

Maple was tired of him beating around the bush. "Kenny, you clearly have something more you want to say. Would you spit it out already?"

"Okay, fine: you're biased. You'd love it if Ginger Comstock was involved in something illegal, so maybe you're giving more weight to the idea that she's involved because it's what you want to be true."

Maple told herself to take several deep breaths before she responded. She only made it halfway through one. "And *you*, for some reason, are determined for *me* to be wrong! You're giving more weight to any idea that contradicts any of my ideas!"

Kenny tossed his hands up in disbelief. "You're the one who threw away perfectly good cookies! Can you blame me?"

Maple mirrored his stance, throwing her own hands in the air. "*That's* what you're concerned about?"

But then she saw Kenny's slightly mischievous half smile. Staring at each other across a table strewn with granules, torn paper, and spilled cookies, they both lowered their arms. Maple, breathing heavily, wondered where they stood in their relationship. She had trusted Kenny and he'd trusted her, but he'd been so distant and hostile toward her today, just when she'd needed him most. The intruder's presence in her home and the grisly message he'd left on her porch had rattled her to her core. The intruder had changed the rules of the game. Upped the ante. This wasn't just a cold case anymore. Maple was now the victim of a crime herself, the recipient of a threat on her life.

And Ginger Comstock was still missing.

Maple voiced what she was sure was on both of their minds. "What if Ginger's still alive? What if he's holding her somewhere?"

Kenny, looking grim, sighed. "Okay, let's go check it out." He pointed at her sternly. "But we're just doing a drive-by, that's all, to get the lay of the land. Then, we're going straight into the office to file a report on your break-in and tell my uncle and Deputy Rawlings what we think."

She nodded her understanding, and he pulled his keys from his pocket.

"I don't suppose there's any point in telling you to stay here." He said it as a statement, not a question, and looked almost bemused. Maple shook her head.

"That's what I thought," he muttered.

A minute later, they were in the car, headed to Mooreland's house. Dusk had settled over Elderberry, and the silence between them in the car was tense. Maple wondered again what accounted for Kenny's attitude change. Was it that Maple had failed to get insurance coverage for his father? She felt bad about that, but it certainly wasn't her fault. No, she realized—Kenny's tone toward her had changed before that visit, when she'd met him and his mother prior to the trip to the insurance company. She glanced at Kenny's profile. His eyes were on the road, and a tiny muscle in his jaw clenched and unclenched. Maple clenched and unclenched her fists in the lap, unconsciously matching her rhythm to his.

For the first time since they'd left Maple's driveway, a set of headlights appeared as a vehicle approached from the opposite direction. The lights were set too far up to be a car, and Maple wondered whether it could be Mooreland driving his truck away from his farm. Immediately, her mind raced to find a way to convince Kenny they should snoop around if no one was home. She craned her neck to watch the vehicle's approach, but it wasn't Mooreland. A large truck piled high with hay bales passed by them. The driver never took his eyes off the road. Maple frowned.

"Something's wonky," she said.

"What?" Kenny asked.

"I don't know. I just have a feeling."

He shot her a sideways glance, then looked forward again, gripping the steering wheel a little tighter. He slowed down a minute later when they got near Mooreland's farm, his headlights bouncing as the car navigated the potholes. A rabbit skittered across the road. Maple peered out the driver's side window while Kenny glanced back and forth between the road ahead and Mooreland's property.

"I think I see something—can you swing around?" Maple asked. "There's a big pile of something right in front of the barn."

Kenny pulled a U-turn and headed back for another pass by the farm. An exterior light flicked on and Mooreland's hulking frame emerged from the house into the driveway. He was headed for the barn when he stopped and squinted into Kenny's headlights, his expression alarmed. At that moment, Maple could make out the shape of the pile.

"Kenny, it's bags of sugar! I can see the Domino logos," she gasped. "I bet you that truck that passed us just dropped them off! We caught him red-handed!"

She could hardly believe their luck. Kenny looked like he felt somewhat less lucky. His expression was grim as he pressed the button that made the siren whoop three times.

"So much for driving by," Kenny muttered.

He swung the car into the driveway, lights flashing, and Mooreland slowly raised his hands into the air.

Kenny parked but left the headlights shining on Mooreland, who squinted but kept his hands up.

"Stay here," Kenny barked at Maple.

The car had barely come to a stop, but Kenny was already halfway out, with his gun drawn. Maple watched as Kenny proceeded to cuff Russell Mooreland's hands behind his back. He holstered his weapon and relaxed slightly, though she could tell from the rigid way he held his shoulders that he was still in a hypervigilant state.

This was the moment Maple had been waiting for. Now that Mooreland was subdued, Maple had no intention of staying put, regardless of Kenny's directions.

"Where is she?" Maple demanded as she tumbled out of the car.

"Who?" Mooreland said.

"Mrs. Bishop—" Kenny said in a warning tone. He was behind Mooreland, holding onto the cuffs, and his thin frame resembled a toothpick in contrast to that of the robust farmer.

Maple turned her attention to the bags. Now that she was up close, she was momentarily stunned by how many bags of sugar were piled on Mooreland's driveway. There had to be close to a hundred five-pound bags. She felt almost dizzy in the presence of five hundred pounds of sugar.

"Ginger Comstock." Maple looked back at Mooreland and ignored Kenny's admonishment. "Where is she?"

Mooreland let loose a string of curse words that made Kenny's ears go pink, concluding with, "How should *I* know where she is? Probably at her house, talking her husband's ear off. The poor bastard," he added almost as an afterthought.

"Okay, that's enough. C'mon, Mooreland, we're going over to the car."

Kenny guided the farmer with one of his hands on the cuffs and the other on one of Mooreland's shoulders.

"Maple, get back in the car and hand me the radio through the driver's side window," Kenny instructed.

His use of her first name was not lost on Maple, who wondered whether this was a sign Kenny was starting to see her as a partner again. She did as he asked, rolling down the driver's side window to pass the radio to him, and listened as he radioed in the bare details of their situation and requested backup. Kenny winced as his uncle replied in a voice teeming with cold fury that he'd be responding to their location stat. Clearly, the sheriff would demand a further explanation in person, but didn't want to get into it over the radio. Maple was resigned to the long process of explaining themselves that awaited her and Kenny when the sheriff got there—but first they had to see what Mooreland knew.

When Kenny handed the radio back to her, she opened her mouth, but he cut her off.

"I'm going to question him. You stay in the car. No arguments. I'm a responding officer with an arrest and a civilian. This is far from an ideal situation, and I'm not putting you in any more danger tonight."

Maple appraised him and decided this wasn't a battle to fight. "Leave the window open," she finally said.

Kenny sighed but didn't insist on the window being rolled up. He turned his attention to his prisoner.

"All right, Mooreland, obviously you're smuggling sugar here. No point denying that. Now tell us where you're keeping Ginger Comstock."

Mooreland shook his head. "Where'm I keeping her? Boy, are you drunk? I can barely stand that woman. I'm not keeping her anywhere." He began rolling his shoulders around, seemingly trying to get comfortable in the handcuffs.

"So, if I search the premises, I'm not gonna find her tied up in your barn or anything like that?"

Mooreland went still. "What? No."

"Because I'm going to have a look around as soon as the sheriff gets here."

Because Mooreland was facing Maple, she could see the shock on Mooreland's face as he replied. It looked genuine to her. Ginger wasn't here, and Mooreland didn't know she was missing.

"Look around all you want," Mooreland said. "You won't find any woman here, let alone Ginger Comstock. You accusing me of kidnapping?"

"How about murder?" Maple piped up before Kenny could respond. "What do you know about Elijah Wallace's death? This is his sugar ring you took over, isn't it?"

Mooreland's body language changed at this. He straightened up and his face went white, accentuating the red welts that now stood out even more brightly against his otherwise pale skin.

"Now, hold on just a minute," Mooreland said, his voice low and a little shaky. "I'm no murderer. I hated Elijah Wallace, sure, and I'm not sad he's gone. And I did take over the sugar, but I didn't kill him."

Mooreland's entire persona had transformed. Gone was the silent fury he'd exuded since they'd caught him with the sugar. The intimidating presence that had confronted her during that first trip to the Wallaces' farm was a distant memory. Even the defiant posturing of a few minutes ago had vanished. The man before her now was a cowering shadow of his former self. She, so often accused of being *too honest*, recognized deep down that Mooreland was telling them the truth about the murder. She would've bet her house on it.

All of her houses, actually.

Maple felt dizzy. Ever since she'd discovered Wallace's body, Mooreland had been her prime suspect. Now . . . what?

The sheriff's car came screeching into the driveway, skidding to a halt next to Kenny's. Sheriff Scott climbed out with impressive speed for a man of his girth and looked from Kenny to Mooreland, to Maple.

"Explain."

"Mr. Mooreland's running an illegal sugar distribution center on his property, Sheriff," Kenny said. "It's in violation of rations rules, obviously. We discovered upward of a hundred bags of sugar he was preparing to resell on the black market."

The sheriff's jaw twitched. "We?" he echoed, looking from Kenny to Maple and back again.

Kenny flushed. "We were on our way to the office to report a break-in at Mrs. Bishop's house when we saw Mr. Mooreland here unloading these bags that were just delivered."

The sheriff waved a hand. "Hold on, hold on. What break-in? And there's no scenario in which *this*"—he gestured to Mooreland's property—"is even vaguely on the way from her house to the station."

While the men were occupied talking to one another, Maple took the opportunity to climb out of the passenger seat. She stood next to the car and watched Mooreland's eyes, frantic and pleading, following the argument between the two officers. They were the eyes of someone accused of a thing he hadn't done.

Kenny, wide-eyed, looked over the sheriff's shoulder as he spoke. "Sheriff, sir, the more pressing issue at the moment is that we think Mooreland might have kidnapped Mrs. Comstock and also that it's possible he killed Elijah Wallace. All due respect, the most important thing right now is to search the premises to see if he's holding her here against her will."

"I didn't! I swear!" Mooreland cried.

Warning bells pinged inside Maple's brain. Smuggling certainly wasn't the same as murder, and if Mooreland hadn't killed Elijah Wallace, then who had? And where was Ginger?

"Elijah Wallace's death was an accident," the sheriff growled.

"Sheriff," Maple said, "I—"

"Enough," he said, and turned to Mooreland. "Do you know where Mrs. Comstock is?"

"No!" Mooreland said. "I don't deny the sugar, but I never kidnapped or killed anyone. You gotta believe me."

"Do you have an alibi for the day of Elijah Wallace's death?" Kenny asked.

Mooreland threw up his hands. "Working my farm like I do every day, seven days a week."

The sheriff's eyes shot daggers at Kenny, but before he could open his mouth, Maple said, "It doesn't matter."

Kenny and the sheriff both whirled on her. The world had turned upside down. How was this possible? Maple had been so sure it was Mooreland. It had all made so much sense . . . until it didn't.

Maple looked into Kenny's eyes. "He's telling you the truth. We were wrong. *I* was wrong. He's not the killer."

Kenny studied her for a long moment, and Maple wondered what he was thinking. Would he berate her? Argue with her? Or did he believe her that she believed Mooreland?

"Go search the premises," the sheriff snapped at Kenny. "I'm loading him into the car, then you're gonna take him downtown to book him."

"For what?" Mooreland asked.

The sheriff moved behind the prisoner and took control of his cuffs from Kenny, who dashed off, flashlight and gun drawn, to search the farm.

"That depends," the sheriff growled, shaking the chain connecting the cuffs so hard that Mooreland stumbled. "We're gonna wait here in silence until my officer returns. We'll see what he finds, or doesn't find"—at this, he looked meaningfully at Maple—"and then I'll let you know what I'm charging you with."

Minutes ticked by. Maple was highly aware of the beating of her own heart. Finally, Kenny returned and shook his head once. "Nothing else."

"Okay, Mooreland, it's your lucky day," the sheriff said, opening the back door with one hand and maintaining the other on the cuffs.

"Yeah, I'm feeling really lucky," Mooreland muttered.

"Well, you should, because you don't deserve luck," the sheriff spat. "You're an unpatriotic lawbreaker, and you disgust me. You know that poster downtown? The one with a giant thumb pressing a stamp down on top of a tiny man?"

Maple could picture it. The tagline underneath the image read "Stamp Out Black Markets."

The sheriff shoved Mooreland unceremoniously into the car. "Well, that thumb is *me* pressing down on *you*, pal."

Even amid her emotional turmoil, Maple felt a flicker of satisfaction at this.

As he slammed the door, the sheriff grumbled, "That bum. I haven't had sugar in my coffee in *years*."

Chapter 30

With Mooreland stowed in the backseat, Sheriff Scott turned his attention to Kenny and Maple.

"I have a lot of questions for you two," he said, glaring from one to the other, "but my first is, what's this about a break-in at your house?"

Kenny explained what he and Maple had discovered at her house. The sheriff listened, dead-eyed, and then shook his head.

"Here's what I need you to do. Take him back to the office, book him on charges of smuggling, and lock him up. We'll see if he makes bail. File a report on Mrs. Bishop's home invasion. Then, go catch a few hours of sleep. I'm going to need you in early tomorrow."

Kenny gulped. "I'm not . . . fired?"

The sheriff's nostrils flared. "Somewhat against my better judgment, no, you're not. But you are creating an awful lot of paperwork for me."

"Yessir."

"And you know how I feel about paperwork."

Seeming to think it was best to act before his uncle could change his mind, Kenny hopped into his car and backed down Mooreland's driveway.

The sheriff rubbed his mustache and said, "I don't know what to do with you."

Maple cocked her head. "Excuse me?"

"He wasn't like this until you came around."

"Like what?"

"Trouble." He pulled his keys from his pocket and nodded at the car. "Let's go."

The drive back to Maple's house was quiet. Maple churned over the events of the evening, trying to figure out where the new puzzle pieces fit. She was convinced, now, that Mooreland hadn't killed Wallace or kidnapped Ginger. However, had he been the one who'd left her the threatening note and doll? She supposed it was possible—perhaps he'd feared that she was getting too close to the truth about his sugar-smuggling operation. But she was forced to admit it was unlikely. No, whoever had killed Wallace and taken Ginger had the most to lose and was therefore more likely to take the risk of breaking into Maple's house in broad daylight in order to warn her off. But her suspect list had only really had one name on it. Now that that name was crossed off, she wasn't sure what to do. Maybe she could try to get to Mooreland to ask him some more questions tomorrow. If he didn't make bail, he'd still be locked up. She just had to figure out a way to get the sheriff to let her speak with him.

She glanced sideways at the sheriff, who stared straight ahead.

"You did good finding out about the sugar smuggling," he said.

She pulled back in surprise. She and Kenny had broken about half a dozen protocols—if not outright laws—tonight, and a compliment was the last thing she'd been expecting from the gruff sheriff.

"Thanks," she said tentatively. Then, she added, "You . . . don't think I really had anything to do with Ginger's disappearance, do you?"

"No," he said slowly. "No, I don't suppose that I do."

He turned into Maple's driveway.

"Well, good, because—"

"Hold it right there. Don't push your luck."

"You're not going to stop looking for her, are you?" Maple asked.

The sheriff shook his head, but he had a resigned look on his face. Maple had a bad feeling about what that look meant: the sheriff didn't think he had much chance of finding Ginger—at least, not alive.

The sheriff walked inside with her to ensure the intruder hadn't returned in her absence. Everything inside the house was just as it had been when she and Kenny had left it, so Maple walked the sheriff back to the front door and bade him goodnight. As he pulled away, his headlights illuminated her mailbox, and she realized she'd forgotten to check the mail that day. She walked to the end of her driveway and opened the box. On her way back to the house, she shuffled through the pile of typical bills and advertisements. As she reached her front steps, she noticed a sealed envelope with just her first name scrawled across it. With no address or postmark, someone must have dropped it off. Cold flooded her veins as she wondered whether it'd been the intruder. She wondered whether she ought to try and flag down the sheriff before she opened it, but immediately realized he was too far gone.

She moved into the kitchen, absently placing the pile of normal mail down on the counter, and sat at the table, still clutching the envelope. If the intruder had wanted to leave something for her, why would he have put it in the mailbox, where she wouldn't be likely to see it right away? Why not put it somewhere prominent inside the house?

Maple decided she wasn't going to answer those questions by staring at the outside of the envelope, so she tore it open, taking care to touch it as little as possible, in case fingerprinting was necessary later.

A note fell out, penned in the same loopy scrawl.

Dear Maple,

You'll know what to do with this. It was my "insurance policy," and I'm entrusting it to you. Please know how sorry I am. You can find her if you act fast. I can't have any more deaths on my conscience.

Sincerely,

Patrick Murphy, M.D.

Maple blinked. It seemed incongruous—no, impossible—that cheerful, elderly Dr. Murphy could've written these words. Insurance policy? Deaths on his conscience? She must be misunderstanding something . . . but when she saw what else was in the envelope, a horrible sinking feeling accompanied her realization that she had not misread his letter.

In her hands, Maple held two documents: Elijah Wallace's autopsy report and his life insurance policy.

She sank into a chair and started reading. She read both documents through once. Then, she read them again. She sat thinking for several minutes; some pieces clicked together in her brain, and others she needed more information to connect. She retrieved several medical textbooks from Bill's office and spent the next two hours poring over them, cross-referencing details and underlining key concepts. It felt a little bit like she was in law school again, delving into briefs and sifting through precedents in preparation for a mock hearing in class.

But there was nothing "mock" about what she was doing now. By the time the sun peeked over the trees in Maple's backyard, announcing the dawn of the day that marked exactly one week since Maple had discovered Elijah Wallace's body in the barn, she knew that the information she'd learned was going to help her catch his killers—and also make her some powerful enemies in the process.

The last time she'd marched into the sheriff's office first thing in the morning, it hadn't ended well. This time, Maple was armed not only with her nutshell but also with the autopsy report, insurance policy, and several medical textbooks. She was well aware, though, that a number of things had to go right in order for her plan to work.

As soon as she stepped inside, she encountered her first win: although the secretary did not appear to have arrived yet, Kenny and the sheriff were both in the office already, sipping coffee and in the midst of a serious-looking conversation. Deputy Rawlings was there too; the three men stood over a table with a map spread out on it. All three looked tired.

The sheriff looked up and frowned when he saw her, but didn't say anything. Maple took this as her second win of the morning:

he hadn't immediately kicked her out. The grudging respect he'd expressed for her the previous night hadn't entirely evaporated.

Good. She needed him to listen to her now.

"Morning, officers," she said, placing the nutshell on the ground near the table. "Is Mr. Mooreland still here?"

Kenny furrowed his brow at her but then nodded.

That was win number three. This was officially a winning streak. Maple blew out a breath she didn't realize she'd been holding.

"What can we do for you, ma'am?" asked Rawlings.

Maple looked each man in the eyes and decided not to beat around the bush. "I can prove that Elijah Wallace was murdered."

Kenny's eyebrows just about flew off his forehead. Rawlings pursed his lips.

The sheriff sighed. "We don't have time for this. We have a missing person to find."

"Well, you need to make time for it, because I think Ginger's disappearance is linked to Wallace's murder," Maple said brusquely, "and there might still be time to find her."

The sheriff squinted at the papers. "How did you get a copy of the autopsy report?" He glared at Kenny, who shook his head, bewilderment splashed all over his face.

"It was in my mailbox." She held up her hands in a placating manner. "It sounds incredible, I know, but I found it just after you'd dropped me off last night."

A storm cloud was brewing on the sheriff's face. "That's privileged! You aren't supposed to—"

Deputy Rawlings held up a hand. "Hang on, Sam. Let's hear her out."

The sheriff exhaled noisily, but didn't protest. Win number four. Now, Maple was going for broke.

"Thank you, Deputy Rawlings," Maple said, very aware that three sets of eyes were boring into her. "Based on the evidence in this report, it is impossible to conclude that Elijah Wallace's death was an accident."

"What—how—"

"But the coroner said—"

They were eyeing her so skeptically that she wondered how she could possibly convince them, but there was no going back now; the horse was out of the barn, so to speak, and there was no chance of putting it back in, even if she wanted to.

"Okay," she started again, "let me back up. When you have a death by hanging, the most likely cause is suicide. That's been well established in medical studies and published reports. Now, there are two main types of hangings—complete and incomplete." She opened one of the texts—*Death, Natural and Otherwise*—and pointed to a diagram. "We already knew that Elijah Wallace's hanging was complete, meaning his body was freely suspended. No part of him was resting on the ground or on a chair or anything to partially support him. Are you with me so far?"

All three men nodded.

Maple went on, "His hanging was also what is referred to as a 'drop hang,' meaning the victim fell from a height."

"Like when they hung those Nazis in Nuremberg," Kenny said.

A shiver ran through Maple.

"Exactly. It's a type of hanging most often seen in executions, but not in suicides." She looked at the sheriff. "You were even surprised about it that night when I found Elijah; you told me as much. Most people who die by suicide use a chair or a box that they position on the floor and then hang themselves from something relatively low, like a ceiling fan."

Maple remembered how the sheriff had callously referred to people who killed themselves as *suicides* and frowned.

"Of course," she continued, "that was back when everyone was assuming it *was* a suicide."

She moved to stand next to him and pointed to a box on the coroner's report.

"From what I've learned, the laryngeal and hyoid fractures are not surprising. They are found in most deaths by hanging." She flipped open the other textbook and pointed to the larynx and hyoid, which she'd circled and labeled on a diagram of a throat. "The cricoid fracture is what's really interesting—and very problematic in supporting a finding of accidental death."

Kenny scrunched up his face. "Why? I mean, he was hung by his neck and dropped from a significant height. Wouldn't we expect his neck to be broken?"

"Well, yes, but not in this particular way," Maple said. "As you can see from this picture, the cricoid cartilage encircles the throat lower down than the hyoid bone. In fact, its name is derived from the Greek word *krikos*, meaning 'ring-shaped.'"

"Spare us the history lecture," the sheriff said impatiently.

"According to this book"—she pointed back at the first text again—"cricoid fracture usually only occurs in cases of manual strangulation. Like this." Maple held her hands out in front of her and mimed choking someone. "Or actually, more like this." She dropped to her knees and pressed her hands straight down onto an imaginary victim's throat.

She looked up and saw all three officers gaping at her. She hurriedly picked herself up off the floor so she was once again at their eye level.

"A rope wouldn't cause that particular injury, even from such a drastic fall. A person's hands would."

Kenny's eyes widened. "It makes sense with the lividity," he almost whispered.

Maple nodded, her heart leaping to her throat. He was with her. "It does. The killer lured Elijah up to the loft, strangled him, and then hung him—but not right away. Elijah's body was lying there dead for a while first."

"Hold on, hold on," said the sheriff.

Deciding it was better to demonstrate using dolls than to act it out herself, she pulled out the nutshell and walked the sheriff and deputy through the scenario she and Kenny had done (had it only been days ago?) in the Quirks' kitchen.

"Elijah Wallace was already dead when somebody hung his body from that rafter," she concluded.

The sheriff rubbed his eyes. "Please explain to me why Dr. Murphy would rule it an accident when the medical evidence directly contradicts that conclusion? It makes no sense."

Maple placed the doll version of Elijah down in the hayloft. "It will make sense in a minute, but I need to talk to Mr. Mooreland first. He can confirm it for us very quickly."

"Now, hold on a minute," said Rawlings, piping up for the first time. "We can't just be letting civilians interview prisoners."

Rawlings's brow was knitted and his eyes narrowed; he looked troubled. Maple held her breath, but she didn't have to wait long for the sheriff's reply.

"For God's sake, Rawlings, you're not the sheriff yet," he grumbled. "C'mon."

Relief flooded Maple as she, Kenny, and Rawlings all followed the sheriff down the hall, past the empty cell Willy occasionally frequented when he needed to sleep it off, to the only other cell. Maple's heartbeat picked up when she saw Russell Mooreland standing up and clutching the bars. His eyes were wild. "Are you releasing me?"

"No," the sheriff barked. "The lady wants to ask you something."

He gestured for Maple to go ahead.

"Mr. Mooreland, whose idea was it for you to take over the sugar operation?"

Rawlings interjected before Mooreland could reply: "I'm sorry, sheriff, but I just don't think—"

"Dammit, Rawlings, let him answer."

"It was *her* idea," Mooreland said, after a pause. "The wife. Well, now the widow, I guess."

"Mrs. Wallace?" Maple asked, just to be sure.

He nodded. "She came over Friday morning and said she had an opportunity for me." He laughed bitterly. "Some 'opportunity' it turned out to be."

That was the morning of the day Elijah had died. Maple glanced at the sheriff. His expression told her that he, too, had realized the significance of the timeline.

"So, you only went over to the barn and took the sugar back to your house at her invitation, then?"

He nodded. "She said Elijah was tired of the racket. He wanted out but was too proud to approach me himself." He shook his head. "I was so excited by the possibility of the money—according to her, there'd be tons of it—and by the prospect of lording it over Wallace, that good-for-nothing bum—that I agreed right away." He paused. "Seems stupid in retrospect, especially from this jail cell."

"And you went over in your truck immediately?" Maple asked.

Mooreland nodded. "Mrs. Wallace said there was no time to waste, that I had to take the sugar right away. So I did."

"And you were in such a hurry that you bumped your truck into the doorframe, creating a gash," Maple said.

Mooreland nodded. "Wallace's truck was gone. The lady said he was off doing errands, and she insisted that I had to get in and get out before he got back. She was stressing me out, and I was already starting to regret my decision. I pulled up in too much of a hurry and whacked the door."

"And then?" Maple prompted.

"Then, it took a while because I got stung by all those bees and also my back was acting up some. Had to take my time up and down that ladder." He winced at the memory. "Mrs. Wallace helped me, actually. For a little lady, she's pretty strong. She seemed real eager to get the stuff out of there. Said she'd take care of letting the customers know who the new contact was going to be and that they'd come to me from now on. Put me in touch with the distributor too, to arrange new shipments."

Mooreland's entire demeanor was changing now. He slumped a little, loosening his grip on the bars, and the relief at unburdening himself was obvious on his face.

Mooreland scratched his chin and looked thoughtful. "You know," he said, "afterward, I wasn't real cut up about old Wallace's death. Good riddance. He did us all a favor when he jumped."

"His death was ruled an accident," Rawlings said.

"Yeah, okay. If you believe that, then I've got an iceberg in Arizona I want to sell you." Wallace snorted. "But, anyway—the new widow? She seemed downright giddy. Can't say I blame her. It was bad enough living next door to him all those years. I can't imagine what it was like being married to him. He treated her worse than he treated those goats."

Maple nodded once, sadly, in agreement. "Thank you, Mr. Mooreland," she said.

"So, the wife did it?" Sheriff Scott asked Maple. "But she's so little. How could she have overpowered him?"

Maple couldn't help savoring, for just a moment, the satisfaction she felt at the sheriff's change in attitude. How far they'd come from a few short days ago, when he'd thrown her out of his office. Now, he was almost deferring to her.

However, Maple knew she couldn't afford to lose focus now. This was a crucial moment. "I have one more thing to show you, and it'll tie everything together," she replied, her neck prickling as the three men trailed her back to the lobby.

"Does this mean I'm free to go?" Mooreland called after them.

"It most certainly does not!" the sheriff shouted back. "Now, pipe down."

"Aw, c'mon! I cooperated."

"I miss Willy," the sheriff groused as they passed the cell where the intoxicated man came regularly. "At least he's quiet."

Back at the table, Maple pushed her nutshell to the side. "You asked me how it makes sense that Dr. Murphy concluded the death was an accident when the evidence *he himself documented* directly contradicted that finding." She pulled out the insurance policy from between the pages of *Death, Natural and Otherwise* and spread the three pages out on the table. "Well, this is why."

All three officers leaned in to read the document. Maple watched their faces carefully. Sheriff Scott squinted in concentration. Deputy Rawlings's mouth was set in a grim line. Kenny's mouth moved silently as his eyes scanned the pages.

Kenny was the first to look up. "Double indemnity," he said. "Son of a gun."

Maple nodded grimly and pointed to the date at the top of the page. "Two months before Elijah died in that barn, Angela Wallace took out a life insurance policy for him. If he were to perish of natural causes, she'd receive the face value of the policy: two thousand five hundred dollars." She moved her finger to a spot on the third page. "However, the double indemnity clause at the bottom states that should Elijah die as a result of an accident, the beneficiary would receive twice the amount of the policy's face value."

Kenny rocked back on his heels and let loose a low whistle. The sheriff looked at Maple, his eyes blazing. "So, in this case, that would mean five thousand dollars."

Maple nodded. "And the suicide clause—" she pointed at a line halfway down the second page—"doesn't kick in for another twenty-two months."

"So, if his death was ruled a suicide, the wife would get nothing." Kenny's eyes grew to the size of dinner plates. "And that means—"

"—that Mrs. Wallace had a strong financial incentive to have her husband's death ruled an accident," the sheriff finished, closing his eyes.

Maple placed both hands on the table and leaned forward: "And Dr. Murphy's own evidence shows us there was no way his death was either suicide or accidental."

Kenny inhaled sharply. "Then—he was in on it?"

Maple nodded grimly. "Elijah Wallace's death wasn't just a murder. It was a conspiracy."

CHAPTER 31

"Well, Dr. Murphy needs to be arrested immediately," Rawlings said. "I'll go."

Maple watched as he sprang to his feet and yanked his car keys from his pocket.

"Hold on, Carl! What about the wife? We need to make a plan here."

Rawlings had already turned away and started toward the door, keys in hand. Maple placed a hand on the sheriff's arm. When he looked quizzically at her, she shook her head emphatically and placed one finger over her lips in a "keep-quiet" gesture. He looked puzzled, but followed her unspoken direction.

As soon as Rawlings was out the door, Maple sprang up. "Let's go! No time to waste!"

"What?" the sheriff's astonished voice rang through the office.

"He's not going to the doctor's house." Maple was already moving toward the door. "Murphy's flown the coop—I walked past his house to check on my way here—and Rawlings knows it."

She could sense Kenny and the sheriff following behind her. "Then where's he going?" the sheriff demanded.

She glanced meaningfully over her shoulder. "I'd bet my house—all my houses, in fact—that if we follow him right now, he's going to lead us to Ginger."

"Lead us to—hold on. Are you saying what I think you're saying?" The sheriff's eyebrows just about shot off his forehead.

Maple nodded. "Rawlings was the mastermind."

There was a long pause, during which Kenny and the sheriff stared blankly at her.

"Rawlings is dirty?" Kenny asked finally.

"Yes! That's exactly what I'm saying, and he still thinks he can get away with it! Ginger's a loose end he needs to tie up before he can pin this whole thing on Angela Wallace and Dr. Murphy. Get your keys!"

"No," the sheriff said, "I don't buy it." But, in spite of his words, Maple saw a shade of doubt in his eyes.

"You don't have to believe me," Maple said, locking eyes with him. "You just have to be willing to run down a lead with me. Let's see where he takes us."

Slowly, the sheriff nodded once. Maple wasted no time in taking action. She got to the front door just as Rawlings peeled out of the driveway. With Kenny and the sheriff right on her heels, she burst out the door just as the bewildered secretary leaped out of the way.

"Sorry!" Maple called over her shoulder.

"Rawlings has been my deputy for over a decade," the sheriff said, opening the driver's side door.

Kenny paused with his hand on the passenger door handle, looking at his uncle with solemn eyes.

"Then we'll let him prove me wrong," Maple said, reaching for the handle of the back door behind the driver's seat.

"No way," the sheriff said. "You wait here. I'm not taking a civilian on a car chase."

Maple had anticipated this response, and she knew that what she was about to propose was a move that had legal precedent and would likely hold up in court if it were ever challenged.

"Deputize me," she said, thrusting out her chin.

Amusement slipped through Kenny's tension momentarily. "Ha! Well, it's not a bad idea, Sheriff. We may need her with us. She's gotten us this far."

Maple felt a surge of pride and exchanged a quick smile with Kenny.

The sheriff rolled his eyes heavenward and muttered something Maple couldn't understand.

"Sheriff! We have no time to waste!" she cried.

The sheriff grimaced and let loose a string of very audible curse words. Then, he said hurriedly, "I, Sheriff Sam Scott, hereby deputize Maple Bishop as a temporary law enforcement officer under my direction."

She thought he might have muttered, "God help me," afterward, but she couldn't be sure.

Kenny grinned over the hood of the car at Maple. "Let's go."

Maple, now no longer a civilian—at least for the time being—hopped in, a thrill of anticipation coursing through her. Sheriff Scott slammed the car's gear into reverse and then peeled out of the driveway. Kenny pulled a set of binoculars from the glove compartment and peered out the windshield. The police station was situated up on a hill, and the only road that led to and from it was a winding one.

"There! I see him!" Kenny shouted. "He's still on the hill."

The sheriff navigated the twisty turns expertly, with Kenny alternating between looking out the side and front windows and calling out every time he saw Rawlings's car make a move.

"He's driving like a bat out of hell," the sheriff grunted.

"So are you, sir," Maple replied, catching the shadow of a smile on his face in the rearview mirror.

When Rawlings turned left, the sheriff shook his head. "No way he's headed to the doctor's house."

Maple nodded in grim agreement; Dr. Murphy's house was in the opposite direction.

They zipped through the back roads of Elderberry, just barely managing to keep on Rawlings's tail; the deputy was driving erratically. Maple figured by now Rawlings must've seen them. Was he desperate enough to carry on the next phase of his plan even with them watching? She was pretty sure she knew the answer, and the atmosphere in the sheriff's car felt grimmer as she realized that even though neither of them spoke, Kenny and the sheriff were arriving at similar conclusions.

Soon, they crossed the border into Bloomsville. Somehow she'd expected them to stay within the town limits—maybe even to head over to the Wallaces' farm. The fact that they'd just driven over the border made her go cold as she realized she had no idea where they were headed.

With no warning, the paved section of road ended, and they jounced onto a dirt road dotted with potholes. Maple's head snapped back, and she reached out to both sides to steady herself. Out the front windshield, Maple saw Rawlings's car parked haphazardly, the driver's side door flung open. A few feet in front of it were the Wallaces' pickup truck and another car she didn't recognize.

"The sister," she breathed. "This must be Angela's sister's house."

The house was set back a ways from the driveway, with a narrow walking path hemmed in by overgrown rose bushes on either side. Carl Rawlings strode down it toward the porch, clutching a rifle in one hand.

"That's not his service weapon," the sheriff said, a warning note in his voice. Then, he called out the window to his deputy. "Carl! Talk to me. What's going on?"

There was a hitch in Rawlings's stride, but he continued on his way to the porch. At that moment, Maple knew with certainty that her theory had been correct. Her stomach filled with lead.

"Dammit." The sheriff picked up the radio and spoke into it, requesting backup for an armed and dangerous subject and a possible multiple hostage situation. He barked out the address and replaced the radio receiver.

Thrusting his chin at his nephew, he said, "We can't let him get inside the house. Watch yourself, Kenny. Maple, stay put. That's an order."

That's the first time he's used my first name, Maple thought in a daze. It was also, she realized, the first time she had been inclined to obey him. Fear and dread tingled through every fiber of her body as the sheriff and Kenny threw open their doors and leaped out with their weapons drawn. Rawlings was already striding toward the front porch, seeming—incredibly—not to have noticed them. *Or maybe,* Maple thought, taking in the grim determination in Rawlings's stride, *he's beyond caring.* Her heart raced at that thought. She had a pretty good idea of what Rawlings was capable of when he was flying under the radar. What dangerous depths might he sink to when he had nothing left to lose?

Maple rolled down her window just as the sheriff addressed his erstwhile deputy.

"Carl, put that gun down and come back here. We need to talk." The sheriff managed to strike an impressive balance of calmness and authority in his tone.

Nonetheless, Rawlings's only response was a brief pause. Seemingly driven by invisible internal forces, he continued striding onto the porch and toward the front door. Kenny and the sheriff, communicating with each other via hand gestures, advanced on the house in crouching stances with their weapons ready. Kenny held back, training his gun on Rawlings, as the sheriff advanced down the narrow path behind the desperate deputy.

"You don't need to do this, Carl. You don't want to," the sheriff continued in a steady, pleasant voice. "You made some mistakes, but no one else needs to get hurt."

As Rawlings stepped onto the first stair leading onto the porch, Maple heard the sheriff curse under his breath. Then, he fired a warning shot into the air. That snapped Rawlings out of his trance, and he turned to face his colleagues. His wild eyes flew from Kenny to the sheriff, to Maple in the car. Maple's stomach jolted when he shouldered the rifle.

"Stop," Rawlings commanded. "Stay where you are. I'm going in."

"Can't let you go in there, Carl. You know that," the sheriff said, advancing cautiously. "Let's talk out here. Drop the rifle."

"Can't do that, Sam." Rawlings sounded almost regretful. "This is it. There's no turning back now."

A woman appeared at the door, holding a bundle wrapped in a blue blanket. She looked exactly like Angela Wallace, only with brown hair.

Kenny and the sheriff cursed simultaneously.

The woman looked confused and concerned. "Carl? What's going—"

There was a scuffle behind her, and suddenly she disappeared from the door, and Angela Wallace appeared in front of her, eyes wide with panic.

Without taking his eyes off the officers advancing on him, Rawlings somehow sensed Angela's presence behind him.

"Come on out here, Angie."

His voice was cold and calm. Maple shivered. Angela Wallace turned and said something, presumably to her sister, and then faced the scene in the front yard again.

"Mrs. Wallace, ma'am, I need you to go back into the house and close the door," the sheriff ordered. "Now."

Angela looked from Rawlings to the sheriff and back again.

"I don't want my nephew to be hurt," she said.

An ugly snarl twisted Rawlings's face as he cursed at Angela out the side of his mouth. "Everything's gone to hell, and all you care about is that stupid baby."

Angela's whole body twitched. She stayed put in the door-frame, and Rawlings took several backward steps until he stood right next to her. Maple saw Kenny's shoulders tense and realized that, by moving into closer physical proximity to Angela, Rawlings had just made it harder for Kenny or the sheriff to fire on him since it was now likely they might hit her instead.

"Seems to me her priorities are in the right order, Carl," the sheriff said, taking another step closer. "No one else gets hurt if you put the gun down now. It's in your hands."

Rawlings barked out an ironic laugh. "Not anymore, it's not. I was so close—but *she* wouldn't let well enough alone!"

Maple startled as Rawlings pointed the tip of the rifle directly toward her. Instinctively, she put her hands up as though in surrender. Her teeth chattered. On the porch, Rawlings grabbed Angela with his left hand and swung her around in front of him, pinning her to his side with his arm. Maple saw the sheriff's shoulders tense: Rawlings now had a human shield.

No tension was evident in his voice when he spoke a moment later, though. "Tell me why you did it, Carl. How'd you come up with the idea for this scam?"

Rawlings swung the rifle and his focus off Maple and back to the sheriff. He didn't appear to notice as Kenny moved stealthily to the side of the porch—angling himself for a clearer shot at Rawlings, Maple realized with mixed horror and relief.

Rawlings laughed derisively. "I see what you're doing, Sam—get me to talk, de-escalate the situation. I'm not falling for it."

"How do you think this ends, Carl?" the sheriff asked, his voice low and calm. "You can't get away with it now. If you cooperate with us, I can go to bat with the judge, suggest an easier sentence for you, but you gotta help me out. You gotta let everybody in the house go. You gotta tell us where Mrs. Comstock is."

"I'll tell you how this ends," Rawlings said. "It ends with me driving away. I got a hostage now. You're not gonna risk hurting her. You're gonna let her and me go to my car."

Angela whimpered. Behind her, the door concealing her sister and nephew stayed closed. Maple wondered what the people behind it were doing.

"You know I can't do that, Carl," the sheriff said. "C'mon, tell me—how'd you pull this off? Was it her idea?"

"*Her* idea? Don't insult me," Rawlings scoffed. "You think this was my first scam, old man? I've been lining my pockets for years, preparing to ditch this podunk town and start over. Right under your nose."

Maple saw the sheriff's shoulders stiffen. "Really," he said evenly. "Tell me more about that."

"I'd gotten bored taking petty bribes, and I was scouting out bigger opportunities. I realized the government was overwhelmed with life insurance claims during the war, and I knew the coroner system was rife with corruption and had basically no oversight—ironically, because I attended one of Dr. Murphy's seminars. But it wasn't until I found out Dr. Murphy had a bit of a gambling problem that I realized I could combine the two. That combination—insurance policies and fraudulent autopsies—was my golden goose."

Maple inhaled sharply.

"It was easy to get him to doctor an autopsy," Rawlings continued. "His cut for the first one was almost five hundred dollars—a pretty nice payday for a rural family doctor who likes the ponies. Unfortunately for him, Murphy wasn't nearly as good at picking winning fillies as he was at falsifying autopsy reports, so he kept going willingly for a few more. I'd spread them out across the county, so it didn't look too suspicious, and it didn't matter if I was always the responding officer since I had the good doctor in my pocket. And when he finally did try to get out—right around the time Bill Bishop took over the practice—he was in too deep. I had him by the short and curlies."

A wave of sadness and disappointment swept over Maple as she thought of her mentor and friend reduced to such a . . . cliché. It was quickly followed by a burst of anger at Rawlings for using him in this way and for speaking so casually about blackmailing him.

The sheriff took two more slow steps. Rawlings was looking at him, but his eyes looked dreamy, as though maybe he wasn't actually focusing on what was in front of him. Maple noticed the sheriff had stopped replying to Rawlings, instead letting him monologue as he crept closer and closer.

"And what with all the insurance claims related to the war and the federal government farming them out to little local places, worker bees like Daniel Duncan are too busy scurrying around to give too much scrutiny to any individual claim. I had a good run."

He sounded almost nostalgic. Maple shook her head in disbelief.

"And it turns out there's no shortage of lonely broads who like the attention of a dashing deputy sheriff—and don't object to bumping off their husbands."

Angela inhaled sharply.

"Ha!" Rawlings leered, glancing down at the woman he now held captive. "You thought you were different from any of the others? You really thought I was going to, what, marry you when all of this was over—"

"Bastard!" Angela screamed. Then, she bit Rawlings on the arm, hard, and a string of gunshots echoed through the air. Maple dove to the floor of the car, covering her ears and squeezing her eyes shut tight.

She wasn't sure how long she was down there, curled in the fetal position, but eventually she became aware that the low wail of approaching sirens was punctuating the echoey ringing in her ears. Slowly, she uncurled herself, sat up, and peeked out her window. Kenny was up on the porch, fastening handcuffs onto Angela Wallace. Rawlings lay sprawled, face up and unmoving, on the porch a few feet away. A pool of blood was spreading across his chest. But where was the sheriff? A wave of nausea swept Maple, and she gripped the edge of the car window to steady herself. Kenny, having secured Angela's wrists, scurried toward Rawlings and placed his fingers on the deputy's neck to check for a pulse. He shook his head and bent his ear down close to Rawlings's mouth. Then, he looked down at the footpath and shook his head.

Maple fumbled with the door latch and tumbled out of the car. Legs skittering underneath her like a newborn deer, she saw the sheriff lying on the path ahead, blood pooling around the lower half of his body.

"No!"

She ran to him on her shaky legs and knelt next to him. A bullet had torn a hole in his pants; blood flowed from his left calf. She pulled off her scarf and pressed it to his wound with trembling hands. Then, she looked at the porch, where Kenny had affixed handcuffs to Angela Wallace. Her shoulders slumped and her head down, she allowed Kenny to steer her to the backseat of the sheriff's car, where he deposited her. He then jogged over to check on his uncle. As he took in the sight of the sheriff, his entire face, ears included, was as pale as Maple had ever seen it.

He grabbed his uncle's hand and squeezed. "You're gonna be okay."

The sheriff moaned. "Get in there."

"I know, I know," Kenny said. Then, he turned to Maple. "Can you stay with him? I need to check on the others in the house."

Maple nodded. "I'll stay with him, but he needs a doctor soon."

But how quickly would they be able to get him to one? Dr. Murphy was on the run. Bill's absence throbbed more painfully than ever. The sheriff cursed, but his voice was weak, and his face had gone white. His blood had already soaked through her scarf.

"Officers from the next county are on their way," Kenny said, shooting an anguished look at his uncle before turning and running into the house.

The sirens did indeed sound a little closer. Maple shrugged off Jamie's coat, glancing at the smear of her brother's blood on the inside of the collar before pressing it to the sheriff's leg. She closed her eyes, hoping against hope that the other officers would get here in time—that the outcome would be different for the sheriff than it had been for her brother.

Without opening his eyes, the sheriff asked, "Is Kenny okay?"

"Yes," Maple said. "He's fine. He's doing what needs to be done." She pressed harder on his wound.

The sheriff sighed and mumbled something she couldn't understand.

Kenny emerged from the house and, his expression grim, draped a sheet over Rawlings's body. He darted back inside and emerged again, this time escorting Angela Wallace's clearly terrified sister, who clutched her baby in her arms. He steered them around the body of his fallen colleague, attempting to shield the sight of the dead man on the porch from her view by stepping between them. Dully, Maple realized that the woman's home was now a crime scene. The sirens grew even louder; they'd be here any minute now.

"Ride back with Angela Wallace," Sheriff Scott said, his voice barely audible. "She'll be more likely to talk if a woman's sitting with her."

Maple wasn't sure whether she ought to be flattered or insulted by this sweeping generalization, and though his eyes were still closed, the sheriff must have sensed her skeptical expression.

". . . if *you're* sitting with her," the sheriff corrected himself, and Maple felt a tiny surge of satisfaction at this distinction.

Then he went limp.

"Sheriff?" She kept pressure on his leg and reached over to tap his shoulder. "Stay with me, Sheriff. Help's on the way."

Two police vehicles pulled up, lights flashing and sirens wailing. Four officers hopped out. Two of them came over to Maple, and she quickly explained what had happened. They wasted no time in loading the unconscious sheriff into their car. The other two checked in with Kenny, and within minutes, were stowing Angela's sister and nephew in the other car. Exhausted, she sat back from the crouching position she'd been in while she held the coat on the sheriff's wound.

For the first time since their arrival, she noticed a small shed off to the side of the driveway, partially concealed by two trees. There was a window on the side facing her, and Maple caught a flash of movement through it.

Instantly on high alert, she shouted, "Kenny!"

She pointed at the shed, and he drew his gun for the second time in an hour. They both sprinted toward it. Kenny tugged at the lock, which stayed stubbornly in place, and swore under his breath.

"Stand back!" He aimed his pistol at the lock, and Maple had barely enough time to cover her ears before he fired. The lock exploded, and Kenny pulled open the door. Ears ringing, Maple followed him inside.

Ginger Comstock had managed to get one arm free from the rope that lashed her to a wooden chair and was frantically tugging at her gag, her eyes bulging in panic. Kenny rushed over and untied her. A soon as she was free, Ginger sagged against Maple and sobbed.

"It's okay," Maple said, wrapping her arms around Ginger. "It's over now."

A half hour later, Kenny clasped his hands behind his head and surveyed the scene in front of them. Another police car had arrived, and now four officers from the next county were on the scene. One officer was searching Rawlings's car. Another sat on the ground in front of a tree with Ginger, who now had a blanket wrapped around her shoulders and was sipping from a glass of water. The third guarded Angela, who sat, handcuffed, in the back of Sheriff Scott's cruiser, and the fourth had gone into the house. Maple followed Kenny's eyes to Rawlings's abandoned cruiser, then to the pool of Sheriff Scott's blood on the path. Finally, they landed on the sheet covering the deputy's body. When she looked back at Kenny, his face had crumpled.

"You did what you had to do," she said gently, placing a hand on his shoulder.

Kenny let his hands fall to his sides, looked at her with tears in his eyes, and let out a sigh.

They stood together in silence for a minute, and then Kenny burst out, "Why'd he do it? How could he? We took an oath to uphold the rule of law. Laws and justice—that's what sets us apart, what makes us the good guys. If we don't have that, then what do we have?"

Maple found herself thinking of the Nuremberg trials, where the determination of countries and men to uphold the rule of law on a global scale was groundbreaking—and yet the execution of a handful of Nazis had still left her, somehow, with an empty feeling. Justice had been served when those men had been convicted in a court of law and punished accordingly. But the magnitude of the Nazis' collective crimes couldn't possibly be wiped away with the execution of a handful of the perpetrators. The entire world would certainly suffer aftershocks for decades to come.

She looked from Kenny to the man he'd killed and back again. The young deputy's face no longer looked boyish; his eyes were a little less bright. Kenny would have his own aftershocks to deal with—on a smaller scale, but really no less significant. Uncovering the truth didn't always result in satisfaction or vindication. Often, it seemed to make the seeker more miserable, more jaded, than he'd been when he'd set out.

And yet.

Maple turned so she was looking directly into Kenny's eyes. "We have you," she said simply. "Laws and principles of justice are meaningless if there aren't individuals who stand up and fight to uphold them day in and day out—even when others don't live up to that standard." She grasped both of his hands in hers. "You saved us all today, Kenny. You did that."

Tears rolled silently down Kenny's cheeks as, together, he and Maple watched the fourth officer emerge from the house. He stooped down and picked up the rifle. Maple's eyes moved to the man who was straightening up after searching Rawlings's car. He held a white glove. Maple had a flash of recognition, and then her heart plummeted like a runaway elevator. Was that what she thought it was?

The officer proceeded down the footpath toward them, skirting carefully around the pool of Sheriff Scott's blood. When he got close to Maple and Kenny, Maple held out a hand to stop him.

"May I see that?"

"This?" he said, holding up a white glove.

Maple's knees buckled as she took in the delicate maple leaf embroidered on the wrist.

"Oh," Kenny said as realization dawned on him.

"And . . . may I look at the butt of that rifle?" her voice was shaky as she turned to the other officer, who was approaching from the porch.

The officer obliged, holding it out. She and Kenny both took in the initials *WB* engraved there. Rawlings must've stolen it when he left the threatening note for her.

"Is that . . ." Kenny's voice was hushed.

"My glove and my husband's rifle?" Maple finished. "Yes."

"So, Rawlings was gonna—"

"Kill Ginger and frame me? Looks like it."

"Holy cow," Kenny said.

They both stood there for a long moment. If Dr. Murphy hadn't left Maple that note, she wouldn't have put the pieces together fast enough to halt that phase of Rawlings's plan.

"He was going to kill two birds with one stone," she said. "Get both her and me out of his hair so he could get away with the whole thing."

Her emotions were mixed about being lumped in with Ginger; on the one hand, she felt a surge of kinship with the other woman that was both surprising and disconcerting; she supposed being the co-targets of a murder plot would do that to a person. However, her discomfort at being put into the same box as Ginger Comstock was huge. She remembered the moment on top of the hill when she'd decided to accept Kenny's offer to investigate Elijah Wallace's death, and how she'd wondered whether she was any different from Ginger. She'd decided then that she was, but now Rawlings had tried to force them into his narrowly defined role: troublesome, nosy women.

Maple realized how close Rawlings had come to carrying out his intentions of actually murdering Ginger and framing her. She began to shiver uncontrollably. Kenny, after a brief whispered conference with the other officer, wrapped an arm around Maple's shoulders and steered her across the lawn. When they were far enough away from the hubbub, he invited her to sit on a small boulder facing away from the carnage. Her breathing came in shallow bursts, and she wondered if she might hyperventilate. What was wrong with her? It was very un-Maple-like to have some sort of . . . panicky spell or whatever this was. She was not hysterical.

"Just breathe," Kenny said. "Breathe."

She did, and within a few minutes, she'd stopped shaking and felt her lungs filling and emptying at a normal rate. He rubbed her back until she felt under control enough to shoot him a grateful smile.

"It's going to be all right, Maple," Kenny said. "We did it. We found the truth in a nutshell."

The sheriff's inclination had been correct: on the ride back to the station, Angela Wallace talked, and Maple listened. As Kenny drove, Angela opened the floodgates, telling Maple about her sad childhood, how her mother had married her off to the first man who was willing to take her, about the verbal and physical abuse Elijah had inflicted on her, and of the day she'd begun to fantasize about his death—and, eventually, of killing him herself.

Maple listened with mingled fascination and horror as Angela described the time she'd snuck up behind her husband with a full metal milk pail, how she'd gone so far as to swing it back and had been on the verge of slamming it into his skull before changing her mind at the last moment. She'd dropped the bucket to the ground instead. Elijah, she said, had proceeded to beat her for spilling all that milk.

Angela studied her lap, frowning. "So, I guess it's understandable that when Carl Rawlings started coming around, acting real nice, I enjoyed the attention of a man. Because the only attention Elijah paid me was to insult me or hit me."

Maple wasn't sure what to say to that, so she stayed quiet.

Angela laughed ironically. "But it turns out he was using me too, just in a different way than Elijah." She paused and made eye contact with Maple. "I was in love with him. It's important to me that you know that. And I thought he was also in love with me."

Conflicting emotions swirled inside Maple. She felt simultaneous pity, anger, and even—to her surprise—a sudden surge of sympathy for the woman seated next to her. Angela blinked several times.

"He told me it would be easy. A win–win, that's how he described it. I'd get out of my bad marriage, and we'd get a bunch of money to start a new life together. He had the whole thing worked out. He talked me through the insurance paperwork. He made all the plans. And I was only too happy to go along."

Then, she told Maple what a near-disaster the actual murder had been.

"I had Russell Mooreland come early in the morning to take away the sugar. Then, Carl climbed up there to wait, and I told Elijah I had seen Mooreland leaving our property with what looked like our sugar loaded into his truck. The original plan was for Carl to wait up in the loft and take Elijah by surprise when he climbed up to check on the sugar. Carl would then push him off the edge, making it look like an accidental fall. The hayloft was high, and Elijah had a fake leg. No one would have a hard time believing he'd tripped."

But, as Angela told the story, Elijah was not willing to be subdued so easily when it had come down to it. He'd been so furious at the idea of Mooreland stealing his sugar that he'd stormed up the ladder in a rage to check on the supply. When Rawlings had tried to overpower him, Elijah, with the adrenaline still coursing through him, fought back with surprising strength. With a jolt, Maple recalled the long scratch she'd seen on Rawlings's wrist when he'd come to give her the verbal warning about Harry Needles.

"The two of them were rolling around the loft and very nearly went off the edge together," Angela said. "Carl managed to subdue Elijah long enough to tie his wrists, but then Elijah managed to roll onto his back. They tussled for another few minutes before Carl was able to pin Elijah and started throttling his neck. As he was choking him, though, Elijah managed to get one hand free and took a good swing directly into the side of Carl's head. They both went limp and silent after that. I raced up the ladder to check on them. Elijah was already dead."

Maple marveled at the casualness with which Angela was recounting her role in her husband's premeditated murder. She met Kenny's gaze in the rearview mirror and could tell he was having a similar reaction.

"I roused Carl after a minute, but . . . it was as if he was a different person." Angela blinked rapidly several times before continuing. "As soon as he realized Elijah was dead, he got very businesslike and brisk with me. I assumed we were still going to roll Elijah's body off the loft. I even tried to help, but Carl got angry at me. He said that Elijah's neck showed obvious signs of strangulation now—his exact words were *"Even the sheriff's observant enough not to miss that"*—and we wouldn't have been able to pass it off as accidental and collect the double indemnity."

She sniffled, and Maple wondered whether Angela's tears stemmed from guilt over her role in her husband's murder or hurt that her lover had scorned her.

"And so, Carl said, 'We have to string him up.' Something about how the hanging would conceal the marks."

Angela shrugged. Her matter-of-fact tone as she relayed this part of the plan made Maple's spine shiver.

"What about the rope?" she asked.

Angela nodded once. "That was me. We tried tying Elijah up with some rope from our barn, but it was beginning to rot through. That's what Carl used on Elijah's wrists, and he'd managed to bust free of that, so we thought it might break when we used it to hold his entire body weight." Her eyes darkened. "The last thing we needed was a botched hanging."

Maple thought of the headline about the Nazis in Nuremberg.

Angela continued, explaining that she'd left Rawlings with the body, gone to the hardware store, and stolen the rope right from under Ben Crenshaw's nose.

"But," Maple interrupted, "weren't you afraid someone would see you?"

Angela laughed hollowly. "I've spent my whole life trying not to be noticed. First so my father wouldn't beat me, then so my husband wouldn't beat me. I'm good at being a ghost."

Maple's heart dropped into her shoes. She herself had been in the shop most of that day. She, who'd always prided herself on her

keen powers of observation, who secretly prided herself on noticing what others missed, had missed *this*—and not just seeing
Angela in the hardware shop that day, but seeing her as a possible
suspect at all. Like everyone else, when Maple had looked at
Angela, she'd seen a timid, cowering woman married to a bully.
Like everyone else, Maple had felt a vague pity for the woman,
and that had caused her to underestimate Angela. Perhaps even
more than everyone else, Maple had been in a position to help.
She recalled with shame her choice not to report the woman's
bruises to the authorities, feeling too overwhelmed by her own
personal circumstances and cynical about the likelihood of officers actually taking her seriously to try and intervene.

The question on Maple's mind now was one she didn't say
aloud, but that didn't make it any less pressing: *But why didn't* I
notice you?

"I was back in no time," Angela went on. "And then it was
done."

She raised one shoulder and her eyebrows, as if to indicate
hanging her husband was no big deal—just another item to cross
off her to-do list that day.

"I thought that was going to be the beginning of my new
life—*our* new life. But it turned out Carl had other ideas." A hard
look settled over Angela's features. "At the end of the day, I was
rid of my terrible husband, but I didn't exactly get the fairy-tale
ending I was imagining."

An odd combination of pity and disgust swirled inside Maple
as she realized that within hours of Elijah's murder, she herself
had arrived to make the gruesome discovery of his body. Maple
pulled her coat tighter around herself and shivered.

"Who found my glove?" she asked.

"I did. You dropped it when you came to give me the new dollhouse. That was nice of you." She smiled at Maple, but almost instantly her face went hard again. "But it was Carl's idea to use it to frame you." Here, Angela paused and threw Maple a pleading look, as though checking whether the other woman believed her. "We knew you had the rifle in your front closet because Harry Needles was going around town telling everyone who'd listen how you'd threatened him with it." Now, Angela looked almost apologetic. "Then, when Ginger Comstock became too much of a loose cannon and you kept nosing around investigating Elijah's death, Carl said we could kill two birds with one stone."

Maple—one of those birds—wasn't sure what to say to that. Kenny pulled into the police station parking lot. Suddenly, she became aware of how tired she was and closed her eyes.

"Maple?" Angela Wallace's voice was different. Her tone had a distinct hesitation in it. "Can I—is it all right if I call you Maple?"

"Yes?" Maple said, opening her eyes again with great difficulty and looking at the prisoner next to her. She saw with some surprise that the other woman was blushing.

"I realize," said Angela, moving her gaze to her own lap, "that I'm in no position to ask you for any favors. But I was wondering . . ."

Maple sat up straighter. Kenny steered the car into a parking space and killed the engine.

"Well, I really do love the dollhouse you made me," she said, meeting Maple's eyes with her own once again. This time, they shone with childlike delight. "And I was wondering if you could make sure it goes to my sister. I'd really like for my nephew to have it when he's older."

Kenny climbed out the driver's side door and opened Mrs. Wallace's from the outside. He reached behind her back and grasped her by the handcuffs.

"That dollhouse was just like the one I had as a child, and it was my refuge. My tiny, perfect world."

Maple found herself unable to reply, but it didn't seem to matter to Angela. She'd made her request and seemed at peace with the lack of control she now had over whether Maple actually carried it out.

An officer from a nearby county, who must've been summoned to help when two-thirds of the sheriff's officers became indisposed in one fell swoop, walked over and had a brief consultation with Kenny before taking possession of the prisoner.

Angela went with him willingly, almost docile under his guidance. Her expression was dreamy as she allowed the officer to steer her toward the jail as if she were a doll—one who was used to people bigger than her moving her around—who had tried, briefly, to take control of her own destiny, but failed.

But did she need to have failed? Why had Angela arrived at a place where her sense of the world was so warped that she felt murder was her only option? Maple thought of how she and Ben had shaken their heads in sadness and anger when they'd seen the obvious signs of physical abuse on Angela's body. What might've happened if they'd said something? Could Angela have mustered the courage to leave Elijah? To press charges against him and send him to jail? Would law enforcement have believed her or been willing to intervene on her behalf?

Or had it already been too late? By then, the plot was underway. Maple felt a flash of fury at Carl Rawlings for exploiting this woman. He, even more than Maple, had been in a position of power, a position to take official action to right some of the wrongs Elijah had perpetrated on his wife. Instead, he'd manipulated Angela for his own gain.

There was a knock on her window.

"Want to go in and see this thing through to the bitter end?"

Kenny had come around to her side of the car. His voice was muffled through the closed door. He gestured at the sheriff's office. Maple exhaled, and her breath fogged up the window, obscuring her view of Kenny. She wiped it away.

"No," she said. "Take me home. I'm going to sleep for about a year." Kenny opened his mouth, but she held up a hand to stop him before he could speak. "I know, I know. You're not my damn chauffeur."

Smiling, Kenny opened the door for her and gestured grandly with his arm. Maple walked around to the front passenger side and sank into the seat.

Kenny didn't restart the motor right away. Maple glanced over and saw the exhaustion written all over him. "I'll have to face an inquiry. Any officer who discharges his weapon does. To make sure the use of deadly force was justified."

"Well, if you hadn't shot at him, he'd likely have killed at least one other person," Maple replied. "Sounds justified to me, and I'll say as much to anyone who needs to hear it."

Kenny nodded his thanks but seemed unable to speak for a long moment. Maple saw his eyes brim with tears and glanced away to give him a modicum of privacy. Finally, Kenny cleared his throat. "I was angry with you."

Maple's gaze snapped back to Kenny. Whatever she'd been expecting him to say, it wasn't that.

"Uh—"

He held up a hand and closed his eyes. When he opened them, he looked directly into hers. "When you basically fired me from the investigation that was my idea, I was so resentful. Everything in my life was going wrong. My dad was sick, my mom was sad and exhausted, and I just kept bumbling around at work and annoying my uncle. Then you went and made that decision for me, and it was—"

He took a deep breath and let it go.

"We were supposed to be partners, you know? I felt so betrayed."

"But, Kenny, I—"

"I know, I know. You had my best interests at heart."

He'd taken the words right out of her mouth.

"But partnering with you . . . that was the one part of my life where I had felt in control—like for the first time, I was really . . . I don't know, really pursuing the mission I thought I'd signed up for when I joined the sheriff's office."

"Kenny, I'm sorry." Maple felt a bowling ball form in her gut.

He smiled sadly. "The thing is, after my uncle caught us, I decided that I couldn't in good conscience continue clandestinely working with you. I was going to tell you that the morning after, but I was also going to suggest we meet with my uncle—lay out all our suspicions and everything we'd discovered and formally request that the sheriff's office reopen the case. I know my uncle really well, Maple. He's basically been like a second father to me my whole life. He might or might not have agreed to look into the case again, but he would've heard us out. But before I could say any of that, you shut me down."

Maple was floored. She'd never considered what Kenny had just said: taking the honest and straightforward approach—ironic, considering she was so often accused of excessive honesty. She found herself thinking of the gatekeepers in the legal profession—of how those smug lawyers in town had refused to consider hiring her, their minds made up before she even opened her mouth at the interview. Had she unwittingly done the same thing to Kenny?

"I don't know what to say," Maple said.

He shrugged. "My point is, we could've discussed it like the colleagues we were supposed to be. Like the partners we were."

She looked at her hands in her lap, wanting to sink into the seat of the car and disappear.

Kenny's voice was thick as he said, "I just wanted to say it's been an honor working with you. The highlight of my career so far, actually."

Maple's own throat was suddenly constricted. The fondness she felt for this young man seated beside her was momentarily overwhelming.

"Well," she said briskly, "I'd say thank you, but since your career has been about five minutes long, I'm not sure that's such a great compliment."

Kenny threw back his head and laughed. Then, he drove her home.

A few minutes later, Maple let herself into her house, which was blessedly quiet. She shut the door and leaned her back against it, closing her eyes and letting her shoulders sag.

An insistent meow punctured the quiet, and Maple immediately knew what she needed to do; deep down, if she was being honest with herself, she'd known for a while. She opened her eyes, stood up, and went into the kitchen. She got a bowl out of the cupboard, filled it with water, and placed it on the floor.

Then, she opened the back door. The orange tabby strode in like he owned the place, rubbed against Maple's leg, and began lapping up the water. Maple sat at the kitchen table where, barely ten hours ago, she'd worked out the truth of how Elijah Wallace had died. Mack finished drinking and leaped up onto her lap. He curled up in a tight ball, closed his eyes, and purred.

For the first time in a long time, Maple felt truly content. She stayed there for several minutes and felt her whole body relax under Mack's gentle purring. However, she knew the peace and quiet were going to be somewhat short-lived; soon enough, everyone would find out all about the sugar ring and the murder and insurance scams. Much as it hurt her heart to think of Dr. Murphy's reputation being destroyed, there was nothing she could do about it now. Her blood boiled, though, at the thought of Harry Needles being the one to write the story, which would likely garner regional—if not national—attention.

Maple realized there was actually one thing she could do. She gently moved Mack off her lap and went over to her phone. She asked the operator to connect her to Ella Henderson.

When the young reporter answered, Maple took a deep breath. "Boy oh boy, do I have a scoop for you."

CHAPTER 32

Two weeks later

As soon as Maple stepped into the sheriff's office, his secretary bustled over.

"Mrs. Bishop, you got a new coat!" she exclaimed. "It's lovely. May I take it for you?"

Maple shrugged off the burgundy coat and handed it to Mrs. Langley with a grateful smile. On the one hand, Jamie's shabby blue peacoat had accompanied her brother to his untimely death, and she'd clung to it—maybe too hard—as a last physical remnant of her beloved sibling. However, she hadn't thought twice about using it to staunch the sheriff's blood flow until the officers could get him to the hospital. Maple felt the coat had come full circle, and maybe so had she. She'd found she liked the trim fit of her new coat, which she'd chosen and paid for herself—a luxury that had been almost unimaginable a few weeks before.

Now, Mrs. Langley waved her in, saying, "The sheriff's expecting you, dear."

As she walked toward Sam Scott's office, Maple reflected on how different this visit was compared to the time she'd brought him the nutshell. Then, she'd had to exercise subterfuge to finagle a meeting. Now, she was an invited guest. She passed the door to Carl Rawlings's office, which was shut tight. The next door—the sheriff's—was open, and the area around it was decorated with streamers and "Get Well Soon" cards. She grinned when she saw the sheriff sitting at his desk, his wounded leg propped up on a chair in front of him. He was talking on the phone, but he gestured for her to sit down across from him.

"No," he barked into the receiver. "And that's my final answer."

He slammed the phone down and scowled at it.

"Good morning to you too," Maple said lightly.

"Harry Needles," the sheriff growled, still glaring at the telephone, "is the bane of my existence."

He'd used almost those exact words to describe Elijah Wallace and Russell Mooreland a month ago. Maple tried to hide her smile. "Looking for a quote from the sheriff, is he?"

The sheriff gave her a look that was half exasperated, half admiring. "You really rattled him by giving the scoop to that girl reporter."

"I did," Maple agreed as she serenely smoothed out her skirt.

The sheriff snorted, then faked a cough to cover his amusement.

Again, Maple was struck by the contrast between this visit and an earlier one—that time, she recalled, when she'd come in to report the argument she'd witnessed between Wallace and Mooreland, and the sheriff had tried to rush her out of his office by telling her to go home and take care of her nonexistent children. Now, they were chuckling together at her revenge on a reporter.

It was amazing what a few weeks and a near-death experience could do for a relationship.

"How's the leg?" she asked.

His face grew serious. "I'll live."

They were both quiet for a long moment, and the sheriff's expression was solemn. "I wanted you to hear this from me. They caught up with Patrick Murphy just south of the Canadian border."

Maple's heartbeat picked up. She sensed there was more. Was Dr. Murphy alive? "And . . .?"

"And he surrendered without incident. He'd been staying in a tiny border town called Derby for days, not trying very hard at all to cover his tracks."

Maple processed this information. Having gotten so close to escaping the country—after which it would've been much harder for authorities to overtake him—why had he stopped just shy of the border?

"The troopers said it was almost like he wanted to be caught— that he was relieved it was over." The sheriff cleared his throat. "They told me the first thing he said when they caught him was 'Tell Maple I'm sorry.'"

Maple inhaled sharply, not sure how to feel about this. An investigation was underway, and it looked like Dr. Murphy had assisted Rawlings by intentionally falsifying at least three other autopsy reports. A tornado of emotion—anger, disgust, disappointment—whirled in her. She was devastated by her mentor's actions, but shouldn't Dr. Murphy's regret be focused on the families whose lives he'd helped to ruin?

The sheriff, who observed her with unflinching eyes, leaned his elbows on the table and rested his chin in his hands. "You want my two cents?"

She nodded, taken aback by his candid tone and relaxed posture.

"He has enormous respect for you. You are a person of utmost integrity, uncompromising in your values and unwavering in living a life that upholds your moral convictions. In short, you're the kind of person he'd hoped to be."

The sheriff was kind enough to look away when Maple began to sob. She didn't know what, exactly, pushed her over the emotional cliff—the words themselves or the man who'd said them—but she suddenly couldn't bear the thought of Dr. Murphy slumped in the back of a police car, small and handcuffed and apologizing to her. The sheriff wordlessly passed her a handkerchief and waited for her to get her crying under control.

"May I see him?" she finally asked.

He nodded. "They're on their way. Should be here within the hour."

She squeezed the handkerchief.

"In the meantime, I have two things to give you," he said. "First, this." He reached down to the floor next to him and with some effort picked up the dollhouse Maple had made for Angela Wallace, and plopped it on his desk. "I don't know why you asked for this back, but it's not needed in evidence, so you're free to do with it as you wish."

A lump formed in Maple's throat. "I made a promise, and your returning it to me will allow me to keep it. Thank you, Sheriff."

He acknowledged her thanks with a tilt of his chin. "Next is this."

From a desk drawer, he produced the glove that Rawlings had taken and planned to use to frame her for murder.

Maple's heart lifted. She took the glove from his desk and pulled its mate from her handbag, admiring the colorful embroidery on the last gift Bill had ever given her. The pair was reunited at last, and Maple felt a surge of affection for her husband, tinged with an ache she was beginning to accept would be her lifelong companion.

She blinked away tears. "Thank you."

The sheriff cleared his throat. "One more thing."

She cocked her head. "Yes?"

He took a deep breath. "I'd like to hire you."

"Hire me?" she echoed, disbelieving.

He nodded. "As a part-time consultant. You could keep going with your dollhouses. Mrs. Langley tells me business is booming, and my wife's been singing your praises to everyone she knows or meets about the one you made for Sophie. I'd call on you as needed to assist in investigations or provide legal advice." He looked down at his desk. "There are things we missed." He looked up at her again. "Things *I* missed," he added quietly, "or outright dismissed—but *you* didn't. You notice what other people miss, and I need to do better. Would you consider . . ." He trailed off and looked away, and Maple realized, to her utter astonishment, that the sheriff was nervous.

Maple didn't trust herself to speak. She nodded and reached across the desk to shake hands with the sheriff: her new colleague.

Maple was watching out the front window of the sheriff's office when the car pulled in. The driver, a deputy from a town in northern Vermont, hopped out and opened the rear door. He reached in and assisted his prisoner in exiting the vehicle. Dr. Murphy's disheveled appearance squeezed at her heart. Patrick Murphy had never been a big man, but the doctor seemed to have shrunk since she'd last seen him. His normally neat gray hair stuck up in all directions. His shoulders slumped. Though she had a powerful urge to look away, Maple watched as the officer guided her handcuffed mentor across the same parking lot Carl Rawlings had fled from just two weeks before. As they got closer, Maple saw the smudges on his gold-rimmed spectacles and, behind them, the defeat in his eyes. The deepest sense of pity she'd ever experienced made her knees wobble. She steadied herself just as the men reached the door.

She stood to the side and averted her eyes as the officer guided Dr. Murphy inside. Her heart in her throat, she was unable to look him in the eye. She heard his sharp intake of breath, but he didn't say anything. Kenny emerged from the office to escort them to the cell that awaited him. Maple trailed behind, recalling that day less than a month ago when Kenny had been astonished to discover that the town drunk routinely let himself into the second cell. She wondered vaguely what Willy's reaction would be the next time he stumbled in to sleep it off and discovered the town doctor now occupied "his" cell.

Kenny and the other officer exchanged some words, but there was a rushing in Maple's ears that prevented her from hearing them. Maple looked into the first cell and saw Angela Wallace curled in the fetal position on the tiny cot, facing the wall.

"Mrs. Wallace?" Maple said tentatively.

The woman gave no visible reaction. A line from an Emily Dickinson poem she'd read years ago flashed across Maple's memory: *"Nobody knows this little Rose . . ."*

Maple cleared her throat. "I have the dollhouse. I'll bring it to your nephew."

Angela might never again see the house Maple had made for her, but her nephew would. Maple wondered what Angela's sister would tell the boy about his aunt. Would he play with dolls inside the rose-covered walls, unaware of the violence and corruption that had tainted its previous owner?

Still, Angela Wallace didn't move. The sight of her small, still body instantly transformed the pity Maple had felt toward her erstwhile mentor into cold fury. Though she knew Angela had done terrible things, Maple still couldn't help seeing the woman as a victim in her own right—and she carried a not insignificant amount of guilt for her own failure to help the woman escape the fate that had landed her in this cell.

She had little time to process her own rapid emotional transition, though, because just then Kenny closed the cell door with a clang that reverberated down the small hallway, and Maple, whose legs had continued moving seemingly independent of her brain, found herself standing in front of Dr. Murphy's cell. She felt Kenny pat her shoulder before he and the officer left her there, face to face with the shell of a man she'd thought she'd known. He rubbed his wrists where the handcuffs had, until moments ago, been fastened.

"Maple. I'm so sorry." His eyes filled with tears, but she felt no pity for him now. Anger blazed in her chest.

She laughed bitterly. "That might be the least adequate apology in the history of apologies."

"I know. If you could see inside me right now, you'd know how tortured I am. I can never make this up to you."

"Up to *me*?" she echoed incredulously. "Me? What about Elijah Wallace? And who knows how many others are dead because of you?" He flinched as though she'd hit him, which only made her more furious. "What about that poor woman in the next cell over?"

Dr. Murphy—wittingly or not—had contributed to Angela ending up where she was now. Angela, powerless for her entire sad life, had been at the mercy of the whims of powerful men around her. Dr. Murphy had been in a position to do something about that. He'd chosen not to.

He stared at her with sad eyes. "You're right."

Maple felt some of her righteous indignation evaporate at his agreeing, which only made her resent him more.

"I let everyone down, including myself. I deserve to be in this cell. I deserve to stay in it the rest of my life, however long that may be." He blinked several times, and tears slid down his cheeks. "I was going to end my own life. That was my intention when I stopped in that border town. I was disgusted with myself for all the things I've done in the past few years, and especially for being such a coward: instead of turning myself in and telling the sheriff about Rawlings, I left you a trail of breadcrumbs. I knew it'd take you just long enough to put all the pieces together that I could escape."

She wanted him to wipe away his tears—something about them dripping freely like that was disconcerting—but instead he grabbed the bars of his cell with both hands and leaned closer to her, letting the tears roll down his cheeks and drip off his chin. She took a step back and felt her mouth twist into a sneer.

"You're repulsed by me," he said, his voice wavering. "Good. You should be."

"You're the one who—" Maple pressed the tips of her index fingers into her temples and rubbed them.

"Who failed," the doctor finished for her. "I lost my way after Darlene died. Life lost its meaning. I started gambling and got into debt with the wrong people." He laughed bitterly. "What a cliché."

Maple pointed a trembling finger at him. "You're the one who taught me how to relentlessly pursue truth and justice. Your corruption taints everything I learned from you."

There it was. She hadn't really realized it until she'd said it aloud, but that was the core of the betrayal. It wasn't simply that someone she respected had made a bad choice. It was that the person from whom she'd learned the most about truth had turned out to be dishonest; the person who'd taught her how investigators could clear the innocent and help convict the guilty had used his knowledge to break the law. Because he'd turned out to be a hypocrite, Maple was now unmoored, not sure how to navigate with her own moral compass. A sob bubbled up and nearly choked her. Dr. Murphy's eyes shone with his own tears.

"No," he said, pressing his lips together. "You're wrong."

"How can you—"

He held a hand up to stop her. "I don't mean you're wrong about me. You're right about me. I'm a failure and a hypocrite."

Maple felt an odd instinct to deny this statement, so deeply ingrained was her loyalty to this man. Something inside her ripped as she realized almost instantly that he was right.

"But, please," he said, reaching his hands through the bars imploringly. Maple kept her own firmly at her sides. He nodded once, respecting her decision not to touch him. "Please don't let my bad decisions taint everything you believe in. I taught you some things, sure, but you came to my seminars already in possession of something no one could teach: a deeply instilled passion to do right—and that isn't just an aspect of your personality, Maple. It's who you are. It's your core."

Overwhelmed by emotion, she looked down at her feet. Her sturdy brown walking shoes were firmly planted on the outside of the jail cell; they were broken in but still had plenty of miles left in them. Her gaze moved to Dr. Murphy's scuffed black loafers, which would always remain on the other side of the bars. In them, he would shuffle sadly around in the same six-foot-by-six-foot cell until his death. She closed her eyes.

"I know I'm in no position to ask anything of you, but I'm going to ask this: don't give up. I wasn't good enough. Strong enough. But you?" He choked back tears. "You're the strongest person I've ever known, Maple."

Maple heard the sound of footsteps coming down the hall, accompanied by the slow, rhythmic clunking of crutches. She didn't have to open her eyes to know that it was Kenny and the sheriff. She felt them stop by her side. When she was ready, she opened her eyes.

"I'll try."

She looked first at Kenny and then at the sheriff. Then she turned her back on Dr. Murphy. With the officers flanking her, she walked out of the jail.

CHAPTER 33

Thursday, November 21, 1946

Though nearly all the leaves were off the trees and the days were growing shorter, the morning dawned bright and clear. In the kitchen, Maple placed her breakfast plate in the sink. Her eyes landed on the cookie jar, which no longer housed the photo of Maple and Jamie. Instead, a check for twelve dollars and sixty-seven cents was tucked in there—just in case she needed a tangible reminder of her ability to claw her way back from the depths of despair.

Mack meowed. Maple bent down and ran her hand from his head all the way down his back to the base of his tail. He arched in pleasure and rubbed his head against her leg.

She knew exactly how he felt.

The sound of hammering came from her garage, letting her know that her employee had arrived. She walked out the front door and stepped onto her driveway, pausing to pat the hubcap of the car. Dew had formed overnight, and her fingers tingled pleasantly at the cold. In the month since the investigation had concluded, her business had flourished, so much so that she'd been able not only to pay her mortgage and other bills, but also to purchase new tires. The Chrysler Saratoga had been relocated to make room in the garage. Maple had even begun driving it sometimes, though for shorter trips she still preferred to walk.

She looked up to admire the sign she'd hung above the garage door: "Maple's Miniatures." It was the identical twin of the one at the hardware shop, where Maple would continue to work on the painting, wallpapering, and other details. The construction of the actual houses, however, would be happening here—thanks to her new carpenter.

She went over to the open garage door and said, "Good morning."

Ken Quirk, Senior, paused his hammering and smiled over his shoulder, touching the brim of his cap in greeting.

Ken and his carpentry skills had been a godsend. He crafted the frames and exteriors far more professionally than she could have, leaving Maple free to focus on the interior detail work. Kenny and Mary had both privately told her that since he'd started working for her, Ken had a light in his eyes that had been missing since before the war. He still had demons to fight, and some days were worse than others, but working for Maple gave him the flexibility to set his own hours and to work largely in solitude, which he liked. He was able to take pride in a day's work and support his family again.

"Two more orders came in yesterday," she told him. "I'll get you the details later today."

"Sounds good, Maple."

Ken returned to the hammer and the boards. He wasn't one for excessive chatting, which was just one of the many things Maple liked about him.

Maple returned to the house, where the number of dollhouses had decreased significantly. Overwhelmed by demand—even after doubling her staff by hiring Ken—she'd begun selling off her back catalog, so to speak. She kept the one of her and Bill in their house, though; that was one she was sure she'd never part with. She also kept the brown-haired doll who'd gone through the discovery of Elijah's body with her, though she placed it in a drawer. She didn't need to see that one every day.

Somewhat to her surprise, Maple found she liked having more open space. Until some of the houses were gone, she hadn't realized how claustrophobic her home had become. She liked the new, uncluttered feeling. It felt . . . free.

There was one work in progress, though, currently taking up her entire coffee table. Different from the cheerful ones she worked on at the hardware store, this was no less important to her: Carl Rawlings's death scene, in a nutshell. Working through the details of that day was cathartic for Maple, and she'd decided to embrace the exercise rather than worry about it being macabre or disturbing. After all, the creation of her first nutshell had resulted in solving a murder and exposing a black market scam. Even if all this one did was allow her to feel some control over a chaotic situation, or be able to explain it in some way, her work was still worth it.

Her eyes darted to the mantle. Next to Bill's American flag and their wedding photo sat the now-framed photo of Maple and Jamie on the sled. Her heart still ached a little when she saw it, but overall it felt good to have it out in the open.

Outside, Maple waved to a few friends and neighbors as she crossed Main Street, but didn't stop to chat. Ginger Comstock came out of a shop and, upon seeing Maple, waved sheepishly.

While Ginger's kidnapping had engendered sympathy from the townspeople, her involvement in the sugar smuggling had tainted her most prized possession: her reputation. Furthermore, the fact that Maple had been the one to rescue her put Ginger in Maple's debt, which was something Maple doubted Ginger would ever be able to stand.

The names of the other townspeople who'd been sugar customers had leaked too, and their neighbors were angry. Good, patriotic folks who had been suffering through and following the ration rules were furious with those who had supported the black market. The war might have been over, but the deep conviction that everyone had to sacrifice for the greater good was most certainly not. Ironically, sugar rations had been lifted earlier that month—mere weeks after the sugar ring had been busted—so, though it was still in somewhat short supply, Elderberry residents could now enjoy—legally and guilt-free—small amounts of what some of them had taken to calling "white gold."

Maple passed the grocery window where she had witnessed the fight between Elijah Wallace and Russell Mooreland—had it really been just a month ago? It felt like a lifetime had passed since then. She looked at the window where, that day, there had been headlines about the Nuremberg hangings. Today, the top story—written by none other than Ella Henderson—was about the local elementary school preparing to put on a Thanksgiving play.

Maple grinned. The young reporter had gained statewide recognition for her coverage of the dramatic events that had culminated in Deputy Rawlings's death and the arrests of both Dr. Murphy and Mrs. Wallace. Her article, the first and most comprehensive account of the whole sordid tale, had been reprinted all over New England—much to Harry Needles's dismay. Maple had a feeling Ella wouldn't be covering local elementary school pageants for long; she was destined for bigger things. In the meantime, though, even the small, local stories mattered: Matthew and Michael were very excited about their roles as pilgrims in the upcoming play, and Maple was looking forward to attending.

She arrived at the diner just as Charlotte was ushering the boys out the door to school.

"Behave yourselves!" she called.

They watched the boys dash down the street, shoving each other playfully.

"They'll be the end of me," Charlotte said, but she couldn't fool Maple, who heard the note of happiness in her friend's voice.

"I have something to tell you," she said as soon as she and Charlotte were settled in a booth, Hank having promised to deliver their tea shortly.

"Does it have to do with Ben? Do tell . . ." Charlotte winked knowingly.

Maple blushed. She and Ben had been spending more time together recently outside their hours working together at the hardware store. They were both enjoying each other's company, but neither was in a hurry to put a label on their relationship. Charlotte, however, was extremely eager to do just that.

"No. Remember, back before all this started, on the day I found out the money was gone, you came over?"

Charlotte nodded. "I brought you cake."

Maple smiled. "You did. And you also asked me that day if making the dollhouses brought me joy. And I didn't realize it at the time, but I think you were seeing what I wasn't: that I was cranking them out like a machine, with grim efficiency." Maple took a deep breath. "The thing I've realized is I was kind of living my whole life like that—cranking out days with grim efficiency. Maybe because of my childhood and Jamie's death, maybe because Bill was gone or because I was frustrated my law career seemed to be over before it could even begin."

Charlotte was nodding. Maple was nearly overwhelmed by fondness for her friend.

"And you were right: I'd lost the joy. Somewhere along the line, it had seeped out of my life, until I forgot what it felt like."

Maple thought of the car sitting in her driveway, the cat who was probably asleep on her couch, and of all the wonderful people who'd become central figures in her life over the past month: Kenny, Ken, Ella, Sam . . .

"But you know what? I'm starting to feel it again. And all it took to get my joy back was murder, betrayal, deception, and an illegal sugar smuggling racket."

Charlotte threw back her head and guffawed.

Hank appeared and placed steaming mugs of tea in front of them. He tossed a bemused smile at his wife, who had tears of laughter rolling down her face.

"Thanks for making my wife so happy," he said to Maple, who grinned in return.

Once she got control of herself, Charlotte stirred a teaspoon of sugar into her mug and then slid the sugar bowl over to Maple.

"No, thanks. I've decided I kind of like the bitterness after all."

Charlotte lifted her mug, and Maple clinked her own against it.

Twenty minutes later, Maple continued down the sidewalk. Her mood ticked up another notch at the thought of seeing Ben and carrying on with the work of her next dollhouse. Creating the traditional houses felt less hypocritical to her now. After all, the dollhouse business had allowed her to accomplish great things. It had made it possible for her to keep her own house, restore Bill's car—*her* car—to drivability, and provide much-needed employment to Ken Quirk.

Angela Wallace's description of how important her own childhood dollhouse had been to her had resonated with Maple, too. Perhaps, she thought, she was creating a necessary escape for some children. At the very least, she'd come to see her houses as vessels for children's imaginations rather than as solemn memorials to unrealistic domestic ideals. In fact, she'd realized, her miniatures, whether they were nutshells that might be used in crime scene investigations or pleasant houses meant as children's toys, were springboards of possibility, offering opportunities for the people who used them.

Glancing to her right, she saw that she was passing the lawyers' office, and smiled ruefully when she noticed the sign announcing the hours it would be closed for lunch. It seemed like a lifetime had passed since she'd been unceremoniously dismissed from that office with her meager check. Perhaps, she thought, recalling Mr. Cross and Mr. Higgins's offended expressions, she had been too quick to criticize herself for calling them out on their lie.

After all, there were worse things than being too honest.

AUTHOR'S NOTE

Maple Bishop exists because of NPR.

Well, she really exists because Frances Glessner Lee existed, but I had never heard of Captain Lee until I was scrolling through my phone one afternoon in 2017. When I saw an NPR article titled "The Tiny, Murderous World of Frances Glessner Lee," I was captivated. An heiress who co-opted the traditionally feminine art of miniature making to create tiny replicas of death scenes? A lady who used her "nutshells of unexplained death" to train police officers in crime scene analysis, thus advancing the field of legal medicine? And now those nutshells were on rare public display at the Smithsonian?

Yes, please.

I marched into the next room and told my husband I needed to travel to Washington, DC, to see an exhibit called *Murder Is Her Hobby*. He said that sounded great, and now you know why I married him.

Thus began **my** new hobby: stalking a dead heiress. Not only did I see the nutshells at the Smithsonian that winter, but over the next several years I traveled to both of Captain Lee's homes: Glessner House in Chicago and The Rocks estate in New

Hampshire. I watched and read everything I could get my hands on about her, including Corinne May Botz's *The Nutshell Studies of Unexplained Death* and Bruce Goldfarb's *18 Tiny Deaths: The Untold Story of Frances Glessner Lee.*

Appropriately enough, Maple herself was born—just like Captain Lee—in Chicago when I traveled there to participate in the "5th Semester" residency led by Ann Garvin and Erin Celello. I sat at the huge dining room table staring at pictures of the nutshell called *Barn* and imagining a WWII widow with a strong moral compass and a need to reinvent herself.

Erin coached me remotely as I drafted over the next year. Eventually, I signed with my agent, Chelsey Emmelhainz, whose brilliant insights made the book better and who ultimately found it a great home at Crooked Lane. In 2022, I returned to Chicago to attend Captain Lee's birthday party. In 2023, I visited her grave in New Hampshire.

What started with an NPR story evolved into lifelong passion. I'm left with wonder and gratitude that I've learned so much about this endlessly fascinating woman and that I've discovered the incredible generosity of the writing community.

Frances Glessner Lee mastered the art and science of thoughtful examination, of holding things up to the light and considering *why* and *what if* . . .

I hope, like her, to continue doing just that—to carry on her legacy of finding what's big in what's small.

ACKNOWLEDGMENTS

I am overflowing with gratitude.

Ann Garvin and Erin Celello, I can never thank you enough for helping me develop Maple's story and for coaching me in the nuts and bolts of publishing with a perfect combination of humor and honesty. That "5th Semester" retreat in Chicago and the year of mentoring that followed changed my life.

Thanks to Doe Boyle and all the kind folks in the Shoreline Society of Children's Book Writers and Illustrators (SCBWI) group and Tassy Walden Awards for radiating positivity and offering such a warm, welcoming local writing community. You show me the kind of writer and person I want to be.

I'm incredibly grateful to the writing community I discovered online. Anna Kaling, Nishita Parekh, Megan Records, Kellye Garrett, and Mia P. Manansala all gave me generous feedback and advice. I continue to learn every day from the 2024 Debut group and from Sisters in Crime.

I still marvel at my good fortune that my agent, Chelsey Emmelhainz, plucked my manuscript out of the slush pile. Thanks for your excellent editorial skills, great sense of humor, and for just generally being my partner in (fictional) crime.

Thank you to my editor, Faith Black Ross, and the entire Crooked Lane team for all your hard work. I'm delighted that Maple found a great home with you.

I'm blessed with an amazing extended family, including aunts, uncles, cousins, nieces, a nephew, and in-laws. Thanks for always having my back and lifting me up. I'm grateful to my friends who show up, listen, and are just generally always in my corner. Several of them helped with specific aspects of this book's journey. In particular, thank you to Dayle for answering my law enforcement questions, Delia for coaching me in social media, and Karen for taking such a great author photo. I also highly recommend having friends who, while on vacation, will cheerfully spend an entire morning helping you hunt for an heiress's grave. Alexis, Mike, Jillian, and Kora: thank you for that day and countless others.

Thanks to Izzy, Gomez, Maisie, and Benson for all the walks and snuggles.

For as long as I can remember, I wanted to be a writer. Thank you, Mom and Dad, for your lifelong guidance and encouragement; being raised by two English teachers definitely gave me a literary leg up! Phil and Kelley, you are the most loyal and supportive siblings I can imagine.

And, finally, thank you to my husband and our sons. Matt, asking you on a date back in high school remains the best move I ever made. Thank you for twenty-six years (and counting). Liam and Sean, I'm so honored to be your mom; you're lively, curious, and kind (and avid readers!). I am the luckiest person to have you three as my best guys. I love you so much.